The Secon[d]

A Novel By:

To Tammy

My Family

[signature] L. J. McClain

L. J. McClain

To Tammy

This book is a work of fiction. All names, places and events are fictional and are products of the author's imagination. No portion of this book may be reproduced without permission from the publisher except by a reviewer who may quote brief passages in a review.

I would like to thank my Lord and Savior Jesus Christ, my family and closest friends, as well as my editor and friend a I would love to thank the Native American People for staying resilient, I would love to thank the African Americans for still fighting for justice and to the Jewish People Numbers 6 24-27. The Lord Bless thee and keep thee. The Lord make his face to shine upon thee. The Lord lift up his countenance upon thee and give thee peace, and they shall put my name upon the children of Israel and I will bless them.

Prologue

It was Friday afternoon in Palm Springs, Florida. Nate Barkley and Jason Biggs were listening to heavy metal music. Nate was cleaning an AK-47 assault rifle and Jason, suiting up in bulletproof assault gear. This agenda was being followed across the nation. In 7 other major U.S. cities, 21 other individuals who were part of a terrorist group targeting Jewish people, were also preparing. The mission: To kill as many Jews as possible.

This group of young men belonged to a group known as The Brotherhood that had been recently disbanded by Homeland Security for being a hate crime organization. The 23 members had created this mission not only to be rid of more "dirty Jews," but as retaliation against DHS.

At 7 pm on Friday evening, three gunmen in 7 cities burst into temples and opened fired killing over 5,680 Jewish people. The gunmen engaged the police in a gunfight leaving first responders paralyzed in their attempts to rescue the wounded. The gunmen were killed. 'Suicide by cop' the news stations were calling it. The task of tending to the dead and wounded began. The estimates were somewhere around 6 thousand killed and another several thousand injured across the nation. No other act of terrorism on American soil had claimed so many lives; not the Twin Towers or Oklahoma City.

A Miracle

On a warm day in October, 13 school buses filled with 40 students each, headed to the Atlanta Aquarium on a field trip. En route, the buses were attacked by unknown assailants who opened fire on them. The weapons used were powerful enough to flip two of the buses and rip massive gashes in the metal. Dozens were killed instantly while the screams of the frightened and wounded filled the air.

The gunmen ran off screaming something in their native language but came back when they heard the screams. They opened fired again and did not stop until all screams ceased. Before retreating, they checked the buses looking for any signs of life. Satisfied all were dead and their mission complete, they made their escape. The assailants made a perfect get-away. In the ensuing chaos, no one had seen which way they went.

A small convoy of minivans arrived on scene. These were the parents who were also joining the field trip but not on the buses. They had been held back by a long train, so had been separated from the buses. The parents ran to the bullet-ridden buses desperately trying to find survivors and their own children. One parent called 911.

The scene was gruesome even for seasoned first responders who ran from bus to bus checking for any signs of life. The news media had been tipped off by the police scanners they monitored for news. They had lined up and begun reporting as soon as the emergency crews had arrived. Homeland Security, the FBI, CIA and local law enforcement were all on the scene as well.

News of the attack spread across the city. Parents of the school children began to show up crying hysterically adding to the chaotic scene. Emergency personnel kept parents behind the yellow tape barricade so that the scene would not be contaminated. The attack had not been witnessed, and there appeared to be no survivors. So far, all the leads they would get were on the scene.

Parents cried and hugged each other as they watched the body bags being carried out one by one. No one knew which student it was. The news crews filmed as rescuers cried side by side with the grieving parents. Once again, the country sat in front of their television sets paralyzed in horror, watching the scene unfold. At one point, the news stations aired footage of the parents kneeling in prayer which had turned into a worship service in the middle of the massacre. First responders were filmed giving their lives to God alongside members of the investigative agencies on the scene. The nation was in mourning, grieving the needless loss of innocent lives. The parents called for corporate prayer for the slain students, teachers, and drivers.

The nation watched, parents prayed, and the cameras captured it all. Suddenly a cameraman screamed, "Somebody is alive in one of the buses!!" Cameras quickly turned, sweeping the buses for any signs of life and began to zoom in on movement. Children were moving, and soft whimpering was heard.

Parents along with many across the country had been praying for about 45 minutes by that time. Now children were beginning to exit the buses to screams of "Hallelujah!" and "To the most high, God."

Children ran to their waiting parents as more parents arrived on the scene to find their children had survived. TV reporters had regained their composure and begun reporting on the miracle.

The children were all accounted for and all alive in spite of the bullet-riddled buses. Other children who were trapped were being pulled from the buses and carried across the glass-strewn ground. It appeared none of the children had any wounds at all–not so much as a scratch. Their clothes were bloodstained, yet there was no source for the blood. The reporters called it a resurrection miracle. A miracle all caught on film and viewed by the world.

~~~~~~

Chapter 1

New York City in the year 2021, the crash of the stock market had occurred. It was worse than the crash of 2008. The crash created pressure on the government to pay its outstanding debts. China had called in its loans totaling in the trillions of dollars. Taxes had been increased by 25% for the rich and poor alike.

Foreign governments caused the collapse of the dollar by purchasing oil with gold instead of dollars. This reduced the value of the dollar. Unemployment was at an all-time high of 38% with few job prospects. No new jobs had been created since 2019. The only jobs were in the healthcare field. The Healthcare Initiative had passed, and Medicare and Medicaid revamped creating a plethora of jobs. College graduates were pushed in the direction of healthcare regardless of their degrees. It didn't even matter if they didn't have the temperament for working with the sick.

Marijuana was legalized in all 50 states. The Feds followed suit allowing for taxes to be collected which in turn allowed greater payments to be made to China. Legalized marijuana pharmacies were as respectable as Walgreens or Rite Aid. The drug cartels, of course, were still active with the smuggling of heroin and cocaine. All around the country medicinal herbs were grown on plantations and were just as much a part of the economy as a crop of corn. Marijuana brought in more tax revenues than any other crop, alcohol, or cigarettes.

Marijuana was singlehandedly responsible for saving the U.S. Postal Service. Hemp could only be sent via mail. This pushed the service to be open 24/7 as it once had.

Taxes were no longer an April 15th deadline. Now, 25% was taken directly from the wages each pay period. The tax hike was instituted to recoup the 6.5 billion dollars the IRS had lost in fraudulent tax returns and identity theft.

The government now handled healthcare. Each citizens' information was kept in central medical data banks. These data banks also had massive files on every disease known to man, every cure, and even had a DNA file. DNA samples were now required for each person in the U.S. DNA was used to identify all descendants of any ethnicity including the American Indians. They had databases as there were specific diseases that affected them. Alcoholism was one that was particularly difficult for them. The Indians were not able to process alcohol and were severely affected by it. Other steps had to be taken to help alcoholic American Indians. Tribe leaders felt they knew how best to help their own, on their lands, in their hospitals.

The downsizing of the economy quadrupled the revenues of the American Indian casinos. Now they had established their own cancer research center that rivaled John Hopkins, Bethesda, and other top-notch research facilities. Indian medical research centers were able to hire the best doctors money could buy and had financial backing the government didn't.

The massive increase in revenues positioned the Indians to be able to purchase their land, including all real estate, water, and mineral rights, from the U.S. Government. Because the government was desperate to pay back the multitude of debts that had been called in, they could not refuse. A trillion-dollar deal was made, the purchase completed, and a huge payment was sent to China the following day.

The war between Iran and Israel never materialized even though many thought it inevitable. Israel had stopped the Iranian nuclear weapons programs by sabotaging the enrichment facilities. This debilitated Iran and its nuclear program for years.

Terrorist intelligence was able to determine that the U.S. was instrumental in helping Israel with the sabotage. They were infuriated with the U.S. and vowed revenge against the Great Satan, as the U.S. was known, by staging more attacks on U.S. soil. Attacks were carried out at theme parks and various other public venues throughout the U.S. In one instance, a dirty bomb was detonated in a theme park in Florida, killing thousands and exposing many more to the radioactive waste used in the bomb.

The terrorist group proudly claimed responsibility for the heinous act, stating it was retaliation against the U.S. for assisting Israel.

Again, the country mourned even deeper because so many children had perished. In the end, the death toll was over 7,800 including those who had suffered ill effects from exposure to the radionuclides. It took years to clean up the destruction, and the land around the detonation could not be used until radiation levels were safe.

It took several weeks for the report to come from Homeland Security as to how the plan was hatched. This gave the terrorist enough time to release another dirty bomb during the Tournament of Roses Parade in Pasadena, California. Terrorists also took credit for the bomb and the devastation left on the city. Twenty thousand people were killed and another 12,800 wounded.

Again, the military was called in to assist with the cleanup. America was inconsolable over the death of her people. States across America came to the aid of California. Different utility companies assisted in restoring power and relief agencies brought food aid to the people of California. The country was pulling itself out of the crisis.

The Red Cross no longer existed because of the misappropriation of funds from the Haitian Earth Quake, Frankenstorm, and Hurricane Harvey. The Red Cross was financially strapped after Hurricane Katrina 2005. No audit was conducted of the finances for the department, and the department was found to have had millions of dollars embezzled from the company from higher-ups within the organization.

Due to the attacks in California and Florida, anti-Jewish Semitism had increased as well as violence. Anti-Jewish Semitism had not been this high since World War II. Jewish synagogues were being desecrated and tagged with swastikas. Law enforcement hands were full because of terrorist attacks, creating the perception that complaints by Jewish-Americans were not being taken seriously. Many more were not making formal complaints in fear of drawing attention to themselves. They felt it was better to suffer in silence. Their religion taught them to turn the other cheek, so they suffered in silence in hopes of things getting better.

Passports were slow to be approved, most being denied. This was a result of what came to be known as Green Flight. Early in 2019, a lot of multi-millionaires renounced their American Citizenship and moved to foreign countries to keep from being taxed heavily. The last four years saw green flight from America.

The United States Government concluded that legalizing the sex trade would create taxable income. Homeland Security was not able to stop sex-trafficking and women were dying by the thousands. Prostitution was legalized to prevent the deaths of innocent women and young girls.

There were legalized bunny farms all across the United States; more bunny farms than Casinos. The women were tested through the government once a month to prevent widespread diseases. The women earned a comfortable income and were able to take care of their families well. They worked without fear of the horrors of the illegal sex trade.

The Brotherhood of the Valhalla was at an all-time high with new membership recruitment. Homeland Security tagged the group as a racist, neo-Nazi organization. Membership had grown at a rate higher than the National Rifle Association and the N.A.A.C.P. combined. The Brotherhood conducted nightly patrols of the woods of West Virginia which put them in the crosshairs of Homeland Security, FBI, and CIA. The group was heavy in gun running from the former drug cartels of Mexico. The cartels had subsidized their loss of revenues from the legalization of marijuana by increasing illegal arms trades. It was now at an all-time high for groups like the Brotherhood and doomsday preppers.

✡✡✡

The background and daily attributes of the Brotherhood were dismissed or overlooked by society in general because of the terrorist attacks and the high rate of anti-Semitism. Truth be told, the relationship with the Jewish community was deplorable. The treatment of the Jewish community could only be described as hate crimes. Other minority groups complained, but the Jewish community seldom did.

Money that was stolen from the Jews during World War II had been sitting in banks in Switzerland had now multiplied from millions to trillions of dollars. The United Nations ordered the money to be given to descendants of the Holocaust Victims and Survivors. The tracing of the descendants had begun in the early 1990s only to be delayed by the Swiss Government time and time again. Now that there was a global recession and the money was sitting in the banks, the United Nations ordered the banks to make good on tracking the descendants or lose all national and international banking accreditation, which would mean the collapse of the Swiss and Eastern Union economy.

Needless to say, that the banks were making great strides in finding the descendants and their next of kin, at a much quicker pace. This was where the End-of-Time Wealth Transfer came into play. This was a popular component of the prosperity gospel where the church would become rich and would then be able to spread the gospel. It was a prophecy from Isaiah that pastors and evangelist had been preaching about for years and now it would come to pass.

✡✡✡

RH negative blood was considered to be the Jewish Priestly gene that could be found in many different nationalities and races. Known as the Cohen gene, it was believed to have been passed down from the tribe of Levi or the son of Levi. The sons of Levi took care of the vessels and objects within the Sanctuary; the Ark of the Covenant, Menorah, Table of Shewbread. The offsprings were thought to know about the Ark of the Covenant. The descendants were pursued for this reason as well as hunted for annihilation to prevent the collection of money from the Bank of the Alps.

The Swiss Alps Bank and Trust was in Switzerland where high-ranking SS Officers had stored the stolen money. Since Hitler and most high-ranking officers were killed or unable to claim the money for seventy plus years, 30 million dollars with interests had turned into 30 trillion dollars. Bank of the Alps had a list of Jewish Holocaust victims and their descendants. For the victims who died without descendants, their blood next of kin would be awarded their share of the 30 trillion dollars. Jewish ancestry had to be proven through DNA.

News Flash

Another series of earthquakes with magnitudes of greater 6.5 have been recorded along the Ring of Fire. Geologist and geophysicists are concerned about the increased activity along this horseshoe as it could also be an indication of increased volcanic activity. Areas hit with large magnitude quakes in the last two months include Japan, Indonesia, the Philippines, and New Zealand.

Chapter 2

The Brotherhood of Valkyrie, or BTV, were on nightly watches that consisted of patrols and guarding the backwoods of the Virginias. One night a group of middle-eastern men were visiting a cabin in the woods owned by a prominent family. The cabin was not a typical cabin; the Jefferson family owned the land deeds. It had been purchased right after prohibition, and the property had been passed from generation to generation. The cabin's current owner was the daughter of a plastic surgeon. It had been given to her on her wedding day as a gift. The groom, a doctor of middle-eastern descent, was born in the United States.

One chilly night in early March, twin brothers Zachary and Romero were out on patrol in the hills of West Virginia, discovered a group of middle-eastern men loading some crates into an SUV. Romero, being the older of the twins, was more aggressive. He chose to watch the men out of pure racism. Zachary wanted to know what was in the wooden crates. The crates were three and a half feet long and twenty inches wide.

The twins approached the five men and unloaded their assault rifles into them. No words or looks were exchanged. Zachary and Romero just walked up and emptied their rifles into the men. After going through the truck, they found hand grenades and bomb equipment. While the killings had been purely racially motivated, the discovery of the contents was a bonus.

From the maps and paperwork found in the truck, it was later determined the grenades were connected to Hezbollah. The plans outlined an attack on the White House. The Brotherhood turned everything over to DHS to regain their credibility as a viable organization.

The American public congratulated them and heralded them as heroes for saving countless lives. The FBI kept tabs on The

Brotherhood, but because of the foiled attack, they chose to look the other way, and the files that were kept on the Brotherhood faded into the abyss. Homeland Security did keep up with the enrollment of young men into Brotherhood and the millions of dollars that were donated to the group by a company traded on the New York Stock Exchange.

✡ ✡ ✡

Benjamin was of Jewish ancestry. His father was an accountant for big insurance companies in the 80's. His Uncle, Gabe Zigburgh, was a Rabbi for the largest synagogue in New York. His grandfather started a CPA firm in Brooklyn, growing the business and the family prospered. His grandfather, Heimlich Zigburgh, lost his family in the Holocaust; his mother, father, three sisters, and two brothers.

Heimlich and his younger brother, David, were infants when they were sent to live with a great aunt in America in 1939 before the war took over most of Europe. His other five siblings were older and chose to stay. They assumed someone or some country would stop Hitler, and it wouldn't get any worse. They were wrong; dead wrong. Heimlich only spoke of his siblings at Passover and Hanukkah. Benjamin's Great Uncle David had given up all his Jewish religion and lifestyle years ago. The only thing he kept was the name Zigburgh. His grandfather only saw his brother David occasionally in passing him on the streets with a quick acknowledgment–that was all that was left of their relationship. David denied all of his Jewish heritage because he felt there was no use in believing in a God that would let the Holocaust happen. David kept his Jewish name in case his brother chose to contact with him.

David lived completely different from Heimlich. David was gay and had no family. As a child, he never thought he'd be single and not have a family. He grieved uncontrollably after his great Aunt Myrna told him of the death of his entire family. David hardened his heart and vowed never to fall in love or have a family. He didn't know the repercussions of that decision.

The 1940's and 50's were no problem because he was still a child and his studies came before anything else. School and

Temple were all that were required of him. America was on the move, recovering from the war. He spent his free time going to the movies. They became his passion. David found himself in love with screen characters like Rock Hudson and Tyrone Powers. No one knew his little secret. How he envied Doris Day! The 60's and 70's were a colorful blur, but now in his late 30's, David had some eye-opening experiences into his sexuality. There was a term for it; he was called gay, and he liked it. He often said it to himself quietly. At some point, Barry had come into his life.

Barry was the light of David's life. He was quite handsome and knew it. Barry had an outgoing personality and wasn't ashamed to be gay. Barry had known at a very young age who he was and having grown up in the drug culture of the late 60's, he was allowed to be more himself. With Barry's handsome looks, he had many lovers. When he met David, he knew that no other man could hold a candle to his "David," his own personal Michael Angelo.

David had worked every day for twenty plus years as a CPA, weekends included, to avoid life. He created a significant nest egg with nothing to do with it until Barry came along. Through the years, David and Barry traveled around the world. David never minded spending the money because he had never been happier in his life. It took the long dark thoughts of suicide away, and he loved that. After several vacations to Europe, David and Barry decided to buy a vacation home in Greece. David loved to spoil Barry–whatever Barry wanted, he got. Barry loved to cook. He was a Chef, so of course, the kitchen had to be turned into a chef's kitchen to which David spared no expense. The kitchen and home were constantly filled with friends and patrons from the restaurant that David bought for Barry. Barry believed in feeding people. On certain nights, Barry would invite everyone from their brownstone building to have dinner with them. Life was good, and as long as Barry was happy, David never considered the money. Hell, it was only money.

In the spring of '86, Barry caught a cold but never quite shook it. When David finally talked Barry into letting him take him to the hospital, it was too late. Barry died six weeks later from pneumonia brought on by the complications of AIDS.

David's world was shattered, and he struggled to breathe. He had lost his life mate. He felt alone in the world, and for the first time, in a long time, he thought about his brother.

The loss of his brother's friendship was not lost on Heimlich. He never understood David. David was quiet, and Heimlich thought it was because of the death of his family. They never talked about the murders. That was a painful subject that neither wanted to pursue, so they didn't. Saul Zigburgh, their father, was a wealthy doctor in Germany before the war. His wife, Ida, had wanted to leave earlier when anti-Semitic activities first started. His father said, "It was just young boys creating chaos in the country. They need to get jobs to keep them busy instead of becoming Hitler youths and sending young girls to the woods to become better women for the German country."

Saul Zigburgh, a prideful man, refused to move to the ghettos, so he stayed in his home. Ida begged him to send the children to America to stay with his Aunt Myrna. He refused at first then decided to let the older siblings choose. Of course, they chose to stay with their parents; the younger siblings were sent to America.

Two weeks from the day the younger Zigburghs were sent to America, Nazi Officers came to the door and loaded the family onto trains to a concentration camp never to be seen again. Heimlich grew up in the shadow of losing his entire family to the Holocaust. Because of this, he was very mature for his age. He never played outside, was always in the house learning something or practicing something. He thought if he could learn everything, no one could trick him into believing in something that didn't exist. Heimlich always believed that his family was tricked into getting on the train. There was just no way they went of their own free will! What he didn't understand was that the family decided whatever was going to happen to them, would happen to them as a family. They entered the train cars as a family, girls hand in hand in one car, boys hand in hand in another.

For Heimlich to be successful at not being tricked himself, he spent his lifetime deceiving others. He grew up to become a CPA. He was very good with his clients and built a successful firm from word of mouth. He was so good in fact that the mob came to him for help.

One day while sitting in his office doing an audit for a client, a short, welled dressed man walked into his office unannounced. He was an extra short man, who managed to get past Heimlich's longtime secretary, Barbara. When Heimlich went to see how Barbara could have allowed this to happen, he discovered she was gone. The little guy explained to Heimlich that he felt Barbara deserved an early day, so he took it upon himself to make sure she got one.

Heimlich's client became uncomfortable and excused himself from the meeting mumbling that he would return at a better time. This left Heimlich in the room alone with the small, intimidating man. The man introduced himself as Author Winthorpe.

Heimlich thought he was joking about his name but, he listened very carefully to everything the man said.

"I am a small person, not a dwarf, not a midget... a small person. You got that?"

"I understand sir," Heimlich answered, cautiously.

The little man handed Heimlich a bag containing $25,000.00. He told Heimlich that he would bring 25,000 every two weeks and that Heimlich could keep five grand for himself. Heimlich would write him a check for the remaining twenty thousand dollars that he deposited or cashed in another account that Heimlich would invent for him, no questions asked.

Every two weeks for twenty-five years, Author Winthorpe showed up, and Barbara got an early vacation day like clockwork. Heimlich kept five grand for himself. The money had come in handy through the years.

Heimlich met his wife Ellen in 1960. They were married later the same year. Heimlich wasn't a very social man nor was he handsome by a long shot. They met at a social gathering and his gentleness and intelligence enamored Ellen. She was also a CPA. The wedding made the socialite columns in the New York papers. He would have never thought he would have made the socialite column, but Ellen was from an aristocratic Russian-Jewish family. Her family had been in America thirty years before the war started and were well established in New York society. Her family helped settle Jewish immigrants after the war.

After the wedding, Ellen and Heimlich got busy making a family. Ellen blessed Heimlich with three children; two boys and one girl. Adam born in 1961, Alexandra born in 1963 and Gabe born in 1972; he was a surprise. They lived and grew up in Manhattan and went to private schools and then on to Syracuse University. Adam would become an accountant with the family firm, Alex a photographer and journalist, and Gabe would become a Rabbi.

One afternoon in late 1988, Heimlich expected to see Author Winthorpe with his usual transaction. For the first time in some twenty-five years, Author did not show up. Weeks passed with no word or cash from Heimlich's mysterious client. He also noticed that the money was missing from the account he'd set up. A couple of weeks later, Heimlich saw that there had been a big bust of mafia gang leaders and mob types up and down the seaboard. He wondered if this had anything to do with his friend's disappearance.

Heimlich now realized that he had adjusted his life and family to the extra $250,000 a year income. This money was used for incidentals such a college and upcoming weddings. Heimlich had no worries because he was thrifty with the money he had saved. He had over five million dollars in savings, and he just had met a good friend by the name of Bernie Madoff. It was 1988 and Heimlich had complete faith in Madoff–he would make him a billionaire.

News Flash

CNN reported today that flyers have been distributed to Jewish communities across the United States and other parts of the world, inviting Jewish families to Switzerland to claim their part of the Nazi Restitution. Each family member will be offered a sum of money, free travel to Switzerland, and a new home for each family choosing to stay. The project is funded by The Bank of the Alps who have long been the caretakers of Jewish funds stolen in WWII.

Chapter 3

"Moving is for the birds!" Keisha said to herself as she pushed the last box into her new, three-bedroom apartment in Coral Springs, a small town outside of Savannah, Georgia. Georgia was a life away from New York City. Keisha had spent the last eight years as a New York City police detective. She dated another Detective, Brandon Marshall, for a couple of years and everything was perfect. Well, that was until she realized she was pregnant. Brandon had been very adamant about not wanting to have mix race children. Keisha never told Brandon about the pregnancy. She had an abortion, and now she was moving to Coral Springs.

She refused to allow herself to miss Brandon or even think about him. "What's the use, we will never see eye to eye on anything important. Brandon is still blowing up my cell phone as if he really cares!" Keisha mumbled as she cut off her phone. "This is my first day at work, and I don't need the headache," Keisha exclaimed slamming her apartment door. Small town quiet was what Keisha was looking for and distance from Brandon. Pulling into downtown Coral Springs, Keisha thought to herself, "If I had blinked, I would have missed it."

Entering the police station, you would think you had been transported back to the 1970s. From the look of the buildings, the whole downtown area could have used a facelift, at least an update.

"Excuse me, I'm looking for Chief Merkerson?" she said to a ruddy-faced woman with a beehive hairdo sitting at a desk.

"Hello, I'm Gladys Spaulding, the unit secretary. You must be Keisha Williams from New York City. Welcome. Chief Merkerson is in his office right down the hall to the left."

"Thank you, ma'am." The stale smell of cigars hung in the air as she approached the Chief's office. She thought to herself,

"People still smoke cigars with the new health care initiative? I believe you get an extra fifty dollars a month to quit. Maybe not enough money for him to quit." Keisha stopped at the door, knocked and took a deep breath. "Bad idea," she thought to herself.

"Enter," said a deep voice from the other side. To Keisha's pleasant surprise, Chief Merkerson was an older balding, Asian man.

"Chief Merkerson?"

"Yes?"

"I'm Keisha Williams."

"Hello, Keisha. Welcome to the small, sneaky town of Coral Springs."

"Thank you, sir. I notice you have a southern drawl."

"Born and raised right here. That's why I know it is a sneaky town. Don't let it fool you–it's hiding all kinds of secrets." He took the time to put down his cigar. "Oh yeah, I still smoke– don't believe in the smoking initiative. I use the money to grow my own tobacco. I tried to quit, but the free money made it easier to grow my own. Let's keep this just between us. As I said, Coral Springs is one sneaky little town." Keisha smiled to herself

"What brings you to Coral Springs from the big city?" Merkerson asked without looking up.

Keisha sighed to herself–she knew he wanted a real answer. "Relationship gone wrong, sir. Just need some space of my own," she replied looking him straight in the eye.

"I thought as much, a pretty young girl like yourself. Detective Williams, keep your nose clean, and you could have my seat in a few years. You only have to beat out six other detectives, and three of them started when I started. Coldheart, Blunt and Kewaski." Keisha caught herself giggling. "No, seriously, those are their names. Coldheart is Native American, Blunt is a black ex-desert storm soldier, and Kewaski is an implant from Philadelphia about twenty- five years ago. They're a little hard on the outside but darn good detectives–worth their salt," Merkerson explained beating his chest. "Go to war with any of them at any time, just won't let them drive my police cruiser and I suggest you do the same. They're a bunch of car killers," he said with a wink and a smile. "You will find out soon enough that half of the department funding has gone to replace cars for those three for years. At one point, they had to hitch rides with each other and, they don't always get along. You can pick up your paperwork from Gladys out front and the keys to your cruiser. Here are your badge and sidearm. You can carry your own as well. Start at 8 am bright and early tomorrow morning."

"Thank you, sir, I appreciate the opportunity," Keisha said, rising from her seat.

"No problem. The town can always use fresh blood and a new set of eyes. Welcome to sneaky town." With that, Merkerson turned his chair, put his feet on the desk, and looked out the window.

On the way back down the hall, Keisha thought he had said six detectives–he only named three. "I guess I'll meet the rest later on in the week," she thought to herself.

Keisha patted herself on the back for moving to Coral Springs, "Oh, my bad, I mean sneaky town," she laughed out loud to herself. Keisha pulled up to her apartment which was more of a condo. It was in a building with six other occupants and had two parking spaces. It was a nice spacious two-bedroom with marble floors and granite counters. Keisha thought to herself, "If I had known it would be this nice and cheap, I would have moved years ago." Quick thought but no, she wouldn't have, she was too in love with Brandon to leave.

Keisha walked down to check the mailbox. She was waiting for her 401k check from her previous job but only found bills. "Bills already," she thought. She thumbed through the mail and noticed something from Swiss Bank and Trust. She'd never heard of them before and thought it was a new bank. She checked the address, and it was indeed to her. She laughed to herself thinking that the post office didn't play in sneaky town. She'd only been there a week. She opened the letter from the Swiss Bank and Trust at the same time her home phone rang.

"Hello?"

"Hey Girl."

Keisha knew from the reggae music in the background that it was her best friend from college, Shea Brown. Shea was an Asian American–that's Asian in eyes only.

20

"What's going on with you?" Shea asked. "Like the country yet?"

"This is not the country!" Keisha answered with some hostility.

"Whatever you say. If you are past me in South Carolina and it ain't Miami, it's the country. So how are you liking it?" Shea asked eagerly.

"It's starting to feel like home. It's a lot warmer here," Keisha replied.

"Oh, you know you're in the south now! Have you been to your headquarters and met your team yet?"

"I don't have a team, and yes, I have been there."

"Why your cell phone turned off?" Shea asked, sounding oriental for a change.

"Brandon keeps calling me!! He's called six times today already."

"He came down last weekend and had dinner with Ira and me and played fifty questions about you!" Shea squealed. "When are you going to tell him about the baby?

"Brandon can't handle the truth about the abortion, so let's not talk about it okay?" Keisha said uneasily.

Knowing one more word about the abortion would bring her to tears, Keisha changed the subject. "How's Ira doing?"

"Ira is Ira–coming up with different names and grades of marijuana for different effects. I think if they hadn't legalized marijuana in 2012, Ira would still be in the trafficking game."

"I don't think so Shea, he got out and married you in 2011. He was sincere about quitting the business. The two years he worked for Con. Ed were the worst years of his life. You knew he wasn't happy, but he changed for you, Shea!"

"Yeah, I know. It's great they decided to legalize marijuana and save my marriage at the same time. I was surprised the government legalized it," Shea replied.

"Well, China decided they wanted the trillion-dollar debt paid off because the government kept having shutdowns. A lot of stuff got legal real fast, so it could be taxed to pay the debt. Good thing your parents agreed to make you and Ira the loan to open your own medicinal herb business. With the stuff Ira grows, you were able to pay them off in the first three months you guys were in business. Also, I must thank you and Ira and the United States Postal Service for making me a little richer. I was able to buy that condo in Hawaii because of you guys!" Keisha screamed.

"Well, the United States Postal Service can thank the legalization of marijuana for saving their jobs. You can't send weed through the internet now can you Detective Williams?"

"Investing in your shipping department helped my finances, and I'm glad I came up with the idea of insuring it with the postal service. You gotta love their flat rate shipping. Because of weed, the postal service became a fortune 500 company again!" Both ladies laughed.

"I haven't heard you laugh in so long. It's good to hear it again." Shea laughed and coughed at the same time.

"Are you smoking now?" Keisha asked.

"Yeah, you know Ira uses me for his guinea pig," Shea replied laughing and coughing.

"No, I believe you volunteer!" Keisha said cracking up. "I have never met an Asian that can smoke a Jamaican under the table!!"

"Girl, I swear!! That's why we have stayed married so long."

"Girl, I've got to go! I'm hungry for some of your sesame chicken!"

"I'll mail you some later, Love Ya."

"Smooches," Keisha replied as she hung up the phone.

✡✡✡

Benjamin Zigburgh graduated ahead of his class in 1984 at 16 years of age. He majored in economics at Syracuse University. After graduation, he started working for a big bank on Wall Street. Everything was great. He led a jewel of a life; married his high school sweetheart, Bridgette at eighteen years old. She was the love of his life.

Bridgette came from an ethnic melting pot. Her father was Jewish and a Professor of Jewish History at NYU. Her mother was a black stage actress who occasionally worked on Broadway. Bridgette was not wealthy, but well to do and knew what she wanted. She wanted to help underprivileged people and kids–she fought for the underdog.

Benjamin hated to have to tell her he'd lost his prestigious job at the bank. He had worked what felt like eighty hours a week. He didn't complain–that was the way he liked it. Bridgette hadn't appreciated though. Luckily, he had a wealthy grandfather who owned an accounting firm. He could always drop by his dad's house and talk to him about it. They would find work for him. Benjamin was going to meet Bridgette for dinner. He decided he would tell her then.

Entering the restaurant, he saw Bridgette right away with her big hair. He loved to touch her hair. He often teased her that if she cut her hair, it was a deal breaker–their marriage would be over. Seeing her sitting there still made his heart jump. She was biting her lip and reading the newspaper. She looked up and smiled.

"Bernie Madoff? You ever heard that name before?"

"Sounds familiar," Ben said kissing Bridgette on the forehead. "Not quite sure where I heard that name," Ben replied picking up a menu.

"Well, the papers said he was running a billion-dollar Ponzi scheme, and a lot of people lost a lot of money; some lost their life's savings," Bridgette said turning to the waiter. "I'll have an extra-large plate of Italian sausage and cheese ravioli."

Ben smiled. "You always could eat like a horse and stay a size six. Me, if I eat a large plate of anything, I have to get up an hour earlier and go to the gym," Ben said passing the waiter the menu. "Got a bit of bad news today," he continued, peeking over his whiskey sour at Bridgette. With bad news, Ben decided the best way to tell Bridgette anything was to go ahead and tell her before she started fifty questions with him. "I got fired from my job today," Ben blurted out.

Bridgette turned to him with a grin on her face. "Good! You have given your life to that company with no appreciation. You worked way too many hour weeks sometimes with no days off. Early mornings and late nights. I thought I was going to be a widow before I was thirty. Now you can go to work for your dad and granddad. You know they always wanted you to join their firm, so now is your chance!" Ben rolled his eyes.

"It's what they want, not what I want. I still have my 401k, so that will last us for a while and then if things get tight, I will go to work for them."

The waiter brought the plate of steaming ravioli.

"You know as soon as they find out you lost your job, the pressure will start," Bridgette said with a mouth full of food. "Joe called. He's hosting a dinner next Friday after Sabbath, and he invited us. I want to go. I haven't seen your brother in a while," she said, taking another bite of food.

"We can go. I need to talk to Joe anyway," Ben said looking out the window into the dark, wet New York night.

"You better eat your food before I eat it for you!!" Bridgette squealed at the idea.

Leave it to Bridgette to make you feel reassured on your worst day. Always a positive attitude, always fighting for the underdog. Problem is, I am the underdog now. Hope Bridgette has a super cape, Ben thought to himself.

Ben woke up in the morning feeling foggy and defeated. This was not the way you started a job search off. Luckily with his 401k, he would be just fine. He made a phone call to his financial advisor, his brother, and let Joe know the situation.

"Hey Joe, it's Ben."

"How you doing with that beautiful wife of yours, Scary Spice?"

"Look, you know if she hears you, she is going to bust your chops!"

"She still bushy-headed?" Joe replied.

"Joe, the reason I called is to tell you I got fired from my job. I need to get the money out of my 401k immediately. How soon can you cut me a check?"

"Sorry about your job," Joe sniffed. "I'll have a check cut for you sometimes tomorrow. Want a check out of your stock options from the company?"

"Not just yet. Let me know how much I have to work with. I'll see you Friday after temple."

"Okay, Ben. I have another call. See you." Joe hung up with a click.

Ben thought the only good thing about the day so far was Bridgette was all ready to feed the homeless, so he wouldn't have to play the fifty-question game. Ben decided to stay in. He felt he deserved at least one day.

Morning turned to evening quickly. Joe called to discuss Ben's financial status.

"Hey Ben, you sick or still asleep? Hey, need to talk to you. I have spent the morning checking into your finances and your 401k. It's shot. It took a huge hit about six weeks ago. You didn't get a monthly report about this? Ben, do you hear me, do understand me? Ben? Ben?"

Ben sat up in bed so that he could hear Joe better. "Joe I'm here. What do you mean a hit? A hit to my 401k? I got a summary about three months ago or so."

"Well, Ben you took a big hit. You went from 500,000 to 40,000. They should have sent you an alert, so you could change your stock options before it was too late. I also checked your stock with the company, and it is gone."

"I'm going to talk to dad and see what is going on. This cannot be correct. I'll get some clarification." Click the phone went dead. Ben heard what Joe said clearly. He was broke!

Ben was stunned. His investments had plummeted from half a million dollars to 40 thousand. He was even more amazed that he worked for the stock exchange and hadn't seen it coming. He did not relish the thought of telling Bridgette. He laid back down and drifted off to sleep to wake up some time later to the sound of the shower.

Ben didn't exactly know what she did in there, but he appreciated every aspect. When she came out, the world would be different. That was her haven. Ben hated to have to shatter her world or her trust in him, but she had to be told. She was going to come out smelling like heaven only to be tarnished by the news that he had to deliver. There was an ache in Ben's heart for the disappointment he was going to have to give her. He decided he'd wait a bit. Ben would go to his parents before she exited the shower and find out if there was any hope. Ben knew Bridgette had another thirty minutes in there, enough time for him to sneak out before she emerged. He didn't want to tell her until he knew what his recourse was. With that, Ben was on his way to his parents to see if he could salvage his life and marriage.

"Come on in son, have a seat. Can I take your coat? Your father and grandfather are in the study, they've been in there for hours!"

Ben kissed his mother, Anne Zigburgh, on the check, thinking to himself how good she looked. You could barely tell she had Multiple Sclerosis. Today, she was showing very few symptoms.

"Mom, you look very pretty today."

"Ben, I have my good days, and I have my bad days, but this one is good so far. Go on in and see what's going on with your father and grandfather."

Anne turned to walk away, and Ben could see that her leg dragged a little more than he remembered. The symptoms were increasing, but he liked the fact that she kept her promise–she would fight it with everything she had. Ben ran behind his mom and hugged her.

"Ben, it's okay. I'm still here. God has been gracious unto me, and for that I am grateful!"

Ben held his mother for a few seconds more. She patted his hand, and he let her go. Regaining his composure, Ben heard his mother say, "Your great Uncle David is in there. He still looks good." With that, his mom walked away.

Ben knew if his Uncle David was in there something was terribly wrong. Ben could count the times he had seen his uncle in his life on two hands. Ben tried to remember the last time he saw his him. "Oh! My wedding," Ben mumbled to himself. It was good to see him. His mom was right–he did look good. He hoped he'd inherited those genes. David never looked or acted his age. Hard to believe he was Ben's grandfather's brother. They were so different.

Nothing could have prepared Ben to find out how bad things were.

"Hey Ben, Joe with you?" his father Adam, asked.

"No, he said he was coming by," Ben said looking around the room. Adam Zigburgh was the only one standing, so Ben knew he was trying to make a point. Heimlich and David Zigburgh were looking perplexed at a pile of folders and papers on the table in front of them. They greeted him and continued to look over the stacks of paperwork.

Adam had been raised at the firm. The firm was in his blood. Ben remembered how hurt his father was when he hadn't joined the firm after graduation. Maybe if he had joined the firm whatever mess this was, could have been prevented. Who was he fooling? He hadn't even noticed his 401k going awry. Ben remembered the stories that his grandfather's secretary told him about his father growing up in her office. She was more of a glorified nanny than a secretary. Seriously, his grandfather made her keep him a couple of hours a week, so his father would get used to coming to the office on and regular basis. This is where Ben's work ethic had come from. He tried to explain to Bridgette that it was in his blood. His Grandfather's pride in the company borderlined on worship.

"Sit down Ben. I have some disturbing news for you. Your grandfather has lost the family fortune."

"The family fortune? Last time I checked, my name was on the company door," his grandfather said with a huff. Ben could tell his grandfather was about to lose his temper with his father. "I did not lose the family fortune!" Heimlich barked back.

His great Uncle David held his hand to his head making the gesture that his grandfather had lost his mind. Ben wanted to laugh, but he knew better–that would only make the situation worse.

"He doesn't know where he misplaced five hundred million dollars," Adam barked back.

Five hundred million dollars! Ben thought.

Adam, growing exasperated with his father and uncle turned to Ben. "Have you ever heard of a Bernie Madoff?"

"The guy from the papers?" Ben's heart slowly sank.

"Your grandfather and Bernie have been fast pals for the past twenty some odd years," his Uncle David said with chagrin.

"Yeah, that's him, your grandfather's good ole Bernie," Adam confirmed. Ben could hear the disgust in his father's voice. "About twenty years ago, your grandfather thought it was a good idea to invest five hundred million dollars with him, and now it's nowhere to be found. Gone, disappeared without a trace!"

Ben could tell his father was grinding his teeth. This meant his father was not just mad but pissed off. Ben had only seen his father like that a couple of times in his life, and he didn't like it. Ben turned to his grandfather who only slightly shook his head.

"They're investigating him for fraud!" his great Uncle David said, still making the universal sign of crazy with his hand and pointing at his grandfather when he wasn't looking. Ben slowly dropped in a chair and started silently pouring through the papers himself.

"The company assets are in that pile. Let's hope your grandfather hid some money in an offshore account in the Cayman Islands or Switzerland somewhere," Adam said bitterly.

"It's not looking good at all," his Uncle David muttered.

Ben could feel the knot in the pit of his stomach starting to tighten. He had no idea his grandfather knew Bernie Madoff. Ben could hear his grandfather's favorite line: "Every other penny you earn if invested the right way, you can retire a rich and happy man." Ben sure hoped his grandfather had not invested every other penny. Surely, he didn't believe in that. He shot his father a look and could tell by the look on his face the same quote was ringing in his soul.

It was well after two a.m. before anyone spoke a word or looked up from their stacks of papers. David was the first to speak.

"It's all gone! All of it! Gone!"

Ben's father sat back in his chair and let out a ragged sigh. "Only thing I have found left are the deeds on mine and David's homes. The only two things that were not signed over to Madoff!"

Adam turned to his father Heimlich. "Dad, what were you thinking? I knew after mom died you were thinking about investing some things. I never questioned your decisions because the books were always accurate. The company stocks were always up and flowing. I always assumed we were in good shape. Now, I'm finding out that everything is gone." By now Ben was holding his stomach.

"What about the retirement fund? The homes in Florida?"

"All gone!" David said throwing his stack of papers on the table.

It was so quiet in the room you could hear the hum of the computers. There was a low whimper coming from Heimlich that progressively grew louder. David put his hand on his brother's knee to calm him. Heimlich slowly collected himself and stood to go.

"Heimlich, it's so late, you can stay with me tonight instead of going back to the vineyard."

David helped Heimlich to the elevator and said good night. Ben stayed behind as his father walked them to the door. The men hugged one another and left. Ben noticed how tired his father looked and it was not from the all-nighter. The years of his mother's condition had taken a toll on him. Ben respected that his father stayed with his mother and barely let anyone else take care of her. He admired that and knew he would do the same for Bridgette if the tables were turned.

"Dad, can we really be broke? What about the company? I was running some numbers a couple of months ago, and we were more than okay." Adam dropped his head into his hands.

"We look good on paper and paper only. After the federal government completes the audit on Madoff, we'll know exactly where we stand. From where I sit, it is a complete and utter loss. Your mom wanted us to sell this place and downsize. It looks like her dream will be coming true. I have to break the news to your sister, April. I promised to buy her a brownstone in Manhattan. That's certainly not going to happen now. Son, go home and get some sleep, everything will look better in the morning."

Ben laughed to himself thinking it was already morning. He hugged his father and let himself out. Walking out into the cold, New York air and for the first time, Ben felt like a regular guy. Nothing special, no family legacy, no family history to mold him. Now he was his own man. Ben's brother remained to be told, he would enjoy that as his brother was very spoiled. The one he was concerned about was his sister April. How was she going to cope? *"Poor, kid,"* Ben said out loud while trying to hail a cab.

Another Miracle

Hurricane Elliott hit the Galveston coast of Texas at 4 pm. Tuesday, Sept. 12th as a category five that surpassed Hurricane Katrina's maximum sustained winds of 175 mph winds with 100m.p.h winds. The flood storm surge reached 16ft. The whole town was devastated. Beachfront erosion was up to a mile and a half inland. Home after home were washed from their foundations. Most of the residents were able to evacuate the town before the hurricane hit, and while this saved countless lives, property was not spared.

Property was a total devastation block after block; gone; destroyed; town after town. First responders were on the scene. Lives had been lost among the first responders. The first responders carried on and did the job they were hired to do despite losing their friends.

No RED CROSS or FEMA would be on the scene to help with the devastation. FEMA had been disbanded because of nonexistent government funding and the RED CROSS no longer existed because the American public had lost faith in the organization. The White House made calls to the governor of the state of Texas to tell him that there would be no disaster relief funds available then or in the future.

Galveston had a population of a little less than 50,000 people. All were affected by the storm. There were no storm shelters set-up, there were no refugees stuck in hotels because there were no hotels. No homes where friends could stay with family–the people had nothing. Galveston was gone.

The State of Texas prided itself on the bootstrap population. They believed that if you fell from your horse, you got up, brushed the dirt off, and climbed right back into the saddle. It was no different after the hurricane. What the state and federal governments could not provide, the mega-churches did.

The church had food trucks on the ground serving people three hot meals a day and two snacks. In fact, the church had more food trucks then they had people to drive them. They didn't even have enough people to serve the food. Jobs were being created; truck drivers and food service workers. Within hours of the hurricane, employment was taking place. Forty-eight people were hired on the spot in the rain.

The people were fed, then came the task of shelter and clothing. Eighteen-wheelers rolled into the city filled with every kind of personal hygiene products needed to help the people recover. Portable toilets were available, and even laundry was available; any item needed for the long haul. Two more mega-churches bought out the clothing departments from two different Wal-Marts, providing people with clothes. Medication and prescriptions were bused in from nearby towns and pharmacies. All medicines and medical supplies were paid for by church donations and funding. Tents and supplies were provided for by another church, grief counseling and burial were taken on by yet another church.

The church stood up and assumed the position she was created for. The church had come into the full knowledge of becoming 'fishers of men' and to take care of the homeless, widows and orphans. Again, the church with Homes of Humanity was building and renewing old run down, dilapidated government projects that were boarded up because of lack of funding. Luckily the funding now went to section eight housing. Freddie Mac and Fannie Mae were never able to make a complete recovery after the 2009 housing collapse. Hiring had now begun again for the plumbers, electricians, carpenters and general contractors. Tile fitters, carpet layers general laborers to fix up housing and start new home construction. All this led to jobs and more jobs. The economy was self-adjusting without any help from the government because there was none.

Chapter 4

The Bank of the Alps or its commercial name, Swiss Bank and Trust, was where the fortunes stolen from the Holocaust victims had been kept. The thirty million stolen from the Jewish people during the Holocaust had sat in this Bank for over seventy years. The bank had been sold several times, changing management more than a few times. The money had been used to fund wars in foreign countries, payoffs, and bribes for warlords, and different traitors. The interest had increased the fortune to 300 trillion. The United Nations decided that the money had to be returned to the victims of the Holocaust or their direct descendants. Those claiming to be descendants would have their DNA tested to verify their right to receive the money–50,000 per descendant.

A board of trustees ran the Bank of the Alps. There were five members on the board consisting of Nathan Gardner, Sylvia Stolz, Conrad Brisbane, Eirich Rawlins, and Etienne Morris. Eirich Rawlins was the chairman of the board. The good and gracious people of the country acknowledged the money had been sitting in the bank all those years after the war. Foreign governments had use of the funds to improve their governments and country. The governments of some of the countries that used the money collapsed. War loads that used the money had been assassinated. Most felt the money was cursed.

For this reason, it was decided the money should be returned to the Jewish descendants. The United Nations had decided that if the money was not returned to the descendants, that fines and shutdowns would occur causing the collapse of the European Union. The return of the money was the E.U.'s most important agenda. United Nations had agreed to help the EU if the money was returned. The collapse of the Swiss Bank and Trust would cause a domino effect for the banks of Europe. Eirich Rawlins and the board of trustees had decided that the descendants had to come personally to Switzerland to prove their status. Citizenship in Switzerland, as well as free housing, would be gifted to the descendants if they chose to stay.

The five-member board knew the day would come that the money their ancestors stole from the Jewish people would have to be returned to the people. A long-standing law that was created to hold up the return of the money to the people was that the descendants had to be blood proven. At the time that law was passed, the only way of knowing who the victims of the

Holocaust were, was by the prisoner number tattoo on their wrist received in the concentration camps.

It wasn't until the 1960's that accurate genetic paternity became a possibility. It was called HLA typing and compared the genetic fingerprints on white blood cells between child and parent. While it had 80% accuracy, it could not distinguish how close the relative was. In the 80's the Yad Vashem American Holocaust Museum began to use the technology to reunite families torn apart by the Holocaust. This started in 2005 as the DNA Shoah Project, the brainchild of Syd Mandelbaum, an American scientist and philanthropist with technology developed by world renown genealogist, Dr. Michael Hammer, at the University of Arizona.[1]

It was no longer word of mouth or speculation. The victims had names, faces, dates, and locations of where they lived and where they were last seen alive. The I's were dotted, and the T's were crossed. The Nazi's had no idea that they would lose the war and thought the money would be in the Bank of the Alps for their use after the war. With the gas chambers and mass graves, they knew no one would be alive to claim the money. Seventy years after the war, who would remember the millions tortured and killed? Who would remember their names? Many did live to tell the horror stories, and museums like the Yad Vashem would ensure that no one forgot. Hail to the heroes who lived to tell the tale. The names and the faces of the people who swore never to forget the hellish nightmare they lived through.

There was DNA to prove Jewish ancestry, so the people could claim their birthright. The Swiss Bank and Trust had funded many different organizations chosen by the board and their philanthropic interests. All of that would now come to an end.

Nathan Gardner had a soft spot for race cars and sponsored several races. He financed the invention of new race cars. He even participated in the races himself. Conrad Brisbane supported several charitable foundations whose mission it was to find cures for disease. Brisbane was a known hypochondriac and always swore he was dying of something. Sylvia Stolz tried to

---

[1] http://www.museumoffamilyhistory.com/erc-dna-shoah-project.htm

help the world. She believed in investing in green projects and anything involving animals. She had donated to Green Peace, PETA, and windmill companies to help preserve the earth. Etienne Merris was a homosexual who supported the LGBTQ community and gay rights.

Eirich Rawlin also supported any foundation supporting gay rights. Conversely, he believed in his Aryan heritage and was a well-known supporter of the Aryan Nation. He was the number one supporter for the Brotherhood of the Valkyrie, giving them hundreds of thousands of dollars for military equipment and uniforms. He also funded many of DHS' projects. The government barely invested in different agencies because most of the earned revenues went to pay China. There was a large deposit made to China's account by the U.S. every three months until the debt was paid off.

News Flash

The World Health Organization announced today that there were 30 more deaths from the Ebola virus over the weekend. Concerns are growing as the last major outbreak of the virus was in 2018 in the Congo. This strain does not respond to treatment and may be a mutation. Officials are investigating the outbreak in Saudi, Arabia. Cases have also been reported in Iran.

Chapter 5

The world renown Crazy Horse Cancer Research Institute in the Black Hills of South Dakota was hosting Abraham Reuben, a Jewish research doctor from Bethel, Israel. Dr. Reuben would be doing his research in the U.S. Crazy Horse Hospital, famous for its work in the dreaded area of cancer. The facilities were first class, second to none in the world.

The hospital purchased large quantities of medicinal marijuana from wholesale supplier, Lee Brown Enterprises. Lee Brown Enterprises was owned and operated by Ira James Brown and Shea Lee Brown of South Carolina. In truth, the hospital was 80% of Lee Brown Enterprises revenues.

The medicinal property of the marijuana helped stimulate the appetite while easing the pain of the chemotherapy. The quantity of weed purchased by the hospital was too much to send through the mail, so Ira hired his good friends to make the delivery across-country to Crazy Horse Hospital.

Jeff McAlister was head of logistics for Lee Brown Enterprises. He was a longtime friend and confidant of Ira's. In the days when Ira was a drug dealer before marijuana was legal, Jeff and Ira were in the game. It didn't hurt anything that Jeff was an ex-mercenary in Haiti. He met Ira in Miami, after coming back stateside. Ira and Jeff ran weed from Miami to New York about four times a year. They grew close because they had to watch each other's back. They both saved each other's lives a time a two. It was Jeff that introduced Shea to Ira, resulting in a marriage and a lucrative business.

Shea was in nursing school, and Jeff was her weed connection. Jeff always thought she was a little quirky. He never knew an Asian who smoked that much weed. Jeff assumed that to be that smart you had to have some vices, or you would crack under pressure. Shea called one day for her unique brand, and

Jeff wasn't able to make it, so he sent Ira. Ira and Shea had been together ever since, and that was seven years ago.

Ira and Jeff still had their go-to guys when they needed help on special on projects. Milton Crump, Jordan Baker, and Coyote. Coyote didn't have a last name, and he always had to be paid in cash. Nobody knew where Coyote lived. If you needed him all one had to do was light a campfire in a particular area of the Dakota Hills and use the weed that smelled like Doritos. Coyote would show up about thirty minutes later.

Jordan Baker and Milton Crump were both residents of New York. It was a battle between the four guys when Ira and Jeff decided to leave Miami and settle in New York. After marijuana was legalized, Jordan and Milton lost their customer base, and the bottom fell out of the game. Ira knew how to grow and combine different flavors and blends and also because Shea had been a chemistry major before she went into nursing. They combined their knowledge and came up with a strain of medical marijuana that helped a lot of cancer patients. This kept Ira and Jeff in the game. The only difference was no more dark alleys– the business became almost respectable.

They made so much money that they had to hire good reliable help. That's where Jordan and Milton came into the picture. They already knew the weed game. Coyote knew Jeff from his mercenary days. Jeff knew that Coyote had his own side hustle going. He wasn't sure what it was but, he trusted him to watch his back. The business was secure, and since it was all legal, everybody made money at the now legitimate business.

"Hey Milt, you know any of these cute little papoose nurses?" Jordan asked stuffing his mouth with burritos.

"Man, you a child molester?" Milton asked him seriously.

"Hell no man. I hate a Chester-the-molester. What the hell you ask me something like that anyway?" Jordan gagged back a mouth full of food.

"Papoose means baby, you dumb ass!" Coyote said in his quiet, deep voice

Milton cracked up while driving the semi along a highway outside of El Paso, Texas. "We'll be in the Black Hills before nightfall." Jordan offered Coyote a burrito.

"I don't eat beef, not since mad cow disease and I don't trust the FDA," Coyote answered, shaking his head no.

"Man, whatever," Jordan said taking another bite. "Whatever is wrong with you, Ira can grow an herb that will heal you."

"Unless he has an herb that can cure botulism, your ass is gonna die. I have told you time and time again about eating off unknown food trucks on the side of the road. You're gonna learn the hard way," Coyote said without moving.

"That's why I carry an extra pair of drawers with me where ever I go!" Jordan hollered over his right shoulder, stuffing the last little bit down his throat.

Coyote turned and looked at him, "It's not the black draught that gets you, it's the dehydration and the toxins and fever that fry your brain! You'll have to try a sweat lodge to get the toxins out of your body. Your body is probably crawling with worms the size of snakes from the junk you put in it. Junk in, snake out!"

"Have you ever done a sweat lodge?" Jordan asked loosening the belt on his pants and belching.

"I do one every year to get direction and clear my conscience," Coyote replied, pushing his cowboy hat down over his eyes.

"What do you need to clear your conscience from?" Jordan asked curiously. Coyote was already snoring.

"Damn Milt, he goes to sleep fast!"

"Clear conscience and apparently clear bowels! You better get some sleep, you got first drive back out of the Black Hills," Milton replied turning on the radio.

Reaching Crazy Horse Hospital around 11:00 pm meant that Milton had done a little speeding along the way. He knew the other men didn't mind. He pulled into the parking lot of the delivery side of the hospital. You could feel the was electricity in the air.

"Your chariot has arrived, kind sir!" Milton bellowed in a tired voice.

"And, not a moment too soon!" Jordan said making a mad dash for the public restrooms.

"Hey Jordan, wake Coyote up."

"I've been up the last fifty miles," grumbled Coyote, hat still pulled down over his face.

Jordan came back to the truck doing a weird dance. "Hey, they locked their restroom! I have got to go!" Coyote made a hissing snake sound and reached for the keys to unlock the trailer so that the hospital staff could unload the truck.

"Hey, I'm going inside to use the restroom," Jordan said still doing the little dance."

"You do that Jordan before you have to use that extra pair of drawers!" Coyote yelled from the back of the truck. "I'm sure Milton don't want to be laid up in a ditch somewhere."

"Coyote, next Tuesday, same bat time, same bat channel," Milton said with a sheepish grin.

"Looks like Jordan may be needing those extra drawers you were talking about. Better you riding back with him than me." Coyote tipped his hat pulled, his jacket collar up around his neck and walked into the darkness of the night."

The fat face security guard came out on the dock door blowing cigar smoke and chewing gum. Milton thought to himself the gum must have been the nastiest tasting gum on the planet.

"You early tonight. You must have had good weather all the way from Texas!" the guard said still puffing on the cigar and chewing the gum.

"Yeah, pretty good weather. Had a few high winds coming through Oklahoma but they settled down," Milton answered.

"Where's your other friend?" the security guard asked taking the cigar out of his mouth to spit a brown blob of spit on the ground, passing Milton the clipboard to sign.

"Inside flirting with Nurse Wishingwell I'm sure," Milton said belching trying to keep from gagging on the smell of the cigar.

"He's wishing at the wrong well, get it?" winked the fat security guard heading to the same door he'd just come out of.

Milton didn't reply or slow his pace to consider or answer, he knew the type. Fat boy liked Wishingwell, and old haters were the worst. Stepping inside the hospital, the bright lights and the sick smell greeted Milton, at the door. He was never one for hospitals. He tried to never go inside one as a visitor and definitely not a patient. Under the circumstances, his bladder was tapping his insides. It was as good a place as any to get a free cup of coffee.

He could see Jordan blushing a mile away which made him look younger than his thirties. He hoped he would get enough courage up to ask Wishingwell out on a date. After two years and twenty-four trips, he hadn't seemed to be able to get around to it. Milton thought how odd it was now. Back in the day when he and Jordan were selling weed by the pound, Jordan barely showed up with less than two women on his arms. Now he couldn't get up enough nerve to ask Wishingwell out for a cup of coffee.

After exiting the restroom, Milton gave Wishingwell a nod and winked at Jordan as he exited the building. Wishingwell was full-blooded Sioux Indian. Her father was some big shot with the tribal elders. Maybe that was what kept Jordan at bay. Whatever it was, Jordan got schoolboy polite around her. It was almost endearing. Milton liked the effect Wishingwell had on Jordan, it slowed his pace and calmed him down.

Milton entered the passenger side of the truck and took a snooze. It would be another forty-five minutes before the truck was unloaded and he deserved this sleep.

Coyote liked to walk in the woods at night. It gave him time to think and reenergize after the long drives in the truck. He thought about things he was grateful for–mostly Springlily and the boys. It was a long way from his life twelve years ago. Yet his heart was burdened for his people. His people had come a long way from the scattered, rag-tag tribes of yesterday. They were a proud people and had remained strong because of their pride. Still, they were on the verge of proving themselves to their nation and not just the nation, but the world. Their heritage had afforded luxuries very few people were able to claim. They kept their heritage strong at a great price. They suffered, endured and died to preserve their heritage. Now they had to reveal the secrets that their forefathers had hidden from the beginning of time. Their great forefathers and the Great Spirit knew that if the white man had known or had an inkling, no tribe or red man would exist today. He was grateful for the wisdom of the Great Spirit and the prudence and patience his forefathers had shown in trying times.

Coyote noticed the strong winds blowing that night and the full moon lit a path to his door. He could see that the boys had left their bikes out on the lawn again. Smalleaf was the oldest; his government name was Parker. The youngest, Wandering Bush, always made Coyote smile. Good name for him and he lived up to it. He couldn't be still even in his sleep. His government name was Juan, after Coyote's friend Juan Rodriguez. A very dear and honorable man. Coyote would always be indebted to him. Coyote hurried into the house knowing Springlily didn't sleep until he was home lying by her side. Coyote's last thought before closing his eyes that night was how would the nation, better yet the world, react to the tribal elders' announcement that six of the largest Indian Reservations had the largest untapped oil fields in the world. Coyote was too tired even to contemplate the astounding pride of his people and the shock and horror that would flow through the white men's veins.

Chapter 6

It had been six years since the Jackoff scandal. The Zigburghs had lost everything. The accounting firm had been sold for taxes. The grandkids, Benjamin, Joseph, and April no longer had trust funds. Benjamin was let go from his job at the stock market six years ago, and he had been moving from job to job. His brother Joseph had moved in with Ben and Bridgette after the sale of the accounting firm. April dropped out of college because her parents could no longer afford it. The fact that you work twelve months and three months of your annual salary goes toward taxes didn't help the Zigburghs financial situation. Truth was, America was having trouble adjusting to the new taxes and the financial predicament China had it in. The mess America had created.

"Hey, you up? You told me to wake you at 7:00 am," Bridgette said as she ran to the bathroom. She wanted to beat Joseph. Bridgette had never known a man who hogged the bathroom quite like he did she thought as she turned on the shower. She was grateful to have yoga classes all day so she could avoid Ben. It seemed he'd given up on the job search altogether. All he wanted to do was manage the pizza parlor, drink beer and play video games.

"Yeah I'm up," Ben barked back at Bridgette, even though he was still lying in bed. He knew she was not coming back to the bedroom–anything to avoid sex or the conversation of having a baby. She continued saying it was not the right time.

Bridgette enjoyed her yoga classes. It took the edge off her stress and eased tension in her body. As she headed to class, she thought about how she'd have to ask her younger sister, Keisha, for a loan again. It wasn't the money–she knew Keisha had it. It was that she was embarrassed. She was supposed to be the older sister with everything together. She had it together before Ben had lost his job. Yet, the pizza parlor was a job, but they had bills to pay from before he'd lost his job and they weren't making enough money. Now all Ben wanted to talk about was having a baby. He didn't even know they were three months behind on the mortgage and couldn't go to Joe again. He'd paid the last six months, barely getting them caught up. She hoped the subway wasn't going to be crowded; it was too hot. Bridgette stepped onto the platform and could see that the trains were almost at full capacity at 7:00 in the morning. She wondered where New Yorkers went before 9 o'clock.

After Bridgette had left the house, Ben talked to Joe.

"Joe you up?"

"Yeah, I'm up and have already been out for a run, something you need to try and do."

"Mail in?" Joe asked slurping down coffee.

"It's wherever Bridgette left it," Ben grumbled. "Bills, bills and more bills! We keep mail from the Swiss Bank and Trust. Do we have an account there that grandfather forgot to tell us about?"

"No, and if we did..." both brothers finished in unison, "Ernie Jackoff with it."

"Ben you know it's kind of sick that we can laugh at the fact that this man stole over 15 million dollars in cash and assets from our family."

"He just stole cash, not family," Ben stated turning the bills over in his lap. I think April took it the hardest. She was the little princess of the family." Ben winced at the pain in his stomach. It was flaring up again.

"April just started a new job, but she's thinking about going back to college and get her degree," Joe, replied pointing at Ben's stomach. "You need to get that checked out, that could be an ulcer."

"Nah! I think Bridgette elbowed me in her sleep. I asked her about having a baby before she went to sleep, and she elbowed me out of retaliation."

"Man, it would be nice to have a niece or nephew walking around here," Joe replied rubbing his hands together.

"Bridgette said there is no room to raise a kid here especially with you moving in the second bedroom.

"I'm sorry man."

"Joe, please stop apologizing, you're helping us out. You know we couldn't afford to pay the rent if you hadn't moved in here with us. Man, you're family!" Ben said hitting Joe on the top of his head.

"Well the least I can do is inquire about this Swiss Bank of the Alps. We might be rich bitch!" Joe said throwing his hands in the air. Ben threw a shoe at him on his way out the door to the pizza parlor.

✡ ✡ ✡

April sat on the side of the bed crying hysterically. This was her third attempt at prostituting. Her first two encounters hadn't been so bad. They were young men, and the alcohol and drugs helped a lot. This older man didn't want anything to do with alcohol or drugs. He felt that it interfered with his Viagra medication. His body was old and wrinkly and soft. No muscle tone whatsoever and his breath smelled like coffee and poo. April gagged at the thought of the smell and the sight. He even had the nerve to take the Viagra and then wanted to do it five times. The third time, April felt herself getting queasy, and the fifth time she completely lost it. The old dude left and wanted his money back. April gave him the money and told him to leave.

April stopped crying long enough to try and figure out how she got here. How had her life fallen so far down in the gutter? Yes, her family had lost millions to Bernie Madoff and her trust fund was gone with the money for her college education. She had gotten part-time jobs working for some of her father's associates, but it was never quite enough to pay the bills. She tried to keep the lifestyle she had grown accustomed to, but it was too hard. She couldn't ask her parents for help with her mother's M.S. getting worse. The doctor bills and the rehabilitation therapy were eating her parents alive. Then the company "Flower Petals" she was working for wanted her to sign a yearly contract. This meant she would be stuck in a contract for a year of prostitution working in an apartment or dorm type atmosphere. April thought it was just too much to think about. She ran from the bedroom to the bathroom to throw-up. It took too much of a toll on her psyche. April slowly took out the cleaning supplies and spied a razor. She dragged the blade slowly across her wrist leaning on the bathroom door. April slowly passed out.

✡✡✡

"Hey sis what's going on with you and Benny?" Keisha asked Bridgette.

"Nothing girl, same ole, same ole. Mommy and daddy said hello," said both girls at the same time. "Daddy said Hey, chocolate chips!!" giggling like when they were girls. "Girl, I miss you so much," they said simultaneously and burst into laughter again.

"Seriously, how is Coral Springs or Sneaky Town as you said in your phone calls?" Shea asked.

"Just like I said, slow but fast enough not to be boring," Keisha replied taking some of Shea's frozen sesame chicken out of the freezer. "When are you coming down for a visit?"

"Sorry girl can't afford it, and that's the reason I called, I wanted to know if I could borrow some money? And no, Ben doesn't know I'm borrowing this money neither does he know about the last money borrowed," Bridgette said all in one breath.

"Yeah, Bridge, not a problem. I know things are pretty tight since the market crashed and the Madoff situation."

"I was thinking about the princess, April. Is she okay, after her suicide attempt?" Keisha asked popping her bowl in the microwave.

"Girl hush, nobody in the family wants to believe she tried suicide. They call it her accidental overdose." Bridgette cringed at the thought of having the discussion with Ben again.

"How in hell does anybody think dragging a razor across your wrist is an accident, Bridgette? I mean seriously!"

"Look, Keisha, April is the baby, and you know Joe and Ben are overprotective of her. Some things they are not willing to admit. I did see her a couple of weeks ago, and she looked happy. She is working, so that's a plus. I wish I could say the same about her brother."

"Who, Ben?" Keisha asked with a mouthful of food. "I thought he was managing the pizza parlor?"

"K. he does but even working 18hours days we're still not able to pay all or half the bills. I don't like asking Joe to do more than his share. That way he can save his money and try to get a place of his own. I love Joe. He helped us out a lot. If it weren't for him, we would already be on the street. When I married Ben, I didn't plan to be living with Joe for six years. And, all Ben keeps asking me is when are we going to have a baby? I keep asking him where are we going to put it?"

"Bridge, calm down. Do you know you're screaming right now?"

"I'm sorry. I'll calm down. I need a vacation, and I can't afford one! If I find the money to go on one, Ben will want to go with me."

"Dag Bridge, I'm sorry. It will get better! How much do you need? Is 10,000 okay?"

"K, I can't afford to pay 10,000 back!"

"Stop screaming and calm down–it's okay. I have my 401k so don't worry about paying me back. I'm good, and things down here are a whole lot cheaper than New York. You might want to think about moving here."

"Girl, you know Ben will never leave his beloved New York. K, I'm sorry. I'm just tired. I'm thinking about moving with mom and dad."

"That bad?" Keisha asked swallowing a piece of sesame chicken. "Well, know that I love you and I'll wire the money to you today before I go to work. Love you."

"Love you to K. Thank you!"

Keisha hung up the phone with tears in her eyes. She could hear the pain in her sister's voice. Keisha knew Bridgette was sitting there twisting her hair in anguish. Keisha knew that Bridgette would make the right decision when the time came.

✡✡✡

Joe came out of his office and called Ben, so he would not be heard by his other co-workers. "Hey, I know you're still at work Ben, but I called the number on the brochure we received in the mail from the Swiss Bank of the Alps. They have a very interesting plan. I want to stop by after closing to discuss it and get your opinion. It's quite radical."

"Ok cool, Joe I'll see you soon."

Ben waited on Joe to arrive at the pizza parlor. He knew something had to be interesting because Joe never liked talking about business around Bridgette. Joe knew that Bridgette might stop by but was willing to take that chance. Ben knew that Bridgette had a better head for business than he did even though she hadn't attended college. She had passed college up to dance on Broadway. She was still freaky smart with woman's intuition and all. Joe always thought that if you didn't go to college, you could not understand business. He was a snob that way. Joe arrived with the look of a cat that had just cornered a rat.

"I made a call to the Swiss Bank of the Alps, and this bank has a lot of old money," Joe said removing his jacket.

"What do you mean by old money?" Ben asked taking the money out of the cash register.

"I mean the money that the Nazis stole from the Holocaust victims," Joe said sitting down. "The money that has been sitting in Switzerland all this time." Joe cleared his throat and put on his best nasally voice and the face to match. Ben knew he used this voice and face when he was preparing to talk about a large sum of money.

"So, what does this have to do with us? I know grandfather and Uncle David left Europe before any of the bad stuff happened, but the Nazis killed their entire family."

"This has a lot to do with us. They have hundreds of billions of dollars that was stolen from the Jewish people and the bank has been ordered by the United Nations to give the money back to the descendants or any Holocaust survivors."

"How do they know who is left from the survivors and who their descendants are? I don't know Joe, sounds like a scam to me to get the rest of the Jewish descendants!"

"No, Ben this is the end-time wealth transfer that all the pastors and rabbis are talking about. You know, that the meek shall inherit the earth. It's our form of the reparations."

"Dude, Black people didn't get their reparations, what makes you think we will be getting ours?"

"Ben, we would be getting 50,000 dollars per member of our family with proven Jewish descent! That would be 100,000 for you, my boy. Remember that Bridgette's dad is Jewish and a Jewish professor. So, you get double the money. Don't act as though you don't need the money. This would help everyone in our family! You have to admit that we could use a break. If you don't, then think about April. She needs something to hope for. This may be her last chance to get it together. Ben, you know she needs it more than anybody else."

"Yeah, poor kid. I saw her the other day, and she's not looking good. Joe wait a minute, are you telling me if we can prove, that we are of Jewish descent we can get checks for 50,000 per member of our household? That means momma, daddy, grandfather, and Uncle David for sure. I don't know, sounds too easy to be legit," Ben said slamming the till shut. "Joe, there has to be a catch. Nothing comes that easy. Especially for the Jewish people. . .. hell, for anybody."

"Well Ben, I do know you have to take a DNA test to prove you are Jewish."

"They have a test to prove Jewish descent? Sounds kind of fishy to me," Ben said.

"Ben, you go to Switzerland to collect your money and take the test before you go."

"Why do we have to go all the way over there?"

"From what I understand, they're trying to drum up tourism while the descendants are in the country."

"Heck, the U.N. has already decided that the people will get the money, plus Switzerland is a neutral country and don't have the military to protect this much money, so they're concerned about being able to keep it safe," Joe explained.

"Joe, it can't be that easy. There has got to be a catch. Anyway, I thought Hitler used all that money to fund the war."

"He did use the money to fund the war, but some of it they couldn't get to. This is the money that sat in the banks all these years. The henchmen couldn't get the money unless they came out of hiding and revealed their true identities. Because of the Nuremberg Trials, they were not going to do that."

"All we have to do is prove our heritage, and we get 50,000 to spend any way we chose?"

"Now you're getting it, Ben. At last, the light has shone through. I know you have to go home and discuss it with Bridgette, but I'm going home to pack a bag and get ready to go."

"Just like that Joe, you're ready to leave America?"

"They didn't say I couldn't come back," Joe said putting on his jacket. "Look, I'll investigate this a little more, but it sounds legit. I'm going home to practice yodeling!"

"Dude, you're crazy, yodeling serious?"

"Ben come and let me out," Joe said hollering at the top of his lungs.

"Come on man, that's not yodeling."

"I said I needed to practice. I'll see you at the house later."

As Ben closed the store, all he could do was think about what he and Bridgette could do with 100,000 dollars. They could pay off all their debt and start over fresh in another country–a clean slate. Ben knew Bridgette would be hard to convince. She was no-nonsense when it came to finances. She would have to be convinced it was in the best interest of the family and not just his, but hers too. This was a win-win situation for everybody, and they needed a good break. Not needed, but they deserved this break, better yet, earned this break; it was their blood right.

The next morning Joe called Ben at work early before he even started to prep.

"Did you talk to Bridgette last night?"

"No. When I got in last night, she was asleep. I didn't want to wake her without all the facts. You know this is going to be a hard sell to Bridgette, so I need to make sure I know every detail. What else have you learned?"

"Ben, I'm outside talking to you because I can't contain myself on the inside. I found out more information. Check this out. You can take a cruise ship over to Switzerland free of charge. Entire family cruises for free, for eight days. You pick up your checks, and then you get to decide if you would like to stay in the country where they will provide brand new, free housing for entire families up to 5 bedrooms and 4 baths. You get to pick out what floor plan works best for your family. Did you hear me, Ben? Free brand-new housing. I wouldn't have to live with you

49

and Bridgette!!" Joe said screaming. "Don't get me wrong, I love you and Bridgette but a place of my own? That alone would make me leave the country. Oh, you get passports without problems or interference! Ben, I'm already gone."

"Joe, I was thinking last night that most of the Holocaust victims died and most of their closest relatives are dead. DNA is probably the best way to identify the remaining descendants. We're talking about 6 million people who lost their lives, and this is their money. This is blood money, so it is sacred, and we must if we chose to take it, and pay reverence to it."

"We got to what?" Joe asked.

"It means that whatever we do with it must respect or pay homage to the people who lost their lives to give us this opportunity. It means that we can't just blow this money. We must use it with caution and respect and remember that a good man leaves an inheritance for his children's children."

"That's so deep Ben. Where did you hear that?"

"It's in the Bible somewhere. Just promise Joe, no foolishness."

"I promise Ben! So, when are you going to talk to Bridgette?"

"As soon as you bring some brochures home. I'm going to need all the help I can get!

✡✡✡

Zachary and Romero McEvans boarded a plane to Switzerland. It took two months to get a passport. Once they landed in Switzerland, they met with Eirich Rawlins. Rawlins was a staunch supporter of the Brotherhood and the primary financier of the organization.

"I can't wait to meet with Eirich Rawlins. He says he has good news for the Brotherhood. New ideas that would increase the membership and he has personal news for both of us," Romero whispered to Zachary.

"I hope he can visit the U.S. and give us concrete ideas on how he would like to see the Brotherhood improve and present us with another big fat check," Zachary whispered back. "I'm looking forward to his military expertise. He is a graduate of McIvory Military School in Germany, an astute military academy. McIvory educated some of the top SS officers in Hitler's military," squealed Zachary. "All I know is that this trip is going to be a new look for the Brotherhood and it's about damn time that it gets some recognition from the military exercises we do to help protect this country. We're out there at all times of night, all kinds of weather, doing drills and preparing our soldiers for war. We're watching the backs of Homeland Security. They need all the help they can get. It's our right as American citizens to help defend our country from terrorist and non-American immigrants that plan to cause trouble!"

"Ladies and gentlemen, please fasten your seatbelts and put your seats in the upright position and prepare for landing," came the voice over the intercom.

"Almost home I can't wait," exclaimed Romero.

Romero and Zachary were met at the airport by Rawlins in a town and personal security. They drove immediately to Paradise Cove.

"Let me explain what we are doing here. Here we have a gated community with houses featuring six different floor plans," Rawlins began to explain as he got out of the car. "The homes are 4000 square feet and sit on half acre lots surrounded by golf courses, walking trails and well-stocked lakes. There are also award-winning schools and nearby shopping malls."

Romero and Zachary looked at each other.

"You mean all this for the Jews?" Zachary asked.

"Well yeah, that's what we want them to think. That all this was prepared with them in mind. All their basic needs and dreams met at one time," Rawlins explained.

"I don't understand!" exclaimed Zachary. "The Brotherhood is not an organization that holds Jewish people in high esteem. I thought you understood that when you wrote out a check to our organization."

"Oh, well yes. I truly understand where you stand on Jewish policy. I feel we see eye to eye on the subject," Rawlins proclaimed with a grin.

"Why are you and your bank going out of your way to pamper and protect these people?" Zachary asked sarcastically.

"Glad you asked that question. You see son, this neighborhood is just a prototype that my company is building to take care of the Jews. Under this neighborhood, there is a trash removal system where we take care of the community and keep it debris free. We have underground trash incinerators to burn the trash with a high-tech air filter, where you won't smell any gases or burning of the trash," Rawlins said rubbing his hands together.

"Okay, I'm all about keeping the environment clean, but that's a little much," Romero said.

"No, my dear friend, the trash is the Jews!! I have come up with a plan to rid the world of a problematic people and inferior race. Without them, the world would be a better place."

"Let me understand you correctly. You're going to move the Jews in this neighborhood and exterminate them with an underground incinerator, which in truth is a crematorium, that is smokeless and odorless?" asked Romero in amazement.

"That's exactly right! My boy, I knew you were intelligent," Rawlins said with pride.

"Even if this works, how would you get the people here?" Zachary asked quietly.

"Swiss Bank and Trust has offered every Jewish person an opportunity to receive 50,000 cash and free housing. Every Jewish member of the family receives 50,000 the only catch is, you have to come here to receive the checks. While you're here, you take a tour of the countryside, stay in our housing while you're here. Overnight, before the sun rises, you are gone; vanished into thin air. We send a prerecorded message to your family or friends back home letting them know that you have decided to stay and take refuge in the country," Rawlins explained with a grin.

"Let me get this straight again, bring the Jews here under false the pretense of financial gain and free housing, and when they're not looking, you hit them in the head and drag them to an underground crematorium? Are you serious? That will never work. How would you get an entire family over here and knock them off, family by family and no one become suspicious? That's insanity! It will never work!"

"Well first son, we're going to pick up entire families on our luxury cruise ships. I have at least 12 ships on standby. I want the families to feel that they're on holiday. They'll view the community like a time-share sale. They'll get to stay in the housing to get the feel of the housing, view the blueprints, and chose the home they want or, if not, stay the weekend and attend the grand ball on Saturday night and never re-enter society ever again," Rawlins stated plainly.

"How are you going to hide the missing hundreds of thousands or even millions of people?" Zachary laughed in horror.

"I have a well-paid army that is willing to do their job, so that they can get a share of the 300 trillion-dollar pie," Rawlins said hysterically. "I have voice impersonators. I have people to text. I can Photoshop whatever needs to be done to convince the outside world that the Jewish families are here and enjoying their new lives."

"What about people and live T.V. cameras?" asked Zachary.

"My good friends, that's what flash mobs are all about. Tell them to show up and act a scene, one text and they will come in and do the photo type housing, not a problem!

"What about the ashes?"

"The ashes will be dumped out to sea and will drift in the ocean current."

"What about this big ball you have planned for them?"

"The food is drugged, and the air is filled with an odorless gas to knock them out. Then they're disposed of." Rawlins challenged them to find any hole in his plan.

"What about your country's EPA laws?" Romero asked

"All covered. The squeaky wheel gets the grease," Rawlins said. "I have everything covered on my end. It's your end that I need help with."

Romero and Zachary looked at each other in silence. The twins stood outside in the evening air and tried to fathom the severity of the situation without giving their hand away and still listening to Rawlins. The twins slowly walked around the neighborhood leaving Rawlins in the car. They walked back to the car in silence to hear their involvement in the rest of the situation.

"Now, what I need from you is help stateside. I need you and your organization to step up your program. I need your people to get rid of the shepherds. If shepherds are gone, sheep will scatter and become easy pickings or as my Jewish friends would say, 'lambs to the slaughter'."

Romero and Zachary exchanged a look of amazement.

"We'll discuss more over dinner," Rawlins said opening the car door for them. "Oh, I've had my team watching you guys for a while, and I know about the happy hunting you guys did in West Virginia a couple of years ago. I have a videotape of the hunting. Poor unsuspecting little rabbits in the woods."

On the trip back to the hotel, Romero and Zachary hardly said a word to each other, but they noticed a high military presence all through the countryside. Romero and Zachary dressed for dinner without a word between them. They met Rawlins downstairs in the main ballroom. He introduced them to several people including the four other members of the bank's board of trustees. After a few drinks, Rawlins escorted the twins to an empty banquet hall where dinner was prepared. They sat in silence for a few short moments.

"With all due respect Mr. Rawlins, what is it you need from my brother and me? You seem to have everything covered and under control, so there is no need for us or our organization to get involved.

"You don't understand my friends. You are the finest point of my contribution to the master plan. You and your brother are special–the last of a dying breed."

The boys looked at each other.

"Your mother is Rebecca Winthorpe, a runaway meth addict. She ran away from home at the age of 17 and ended up marrying your father, Earl McEvans." The brothers nodded their head uneasily. "Your father is not Earl McEvans. Your father is Josef Mengele, the great SS officer, and doctor. The twins made eye contact again but remained silent. "Your mother was a chosen vessel to carry the royal seed. This poor unfortunate soul went to a rehab facility in upstate Pennsylvania where she got clean and sober. She was chosen because she had no family, a young woman alone in the world, given a second chance at life. The sperm of Josef Mengele artificially inseminated her, and as

54

expected, twins were conceived. You two boys are blood descendants of Josef Mengele!"

The two boys looked at each other with sick fascination and pride. This would sound so good at their next Brotherhood meeting. To claim real Nazi heritage would only make them stronger leaders! Zachary asked for proof.

"I need proof of our bloodline just to be sure, so we can represent the Brotherhood with all the respect it deserves."

"We can do DNA testing. We have samples of Josef Mengele's DNA and even a few of his descendants here in this country. He has twenty-seven offspring including you two. Artificial insemination has been carried on since the war. He did a lot of work in Brazil. You already met a lot of them at the ball earlier tonight." Rawlins stood up and bowed to the boys. "Welcome sweet princes, welcome home."

Chapter 7

Living in Milan, Italy was Alexandria's dream come true after she graduated from Syracuse University. Everyone thought she would join her father's CPA firm. Alex didn't want a safe job with Adam. She wanted to try something new, and her love of photography led her into a new life. Fashion photography was her road out of New York–it gave her an opportunity to travel and see the world. Alex traveled for years to different countries; Egypt, Russia, Belize, Africa and of course France.

Alex stayed busy. There were a couple of romances, but none turned into marriage. Alex felt her life was too busy for love, so a lot of guys moved on to more serious relationships. The few guys that tried always ended up cheating because of the long-distance relationships. Alex always had photo shoots in some exotic destination where she went and returned alone. Big checks but a lonely heart.

Alexandria always wanted kids, it just never happened for her, so she ended up spoiling her niece and nephews. Through the years $5,000 was not much to spend on each kid. Whatever whim their parents wouldn't support, Alex did. Alex's job was to call and ease their parent into the idea knowing all along she had already purchased whatever the child wanted. By the time April was born, Alex was an old pro at coning their parents. April was especially spoiled because she was the only girl. Alex understood because she was the only girl between two boys– Adam and Gabrielle.

Adam and Ann often quarreled about the gifts that Alex bought for the children. Thousand-dollar swimwear–nothing was too much for April as far as Alex was concerned. With the downturn of the economy, money became an issue for Alex. The economy in Italy was getting tight, and tourism had slowed down quite a bit because of terrorism. This hit the fashion industry pretty hard. Even though she was in Milan, the major seasonal fashion shows were cut way back.

After the financial scandal and trouble her father had gotten himself in with Ernie Jackoff, Alex had to use a lot of her savings to help keep her father afloat. When April called and needed help with her tuition for college, it broke Alex's heart that she wasn't able to help her only niece. She pretended that it didn't bother her that she had to adjust to not being able to afford college. Education was critical to April. She wanted her parents to be proud of her. She wanted to graduate and start a CPA firm of her own to replace the one her grandfather lost. April felt she was letting her family down by not being in a position to fully talk or care for herself. April didn't care what she had to do–she was not going to ask anyone else in her family for a handout. If her Aunt Alex wasn't able to help, she knew no one else could either.

April tried different jobs to help earn her money, but with her apartment, it was hard to be able to afford school and everyday necessities. April didn't want to move back to her parents' house, she was grown and now was the time to prove it.

"Hey April, it's me, your Aunt Alex. I hate calling you on your cell phone, but it seems your home phone is disconnected. I was wondering how you were doing?"

"Alex I am just getting up. I had a late night. It's good to hear your voice. How's Italy?"

"It's starting to get busy here again. I thought that you could fly out and stay with me a while and I could try and find you some work with the company. I'm with... Well, I have a job now, and I'm doing pretty well. I may be able to send you some money now." April chuckled. "How's everybody doing? Your mom, dad and Uncle Gabe?"

"Everybody's fine. I haven't seen Uncle Gabe in a while. I saw Bridgette a couple of days ago, she's good; said the boys are fine."

"Tell everybody I said hi. I'll give you a call later."

Alex hung up the phone with a long sigh. Barbara had called Alex and told her about her suicide attempt and that everyone called it an accidental overdose. No one suggested therapy after the incidence because then they would have to face the truth.

Alex decided to call April back–she had an idea.

"Hey April, it's Alex again. I have an idea. It's a new bank, and they have a good plan. I'd like to run it past you as soon as possible, so give me a call when you can."

Alex called back and left a voicemail. "I have a friend that moved her family to Switzerland and enrolled into a program where she received a lot of money for each member of her family. They also scored brand new housing. I know, new country, new way of life, but I would go with you, and we could start new and fresh together. Think about it and give me a call."

Alex hung up with hope this time. She thought about her friend Elaine Cohen who'd sent her a text telling her how much she loved Paradise Cove, how beautiful it was and how her family was enjoying living there. If she and April could get together and liked it, they would send for the rest of the family.

✡✡✡

Gabe always thought he was special. He knew he was his mother's favorite child as did everyone else. Gabe's world was so wonderful and free, all he did was what was expected of him. He majored in accounting at Syracuse University, and when he graduated, started at his father's firm. He was thoroughly enjoying his work when he felt a pull on his heart to become more involved with the Messianic Jewish Movement. Gabe so enjoyed the teachings that he received Jesus Christ as his Lord and savior. This caused a rift in his family for a while, but eventually, all his family members joined the Messianic Jews and received Christ as the Messiah of the world. It was not hard for them to make the change. They changed temples with relative ease.

The tugging on Gabe's heart increased; he ended up becoming a rabbi for the new temple. Gabe had never been so happy as the day he told his mother. He felt her pride swell every time he saw her in the temple.

Gabe's journey to Israel brought him face to face with the idea of rebuilding a temple at Temple Mount. It was an important holy site for Jews as it was believed it was where Abraham showed his devotion to God but bringing his son Isaac to be sacrificed. Though the area was currently under Muslim jurisdiction and Jewish prayer there was strictly forbidden, Gabriel knew in his heart that one day it would happen, and he wanted to be a part of it. He might not live to see the day it would happen, but he knew it would take place. Gabe believed so much in the temple that he became the leader of the national funding drive for the rebuilding of the temple. He convinced his father to donate to the fund before the Bernie Madoff debacle. Heimlich and Ellen donated a million dollars of their own money and were proud of it. They hoped it would rush the return of the Messiah.

Gabe felt a little guilty that they gave so much, especially since his father and family were now broke. He believed the thought of poverty caused his mother's heart attack and subsequent death.

"Hey dad, Uncle David, are you guys taking care of yourselves? Eating right? Exercising I hope."

"Were as good as two old bachelors can be. I get out and walk," David said. "This one here, not so much!" David said, pointing to Heimlich who was sitting in front of the television shouting at a game show.

"Dad, have you been eating?"

"Yeah," shouted Heimlich who was a little hard of hearing. "I had some soup this morning."

Gabe turned to David who nodded his head.

"I'm healthy as a horse. How's your life at the temple? Still not married I see, no kids either."

"Not yet, dad."

"If your mother were alive, it would kill her all over again to know that you and Alex are not married and have no children!"

"Mom knew there was a possibility that I might not have kids when I went into full-time ministry."

"Oh, Ellen may God rest her soul!" said Heimlich.

"Here we go again!" said David throwing his hands in the air reaching for the remote to put the television on the cooking channel.

"Put that back, I'm watching the Price is Right," snapped Heimlich.

"Oh, I thought you were going to rant and rave for twenty minutes about how you killed Ellen with your poverty," sighed David switching the channel back.

"Dad I have told you that you will never be broke. God will bless you somehow. Maybe not in the form of money, but you will get a blessing. God will take care of you and yours when you least expect it. Well, I was checking on you guys. Do you need anything before I leave?"

"No, no," David and Heimlich answered in unison.

"If we need anything, April will bring it by. She checks on us every day," David said reaching for the remote again.

"How is April?" Gabe asked concerned. He hoped she was in better shape than when he last saw her.

"She's fine," yelled Heimlich over the television. "She has a new job making a lot of money. We're not watching this, let's watch an old cowboy movie from when we were young!" yelled Heimlich.

"I'm going out for a walk," David said getting up from the sofa. "You see why I get my exercise now," said David with a wink and a smile.

"I'll walk out with you," Gabe offered. "Good night dad."

"Goodnight!" Heimlich yelled over the TV.

Outside on the street, Gabe asked David, "Where do you go on these long walks?'

"Oh, just around the neighborhood for fresh air."

"Well, be careful. Things are getting harsh for us here," Gabe said, referring to the increased attacks on Jewish people.

David knew what he meant and said, "Yeshua walks with me. Goodnight Gabe." David watched Gabe walk swiftly around the corner then proceeded on his way. He walked about three blocks to a brownstone and saw a red-haired lady sitting on the steps.

"Are you enjoying your walk tonight David?" Lorraine asked, with her husky German accent.

"Of course, Lorraine, how are you tonight?"

"I'm great. Would you like a cup of tea? Your usual three cubes of sugar?"

"Yes, please. It's a warm night tonight," David said sipping on the warm tea. "Can we pick up where we ended yesterday?" David asked eagerly.

"Why of course." Lorraine smiled inviting David to sit and sip his tea. "Your father Saul and Ida lived an honest life. Your father was a proud man. Maybe too proud is the way my father told me. Maybe it was the pride that got him in trouble. My uncle told me this story through the years and imagine, I have met a real live Zigburgh. Your father saved my family's lives by hiding them. He would sneak food to them every morning by stuffing it in his medical bag. He fed my family for three weeks before your family was shipped off to the concentration camps. After no one came for a couple of days, my family went to your family's home and lived in the spaces between the walls. Your father even told my family where to hide if they were taken. My family would have never known about the space between the walls in your home if your father, Saul Zigburgh, hadn't told them. For this, my family will always be grateful! The security guards would check the home regularly. My family stayed until they heard a new family would be moving in. My family escaped on a supply train through Austria. The train was derailed and inspected by Americans troops. The American troops rescued my family. My family remembers overhearing your mother beg your father to send all the kids to America. When they got to America, they tried looking you guys up, but no one knew exactly where in America you were. It's a miracle that I'm sitting here talking to you."

David sat another 2 hours with Lorraine enjoying tea and listening to the stories of her family and how they made it out of Nazi Germany and lived in the new country. Just knowing his father and family had died heroes and not pointless, gave him some comfort. They died to save his life, Heimlich's life and the lives of the Warlhz brothers. One of the brothers became Lorraine's dad.

David's short walk home was filled with hope and a new-found respect for his father and also to his surprise had a slight crush on Lorraine. This perplexed David a little, but the joy of knowing his family were heroes helped push his walk along.

Another Miracle

In the Congo of Africa, a mine collapsed killing 18 men. It took 36 hours to remove the bodies from the ruins of the mines. Miners had worked day and night to reach the trapped miners who'd gone for an estimated 20 hours without fresh air. The fears were that the miners had already expired.

After 36 hours of straight digging, they finally reached the compartment that held the 18 men. Their loved ones stood by holding their breaths with anticipation only to find out that all the miners had succumbed to asphyxiation. There were no survivors. It took another 12 hours to get the bodies out. The corpses were taken to the morgue for autopsy to determine the exact cause of death.

A lone security guard, Moligi, kept watch at the mortuary every night. Moligi was a child soldier in the war-torn, country of Liberia. He killed his first soldier at the age of 7 and had a substantial body count under his belt; by the age of 10, he had killed over 42 men.

At the age of 10, he had sat in a tree and heard a sermon by Robert Marsales and changed his life. He put his assault rifle down and ran away from the war never looking back. Moligi was now a father of four, and the job of security guard helped him take care of his family.

Late at night, Moligi alone often song praised and sang worship songs to make the hours pass. That night because of the solemnity of the hour, Moligi spirit was heavy, and he decided to listen to Christian television to soothe his heavy spirit.

Moligi awakened to an unknown rustling sound. When he turned down the volume on the television, the rustling sounds stopped. Moligi turned the volume up again and tried to stay awake. He was concentrating on the Christian television program. Moligi heard the rustling again. This time Moligi turned the volume up to drown out the sound then decided to turn it down to hear the rustling sounds better. They got louder. Moligi was the only person in the building. The rustling sound seemed to be coming from the morgue. Moligi pushed the door to go in, and something pushed the door back. He pushed the door again harder to try and enter and the door is again pushed even harder, this time so hard that Moligi fell to the floor. Moligi was surprised but jumped up and tried to pull his service revolver without success. There was an extremely bright light coming from under the door. Moligi attempted to enter the room again, and the force on the other side of the door wouldn't allow him to get in. There was electricity in the air, and the bright light coming from under the door was getting brighter. He now realized the rustling sound he'd heard earlier was the distinct sound of fluttering wings.

Moligi decided to try and enter the room one more time. As he entered the room, he looked up toward the ceiling to see feathers drifting from the ceiling. He stood there with mouth open gazing up into the ceiling as the last feathers slowly floated to the ground. He noticed he was not alone–all eighteen of the body bags that held the dead miners were open and the miners were sitting up staring up at the ceiling. The miners began to sing, rejoice, and praise God all at the same time.

The story of the resurrection spread worldwide. The miners were all interviewed by the worldwide news and Christian televisions. The miners only remembered being in the mine before the collapse then waking up in the morgue halfway out of body bags.

Chapter 8

"Hey girl what's going on? Brandon called today asking forty questions instead of the fifty he usually does," Shea said waiting on Keisha to say something witty.

"Oh, really?" Keisha said dryly.

"Ok K, what's wrong? You usually have something to say."

"Nothing's wrong. I talked to Bridgette the other day. Sounds like she is thinking about leaving Ben," Keisha explained.

"Good! She needs to leave Ben. He boring," Shea said in her Asian accent.

"Doesn't matter if he is boring, Bridgette has been with Ben forever. He was her first love."

"K, sometimes love get boring, and you have to change up."

"Shea you don't change up because the relationship is stale!" Keisha yelled almost laughing because she knew Shea had a reason for why she would. And, she needed Shea to explain why."

"If Ira get boring and he doesn't want to smoke anymore, I leave and take half company and weed. That's what I would do, and he would come find me because he knows I love him long time!" Shea answered squealing with laughter. "You know Luke Too Live Crew, Me love you long time," she said squealing again.

Keisha shook her head and laughed. "Shea, are you high?"

"Yes, ma'am I am," Shea confided laughing. "Man, I was having a bad day, and then you called. Takes my mind off Brandon. Keisha, you need to tell this man about the baby. He is not going to stop calling, and he's flying down there to Coral Springs to confront you." Shea let out a low whistle. "I wasn't supposed to tell you that, but I hate being blindsided myself, so heads up. How's the job anyway?" Shea asked trying to change the subject.

"Sneaky town is sneaky town. Small tourist town. Most of the trouble is caused by out of town tourist. Not too much in town crime, which is good for me. I'm getting a raise."

"Yeah, yeah, yeah. I want to know if you're going to tell Brandon about the baby and the reason you really left. Do you think you would take him back if the feeling is mutual?" Shea asked in anticipation.

"He didn't want the baby. The believes biracial kids have a hard time with their identity and self-esteem issues. I tried to tell him to look at me; my parents are black and white. I'm biracial, and I'm okay normal…at least I think I'm normal! Shea, do you think biracial kids are confused about their identity and have self-esteem issues?"

"I already know if I have a child with Ira, the first four years of that child's life he or she is going to be confused as hell!"

"Why Shea, because they're going to be biracial?"

"No, that will not be my child's problem. The language is going to tangle them up. English, Jamaican and Chinese. There is no way they will not be confused. Poor kid will invent a language all his own called Wu-tang, and I don't mean the rappers," Shea screamed and started cracking up.

"Damn Shea, I forgot I was talking to you high, and I bet you're doing that crazy dance!"

"Yeah girl, I got to go to work," she replied, "drop it like it's hot! Oh yeah, before I go, guess who found out that they're Jewish? Ira just found out he is a Jamaican Jew. Go figure that one out?" Shea said answering her own question; she often did when she was high.

"How did you find out?" Keisha inquired.

"He kept getting a brochure from this Bank of the Swiss Alps or something. Anyway, they said he qualified for 50,000 cash and a free house in Switzerland because he is a descendant of the Holocaust victims! You have to be blood proven to qualify for the money. Ira researched his background information and somewhere back on the island of St. Thomas, his great-somebody got jungle fever and conceived six children by a Jewish rabbi. I told Ira they were in the confessional making babies in that little box. Um huh."

"Shea!" Keisha screamed "The confessional booth is Catholic! How did the bank know to send Ira the brochure?" Keisha asked.

"I don't know, you the police, you find out! Goodbye, talk to you later!"

Shea hung up quickly leaving Keisha to ponder the facts. How would a bank know who was and who was not Jewish? Did they have access to the birth certificate? But even so, did they state whether you're Jewish or not? Maybe the Holocaust museum had a list of the victims and their descendants. That would require a lot of work on the part of the bank to find out. It wouldn't make sense for a bank to go through that much trouble and red tape to find out unless they were getting paid. Keisha decided to call her dad to see if he knew anything. Something didn't sound right to her.

"Hey ma," Keisha sighed. She knew this would be a long phone call because she knew her mother. Her mom and Bridgette could drop 50 questions in 25 seconds or less. Keisha didn't know which one was worse.

"Hey baby girl, how are you? How's the Job? Did you know Brandon stopped by here two weeks ago? What's going on with you and Brandon? Are you guys having problems? Is it because you're in Coral Springs and he's here in New York? Have you considered moving back to New York? Have you talked to your sister?"

"No ma," Keisha replied quickly. "Is dad there?" Keisha asked hurriedly hoping she would get an answer before her mother went on another question tirade.

"No, he went to his office. I don't know why he still goes down there. He retired a long time ago. You would think he would want to spend more time at home, right?"

Keisha interrupted quickly. "Okay mom, got to run; late for work. Tell dad I'll call him later. I love you... goodbye!" Keisha hung up quickly with a smile knowing she had gotten off the phone before her mother got started.

"Hey, Granddad it's me April! Where's Uncle David? I brought you some fresh fruits and vegetables. I'm going to put them in the kitchen," April declared heading for the kitchen. April knew that her grandfather couldn't hear because he had the Price is Right on as loud as a five o'clock whistle. She knew he refused to get his hearing checked; he felt as long as he didn't need a walker, everything else was in good working order. She smiled because he was very wrong about the hearing part.

After finishing putting the groceries away, April went into the sitting area. "Granddaddy?"

"Hey, hon. Where did you come from?"

"Oh, I've been in the house for about 10 minutes. I put the groceries in the refrigerator for you. I could have been a robber, and you would have never heard me with the television so loud," April said kissing him on the cheek.

"I'm an old man. Nobody is going to come in here just to steal an old man's television."

"Where's Uncle David?"

"David goes on those walks twice a day, and the walks are getting longer."

"Why don't you join him for one his walks?"

"I'm just fine with my stationary bike."

"You mean the one that's had clothes on it for the last 6 months?" April asked teasing.

"Well, I plan to start riding the bike, more often."

"Granddad, when you are ready to exercise, you will," April said patting him on the back. "Anyway, I talked to Aunt Alex, and she's looking into trying to get me a job in Italy with the company she works for. I pray she can find me one, so I can leave this place."

"I'm sorry April. I lost all our money dealing with Bernie Madoff. If I could do it all over again, I would change a lot of things. I am so sorry." Heimlich got choked up and started to cry. "The two people I love the most suffered the most from the loss— you and Ellen. I will never be able to forgive myself for the pain I caused the family. Especially you and Ellen... my dearest, Ellen. I'll never forget the day I lost her..."

"Granddad, grandma is in a better place. I miss her too, and I have a new job, and I'm making better money, and I will be able to go back to school. Granddad, don't be upset, it will be alright. Alex may have found a bank that will be able to help us. A bank sent us a brochure that says if you are a descendant of Holocaust victims, you qualify for $50,000. It's not a loan, but it's part of reparations for the money that was stolen from Holocaust victims. They just need a blood test to prove DNA. That sounds pretty good huh Granddad? If we qualify, every member of the family will receive 50,000 dollars. You also qualify for a free 4,000 square foot house in Switzerland. I'm thinking about going!" April said excitedly.

Heimlich didn't move or say anything. He had even turned the television volume down, so he could hear April clearer.

"What's the name of the bank?" Heimlich asked getting up out of his chair, to walk across the room to sit at his desk. He pulled out a stack of brochures he had received from the Swiss Bank of the Alps. "When I first received one, I had a funny feeling about this bank. They sent David a few also. How do they know that we are descendants of the Holocaust victims? This needs to be looked into thoroughly before you decide you want to get involved in it."

"Oh, Granddad it's an honest bank. They are paying reparations to the descendants of the Holocaust victims. They stole millions of dollars from Jewish victims, and now the United Nations is making them return the money to the descendants. I don't know about you Granddad, but I could use the 50,000. It would help me out right now. And, you know everybody in this family could use the money. I need the money and a change of scenery. Just think Granddad, the money could be used to help the family. If you don't want your share, give it to Ben, Joe and me. Don't think of it as blood money or hush money for killing your family. Let the bank pay. Somebody needs to pay for killing a whole race of people. I know 50,000 is not the price of a life, but it's a start. Like I said Granddad, somebody needs to pay. Just think about it, Granddad. I've got to go. I love you, tell Uncle David I will see him later."

April left with Heimlich holding the brochures in his hand and rubbing his head. 'Somebody had to pay,' kept ringing in Heimlich ears. "Somebody had to pay, somebody had to pay."

✡ ✡ ✡

Keisha was dreading going home all day. She had even offered to do Blunt's paperwork. Blunt almost took her up on the offer except it was pretty much completed. The reason Keisha didn't want to go home was that she knew Brandon and Ira were coming by to take her to dinner tonight. Miss Shea decided she had work, that couldn't wait and then decided she was too nosy to stay at home. So, she came at the last minute, plus she cooked Chinese food for two days, and she wanted to see her friend.

Keisha returned to her apartment just in time to shower before anybody got there. Shea had a plastic container the size of a footlocker full of different dinners just for her. She could have opened the meals and served them here, but Keisha knew that wouldn't be fair to Ira who ate Shea's cooking every day. The doorbell rang. Keisha checked the mirror one more time before answering.

"Girl, how are doing? Love your sneaky little town. Love that you're on the ocean and it's quite quaint–old and historical," Shea said in one breath.

"I'm good. I miss you. I'm sorry I haven't been up to see you since I moved down here," Keisha replied.

"What are you saying? You talk just about every day. Like you did in college," Ira said pushing past Shea to get a hug from Keisha.

Brandon moved slowly into the room like each move was a calculated step. "You look good," he said with a long hug.

"You do too," Keisha said blushing, breaking the embrace.

"I like your place, and it's good that you're not exactly on the ocean. Close enough to smell it though," Brandon said looking around.

Keisha thought Brandon still looked good. You could tell he still went to the gym.

"Still go the gym twice a week?"

"Since you've been gone, I'm up to 5 times a week. I'm even a paying member now."

Brandon laughed heartily thinking about all the excuses he'd given Keisha for not joining a gym. Ira and Shea had already started pouring drinks and playing music.

"Let's get the party started," Ira said passing Keisha and Brandon a glass of wine. "I reserved a spot at this seafood restaurant right on the pier. It has great crab legs and cakes; the best in town. It's a little bit crowded at night, so we may need to be on our way."

Keisha smiled putting her wine glass down.

"You did say you had reservations, so we have plenty of time," Shea said glancing at Ira and Brandon. "Show us around your apartment. It's a three bedroom, right?" Shea asked slyly, which meant she had no intentions of staying in a hotel.

"Come on. I'll give you the grand tour." Keisha smiled and winked at her old friend. "This is the deck, right off the living room. Everyone took a seat on the deck. Everyone was sipping on wine and watching the sunset on the warm summer night. It was like old times. After the 2nd bottle of wine, everyone decided it would be a good idea to try the restaurant another night. It started to rain, so everybody went inside. Shea had fixed and packed 26 separate dinners. It was beginning to feel like old times. Chinese food, wine and of course, weed.

"No thanks, I have not been drugged tested for the new job yet, and any day I'm expecting one." Keisha sighed. "It really would be good with this dinner, Shea. Thank you for fixing them for me," Keisha exclaimed.

"Because of you, I still have the feel of cooking. All those years I cooked in my parents' restaurant. I was always told I couldn't cook because I was a girl and I had to prove everybody wrong that I could be a short order cook. It paid to have greedy friends in college. I made almost 800 dollars a week cooking in the dorms illegally."

"The only thing that saved us was that we had a fat greedy house mom who let us cook as long as we brought her a plate," Keisha said cracking up.

"That's how you were able to buy all that weed from me," Ira said pointing to the food.

"Believe me, baby, it was not about the weed it was about those house calls you would make to me," Shea said kissing Ira's forehead.

"So K, how do you like your job? Are you planning to stay down here for a while?" Brandon asked staring at the wine glass.

"I haven't decided yet. I don't think I will retire here if that's what you mean," Keisha replied feeling a bit anxious. "Ira, I hear you can wear a yarmulke now! I also heard you are a few years late on your Bar Mitzvah," Keisha commented trying to change the subject.

"Yeah, I'm Jewish if that don't beat all. I'm a Jewish Jamaican. I've always said you never know who has played in your backyard; especially black people. There are very few 100% black people. Black people are mixed with some of everything. I'm a melting pot. God created it all to blend to become one race. Humankind." He stopped for a few moments before continuing on a different track. "Have you heard that Aliens are landing on earth and putting chips into people and the chips are to allow you to live disease-free for a hundred years and increase your life-span?" Ira asked in deep thought from the weed and wine.

"Doesn't this remind you the old days?" Shea asked, leaping on the sofa and cuddling up with Ira.

"I heard the Aliens are the fallen angels that fell when Satan was kicked out of heaven. If you get the chip, you are changing your DNA, and it's like getting the mark of the beast, the 666 on your forehead," Brandon chimed in.

Keisha moved to the loveseat where Brandon was seated. It was just like the old days Keisha thought to herself. She could see Brandon watching her every move. It felt warm and familiar– a bit too familiar. It was only for one night. Before the night wa over, old friends were toasting a new place, Savannah, and Coral Springs. Keisha also knew her friends would use any reason to make a toast so they could have another sip of wine.

Sometime after 2 am, sleeping arrangements were made. Shea and Ira got the second guest room, and Brandon got the 3rd bedroom. He looked a little disappointed but soon got over it. He was glad to be here with old friends.

Zachary and Romero exited the plane in Pennsylvania.

"There's no place like home even if it's filled with foreigners and Jews," Zachary said stepping out of the plane.

"America, there's no place like her. I can give you a hallelujah to that!" Romero exclaimed.

"You didn't say two words on the plane Rome. Are you thinking about what Rawlins said to us? You can't believe that Josef Mengele can be our father! Rome, you can't be serious… you think…"

"He did a DNA test that matched the other descendants of Mengele."

"Yeah, he gave us a DNA test in his laboratory. This is the same man who plans on fooling the whole world into starting another Holocaust financed with money stolen from the first Holocaust. Come on Rome, you have to admit this plan sounds as crazy as I think he is," Zachary said picking up their bags from baggage claim.

"Zach, all I know is that if we can get this plan to work from our side, we get 50 million dollars. The Brotherhood will get 35million dollars for their participation. We just have to do our parts," Romero explained.

"What is our part, Rome? Do you think I am going to roam the countryside killing Jews because this man tells us that we are offsprings of some Holocaust maniac? Right about now I'm glad just be the son of two meth addicts that loved us enough to give us up," Zachary tried to justify.

"Zachary, it's like the bible says, if we get rid of the shepherd, the flock will scatter," Romero countered. "It's not like our troops are not ready, and they are bloodthirsty. Well, a few of them are, at least enough to get the job done. The rest could be trained with the money we get from Rawlins. Rawlins showed us the video he has of us killing those men in the woods. You know we couldn't make it in jail. We must do this. Zach, if we kill a couple of the shepherds and their families, the rest of the flocks will scatter. This is a race of people whose history has shown will not fight back. This will be a piece of cake," Romero said getting the bags out of the trunk of the cab. "We should start with the largest temples on the east coast, all at the same time. The rest will fall like dominos."

Chapter 9

"Hey, you're up early," Brandon greeted Keisha.

"I still go jogging in the mornings. Coral Springs mornings are beautiful, Brandon. Would you like a cup of coffee?" Keisha asked.

"Sure, a big cup with cream and sugar. Can I go with you K?"

"I guess so. It's no use to wake the smokers–they couldn't run a block if their lives depended on it."

Keisha and Brandon jogged to the beach and ran along the shore enjoying the beautiful day. They didn't speak, only jogged. When they returned to the apartment, Ira and Shea were up.

"Good afternoon late birds." Keisha greeted Ira and Shea.

"I am starving. I want crab legs and shrimp. Can we get into the seafood restaurant in the morning?"

"Shea it is afternoon and yes, you can. I have worked up an appetite jogging."

"Hey! The hot water is not working in your bathroom. Let me show you." Shea snatched Keisha into the bathroom and closed the door behind her. "Have you talked to Brandon yet?" Shea asked quietly. "I saw that you made him sleep in the other room. Did you make him sleep in there by himself all night?"

"Yeah, we haven't had time to talk yet, and it has been a good weekend. I don't want to get into all of that just yet."

"Keisha Abigail Williams, you are going to talk to this man, this weekend or no more Chinese food for you. I am tired of being the middleman for you and him. Grow up and get it together!" Shea was shaking.

Keisha knew Shea was mad; she'd used her entire name. "Ok, Ok Shea, I will talk to Brandon!"

"That's all I ask," Shea said leaving the bathroom.

74

Keisha could count the times Shea had gotten mad at her on one hand. The madder she got, the less English she spoke; so, you knew when you'd pissed her off.

After lunch, it was time to talk to Brandon. Keisha was not looking forward to it, but it had to be done. Shea and Ira went shopping and sightseeing giving Brandon and Keisha time to talk.

"Keisha, you know I love and miss you. I don't understand why you left all of a sudden. I knew we had a few problems but to just up and leave like that?"

"You know I took some time off for a pulled muscle in my back. I didn't pull a muscle. I was six weeks pregnant and had an abortion!"

Brandon didn't say anything. He sat there with his head in his hand. No one said anything for a solid minute. Brandon pulled Keisha to him. Keisha tried to push him away but noticed he was crying which made her breakdown. All the pain, stress, fever and anger came out in a flood of tears. Brandon was sobbing to Keisha's surprise. After ten minutes, they stopped crying and held each other, not speaking a word.

"Why didn't you tell me K? The whole time you knew, and you didn't tell me? What were you thinking? That I wouldn't love you or the baby? I need to know, Keisha?" Brandon wailed through sobs.

Keisha inhaled and exhaled.

"Brandon, how many times have you said that biracial kids are confused and have very low self-esteem? Brandon, I am biracial. My sister and I are both biracial, and we are not confused or have low self-esteem."

"K, how many times have we met kids that were biracial and living on the streets because they're not accepted in either culture?"

"Brandon, all color of kids are on the streets not just biracial. That can happen to anybody. We have seen all races on the streets. I just want to make sure that I'm there for my kids."

"Keisha had I have known, I would have been there for you," Brandon said quietly. "You didn't have to move all the way down here to Cora Springs."

"Brandon, every time I saw you, I felt the need to weep. I was going into a deep depression and wasn't able to shake it. I spent two weeks at Shea and Ira's, and I cried myself to sleep every night. No amount of Chinese food could help or comfort me. I went so dark for a while, I know I scared Shea! If it weren't for the move, I would have lost my mind, and I couldn't tell anyone what the problem was."

"So, you are telling me you moved all the way down to Coral Springs because you were depressed?" Brandon asked sarcastically.

"I moved because I was depressed but it helped my career, and I started to like it. I started to feel alive again, and I started to like myself again. The move was not to hurt you, it was to help me and my life," Keisha declared firmly.

There was nothing more Brandon could say. He wanted Keisha to be happy and healthy, and if Coral Springs did that for her, that's all he could hope for.

"I love you, and I wish you had told me. It was my baby too. I hate that you didn't feel that I could try to be understanding enough to consult or be a part of the decisions. I want you to be happy."

There was a knock at the door. Ira and Shea were returning from shopping.

"Hey baby girl, what is going on in Sneaky Town?" Ira asked Keisha.

"What do you mean?" Keisha said looking through the shopping bags.

"We went for the ride on the edge of town by the swamps before you get to the other side of the island. We saw troops or a gang of people, marching through the edge of the swamps. Do you have Coast Guard or National Guard doing drills this weekend?"

"No, not that I'm aware of Ira, maybe it's paintball, tactical teams playing in the woods."

"Look K, I was a drug trafficker for years. I know when something is not kosher," Ira said.

"Oh, here we go!" Shea laughed. "Ever since you found out you were Jewish, everything is kosher. Kosher this, kosher that."

"Shea baby, serious you know something is wrong. You know that didn't look right. So, we hid about 45 minutes and took some pictures with the cell phone because that's all we had at the time. Here, take a look. What do you see in those pictures? It looks like this person is leading these people through the swamp to go somewhere. They have more than backpacks, so you can tell they're not going on a hike. They seem to be moving or transporting," Ira said.

"They have too many bags to be transporting or trafficking," Keisha noted.

"That's what I said, something's not kosher," Ira exclaimed again.

"If you say kosher one more time, you're walking back to South Carolina," Shea said rolling her eyes at Ira. "I know," Shea said after a pause. "They're those doomsday preppers. A couple of years ago they prepped for the end of the world that never happened. You know, that apocalyptic kind of stuff," Shea said reaching for the phone.

"They haven't done that for years. 2012 came and went with no fanfare," Keisha replied.

"So, what do you think they're doing?" Shea asked again.

"Baby, who you calling?" Ira asked Shea.

"The police," Shea said starting to dial 911.

Keisha snatched the phone from Shea. "Are you still high? I am the police!" she said shaking her head at Shea.

"So, what do you think they are doing? Shea asked again.

"We followed them. They ended up getting on a ferry or riverboat. They're hugging like they had just made it off the television show Survivor Island," Ira said pointing to the outside.

The conversation went on for hours. The two couples decided not to go dinner again opting to stay in watch a movie and grill some steaks.

"Dinner was the bomb, especially since I didn't have to cook it," sighed, Keisha letting out a loud belch. Everyone looked at each other. "Sorry not bad manners but good eating," Keisha said belching again.

"We're going to let the guys wash dishes since you guys cooked," Shea said pointing toward the kitchen.

"It's cool, it's all kosher," Ira responded.

Shea took her shoe off and threw it in Ira's direction. He screamed, "You missed," then started clearing the table.

Shea closed the patio door.

"Did you get a chance to talk to Brandon?"

"We talked and cried for hours," Keisha answered

"So, where does that leave the relationship?"

"I don't know, all I know is that he knows and maybe the relationship will be able to mend. If we end up being friends, I'm grateful. Brandon is a good guy, and I only want the best for him. He wants the same for me."

"Well if you're happy with that train going to crazy town, I suggest you buy a ticket," Shea replied. Keisha jumped because she never knew what Shea would say.

"I love you man," Keisha told Shea.

"It's all kosher," Shea replied, laughing and hugging her friend.

"Hey what are you two laughing about?" Ira asked closing the balcony door behind him.

"Oh nothing," Shea replied. "Everything is kosher," she said again, which caused all of them to laugh.

"How about another glass of wine?" Brandon asked holding up the wine bottle.

"Me!" Shea and Keisha answered in unison.

"Keisha since your father is a professor of Hebrew studies, there is something I always wanted to know, and Shea told me to ask you. It was a story you told her in college about the Ark of the Covenant or your theory of where the ark is."

"Sit down and get comfortable. Get another glass of wine. It's a story my father and I discovered or tried to trace during the summer the movie Indiana Jones the Raiders of the Lost Ark was released. Some of it couldn't be proven back then and some still can't. By you being a new-found Jew, it is good you want to know your heritage."

"Hey, wait, let me grab a seat because I have never heard this theory," Brandon said.

"My theory is there is more than one ark.

"More than one," Ira asked in disbelief.

"The real or first ark I believe is buried under the Temple Mount in Jerusalem. The second ark I believe Solomon had made for the Queen of Sheba and their unborn son, Menelik. When Sheba left to go back to her country Sheba, which today may be modern-day Yemen, Solomon sent Jewish priests to help train Menelik in the religion of his father–the Hebrew religion and its traditions. Some scientists have found a stone with the entire story etched onto it. The etching validates the story of Solomon and Sheba. I heard stories of Sheba and Solomon having a son, and that's how Ethiopian Jews were pulled into the fold.

"The priest married the Ethiopian women," Ira said, "Ok I heard that the ark is an Ethiopian Church."

"Will you be quiet and let her finish. The story gets deeper," Shea said rolling her eyes.

"The story goes that Menelik grows up and hears about the overthrow of the Kingdom after Solomon dies and fears for the lives of his mother and himself, that Menelik decided to lock himself in a room with the God Box. Not sure if he thought the box was going to talk to him or what but stays there until he perishes."

"Mom never opens the door to retrieve the ark, or does she?" Ira asked.

"Before she leaves Sheba, the Queen erects a compound to protect the gravesite and the 'God Box'. The problem of verifying this is that Yemen is a Muslim Country. No Jewish scientist or religious scholars can enter the country or dig up the mound to see if the ark is really there. There are also rumors that the Queen of Sheba took the ark to Ethiopia with her and it is still there now.

Then there's the one that says the prophet Jeremiah took and hid the ark in Mt. Horeb and went to retrieve it after the release of the people from Babylon. He brought the ark to Ethiopia where it is guarded until this day.

There is a newly found tribe called the Lemba tribe that has a drum or had a drum, that was designed after the ark. It is called 'The African Ark'. The drum looks like the ark with pole holders for the drum and has supernatural powers. The drum was played before the tribe went to war–it was carried before the warriors. When the drum was played, the enemy tribes went into a trance or were slightly paralyzed which made it easy for the Lemba tribe to win the war. The 2nd making of the drum, or remnants of the second, were found in a storage house just recently."

"Man, how do you know all this stuff?" Brandon asked with pride.

"My father is a professor of Hebrew and Jewish studies." As children, we were treated to a treasure hunt. We would check out good leads and kept up to date on certain information," Keisha replied blushing because of the pride Brandon had for her.

"You know…. You know…." Ira was getting choked up.

"We know, it's all kosher," they all said together, laughing.

It was the best weekend Keisha had had in a long time. Everybody had a good time. They talked until the wee hours of the morning, and it was like old times again; the 4 musketeers.

Sunday afternoon came so fast no one was prepared to pack and make the trip back.

"It feels funny leaving you behind," Shea said whining. "You live close to me now, closer than in New York."

"I'm glad about that. Now Shea won't feel so lonely when I go on trips. Give me a hug, I love you man," Ira said, starting to put the luggage in the car.

Brandon smiled. "I'm glad you finally talked to me. I still love you. Whenever you're ready to come back or for me to stay, I'm more than ready. Talk to you soon." Brandon gave Keisha a long kiss goodbye.

"See you soon!" Keisha managed a smile. She now realized she missed Brandon more than ever and wanted him in her life; at what point and time she did not know. All Keisha knew was something going on in sneaky town, and she needed to find out what it was.

✡︎ ✡︎ ✡︎

"Good morning Detective Blunt," Keisha said. All she got out of Blunt was a grunt. Keisha knew Blunt had to be smarter than he pretended.

Keisha looked around the squad room more alert now than when she'd first arrived. She got up and looked out the window. She thought about what Shea and Ira had told her about seeing the activity in the woods. She knew they were right–something was definitely wrong. She'd been in an emotional fog since moving to "Sneaky Town" but her mind was clear now, and she needed to figure what was going on.

"Let me ask you a question, does the Coast Guard run late afternoon exercises on the weekend?" Keisha asked Detective Coldheart.

"As far I know weekend drills don't last past 3:00 on Saturday or Sunday. The McCurdy tourism Shop just reported a missing ferry to the Coast Guard," Coldheart replied looking confused.

"What?" Keisha asked looking more confused than Coldheart. "How the hell can a ferry boat be missing?" she asked walking toward the window.

"Hey, you want to ride down to the beach with me to check on this?" Coldheart asked putting on his jacket.

"Yeah, might as well. Could be a college prank. Have any surrounding docks reported anything missing Coldheart? Has the Coast Guard checked into this? Let's stop by their office and talk to somebody in charge. Has this type of situation ever happened here before? I'm driving," Keisha said remembering Merkerson's warning about the other detectives driving.

"Open the car door and get in. You don't even know where the Coast Guard is!" Coldheart exclaimed. "You just want to drive my car!"

"Nope, no how, no way! I have heard about your driving." Keisha finally gave up the keys and entered the passenger side of the car. "Pleases don't kill me!"

Skidaway Island was a well-protected government compound guarded by Coast Guard MPs on every side, with two posted at the gate 24-hours a day, seven days a week.

"It's good to know that Georgia is well protected," Keisha smirked. "They have all this protection, and a ferry boat comes up missing. Has anybody checked with South Carolina Water State Troopers?"

"Look, Williams, you get paid by the day, you do not have to ask all the questions at one time!" Coldheart said looking at Keisha out of the corner of his eye.

"Hey, did you know you give good crook look?" Keisha said changing the subject.

"What the hell is crook look?"

"When you look at a person out of the corner of your eye without turning your head. You know, crooks do it all the time," Keisha exclaimed.

"We're here," Coldheart said. "I'll get out with this crook look I have!"

'He's offended,' Keisha thought to herself, *'good, he won't ask to drive my car again.'*

"Where's your commanding officer?" Keisha asked still laughing to herself.

"Around the corner and up the hill," the MP replied not looking at either of them nor slowing his pace as he walked away.

Sgt. Robinson was a 35-year-old looking gentleman. He was standing up looking out a window with his hands laced behind his back. Looking out of the window seemed to be an all-consuming activity in Coral Springs.

"Working hard there sir?" Coldheart asked in a disrespectful tone.

"I hate to admit, hardly working these days. No budget to cover the things I need to get done and yet they continually ask me why they are not done," Robinson said swinging around to face Colheart and Keisha and shake hands. "How you doing? I'm Sgt. Robinson and you are?"

"Coldheart and this is Detective Williams."

"You sure are purdy!" Robinson said with his most perfect southern accent.

"Thank you," Keisha replied blushing.

"What can I do for you?" Robinson questioned clearing his throat.

"We're here to ask you a couple of question about the missing ferry."

"Damndest thing we have ever heard," Coldheart said shooting a look at Keisha.

"Mccurdy reported it missing early this morning; about 4 a.m. He claimed his last trip across Ossabaw Sound was last night at 11:00. Sunday evening about 7:00 they anchored the ferry down early to allow the crew to enjoy some time off," Robinson said pulling a file out of a drawer. "His son claimed he anchored the ferry down at 11:20 after he counted up the till for the day. He made a bank drop on his way home from the marina."

"Let me ask you a question, have you seen any funny stuff going on in the woods in the late evenings?" Keisha asked in a matter of fact tone. Robinson shot her a look.

"No, I haven't and what do you mean about funny stuff?"

"Unauthorized drills or marches."

"Are you kidding me? They get paid to do drills and marches and then they don't want to do them. So, you know they're not going to do them for free," Robinson scoffed.

"Let me tell you what I think. I think the McCurdy's are struggling financially just a bit, so they decided to sink their ferry to collect the insurance money. You would be surprised at all the abandoned boats people have let sail from New York, New Jersey and tried to sink them to collect the insurance money. So, I believe the ferry is in the same category," Robinson said pointing toward the bay.

"In that case, Sgt. Robinson, we won't take up any more of your time."

"Good day Detectives."

Safely back in the car, Coldheart decided to quiz Keisha.

"Exactly what did you see going on in the woods?"

"I have some pictures if you want to see." She showed him the pictures Ira had texted to her phone.

"They look like refugees. It's old and young women and children. They look like family but where are they going? "Are there cabins in these woods?" Coldheart asked

"I don't think they're doomsday prepping, that's all behind us with the apocalypse not happening," Keisha exhaled heavily thinking she probably could give her mom and Bridgette a run for their ability to question.

Keisha decided she didn't care what Coldheart said, she was going get some answers now that her head and heart were clear. The fog had lifted, and something was going on in the Georgia woods.

Chapter 10

"You talked to April, and she said WHAT?" Bridgette asked again not quite sure of what she was hearing.

"The bank is called the Bank of the Swiss Alps, and if you qualify, you get to apply for 50,000 and a new home in Switzerland," Ben explained eagerly.

"The home is 4,000 square feet, and you get to choose from 6 different floor plans sitting on ¾ of an acre of land." Joe chimed in.

"What are the qualifications for 50,000 again?" Bridgette asked looking from Ben to Joe.

"You have to be Jewish or of Jewish decent proven by a DNA test, given to you by their medical staff. If you are of Jewish descent, you can take a cruise ship over to Switzerland to view and chose from the model homes," Joe explained again.

"How do you get a passport? You know the government banned passports?" Bridgette asked standing up to play a cd, to sort this out in her head.

"The government will allow a 7-day passport to go to Switzerland and chose your housing if you would like. There is a 10% tax on the money up front for each member of the family receiving the 50,000," Ben explained waiting for Bridgette's reaction.

"I talked to my father. He said he never heard of this initiative and the fact that it is just for Jews, I should look into it carefully," Bridgette said cautiously.

April and Alex had both decided that they were going to pursue their option and planned on going in a couple of months. They wanted everyone to go.

"We can make it a family vacation with the cruise ships and all," Joe said agitatedly. "Bridgette, it's a good plan plus you receive 50,000 and a new home in a peaceful country."

"What is it you don't understand or believe in Bridge?" Ben asked begging. "Tell me your fears. Tell me what you are thinking?"

"You're talking about leaving a country I have only known all my life, born and raised here to go to a country I know nothing about, and may not even speak the language. What I do know about the country was during the time of Hitler, and you expect me to decide on April's word alone? You do know that April is two days from a mental breakdown. You know she tried to commit suicide. She didn't accidentally take 40 pills guys, she slit her wrist. Ben, think about this before you make a hasty decision," Bridgette said defiantly.

Joe threw up his hands and walked off in disgust. He knew Bridgette ran Ben, she always had and always would. Ben needed to grow a pair.

"I'm all in, and I'll go without them. I don't care," Joe mumbled under his breath leaving the room.

"Ben, give me the real reason you are leaning toward this and why are you pressuring me to hurry up and make a decision?" Bridgette asked.

"Bridge, I think we could get a fresh start in Switzerland. I think I could get a job with their economic system and not run a pizza parlor for the rest of my life."

"I thought they offered you the opportunity to buy the pizzeria?"

"Bridge, you cannot be serious. I would then own a pizza joint and still be running it. I didn't go to college for four years to run a pizza joint. I know your sister K is tired of lending us money every couple of months. Money we can't pay back!"

Bridgette had never told Ben about the money from Keisha but, she wasn't surprised he'd figured it out.

"Ben, she doesn't, and she has it to give with her investment with Ira and Shea's company. I was hoping you would maybe ask Ira for a job."

"You want me to ask a drug dealer for a job?"

"Excuse you, Ira was just elected to United States Congress, and you know marijuana is legal now. Plus, Ira's thinking about opening another store in Texas and maybe you could run it. You would be making triple what you are making running the pizza store!"

"Bridgette, I'm an accountant. My grandfather had his own firm!"

"Had, Ben. The firm sold for taxes, and you're never going to run that company!"

"Bridge I love you, but I'm tired of running a pizza parlor. I'm going to Switzerland and start my life over again. I hope you come with me!" Ben screamed walking out of the room slamming the door.

"Ben don't go, let's finish this!"

The apartment got quiet. Bridgette could hear herself breathing and the hot tears running down her cheeks.

Ben could feel the cold New York air on his face and decided to go to the temple and talk to Uncle Gabriel. He would know what to say to get Bridgette to change her mind. He had a specialty with that kind of stuff. Ben had to laugh at himself because he just made his uncle sound like a pimp instead of a Rabbi. Still, he would know what to do!

Uncle Gabe was having a midweek service. Ben entered the service and decided he would fully participate. He knew it would make him feel better and help him forget Bridgette for a little while. Out of the corner of his eye, Ben could see Joe already there in worship.

"I would like to announce to the congregation that we have just received another donation for 500,000 toward the construction of the new temple at Temple Mount," Gabe said proudly. "The new temple construction is almost complete. All utensils are ready for the temple except the ark. Well-known Rabbis assure the ark is within reach."

Everyone applauded because they felt the completion of the temple meant Yeshua would be returning soon. The project was expected to be finished within months instead of years.

"I would like to introduce you a very good friend of mine, Rabbi Wesley Schwartz and his lovely family. Their three kids and their newest addition, 3-month old Joshua. Would you help me give them a round of applause?" Gabe walked down out of the pulpit to shake Wesley's hand.

Suddenly shots rang out in the congregation, and two gunmen with yarmulkes and Tallits stepped out and emptied their assault rifles into the Schwartz family. The shooters fled the temple. By-standers were seen screaming and running from the temple. The parishioners that couldn't escape hid under the pews and screamed. Blood splatter covered pews and people. Some of the congregation stood up to see the gunmen fleeing the temple and enter a black SUV.

Ben thought the gunfire lasted an eternity and the silence lasted even longer. All you could hear was the ringing of the gunfire. Ben was able to see the shoes of one of the gunmen.

As he slowly got up from under the pew, he could hear the sounds of fire and rescue in the distance. Ben looked to his left and right and could not see Joe or his Uncle. Walking ever so slowly to where Joe was last seen, he peered across the pews and saw the bodies of the Schwartz family riddled with bullets. All were dead including the infant. Women were weeping–congregants were wailing. People used their tallits to cover the dead.

Joe stood up, and Ben could see blood on his shirt and knew Joe had been hit.

"Joe you're bleeding!" Ben gasped rushing to his side.

"No, it's not my blood."

The young lady sitting next to Joe had been hit by a stray bullet and didn't make it. Joe covered her with his tallit. Their uncle Gabe was sitting on the floor in front of the Schwartz' staring off into space.

"Ben, look Gabe! Let's see if he's okay," Joe said jumping over pews to get to Gabe.

A few seconds later, the first responders entered the temple looking for any injured. Congregants pointed them to the Schwarz family, and all other witnesses were talking to the police and the detectives on the scene.

Ben thought he saw Brandon out the corner of his eye speaking to an elderly lady. They exchanged looks across the sanctuary. Gabe was praying and shaking. Joe tried to calm him down to no avail. Looking at Uncle Gabe, Ben could see that Gabe was only fifteen years older than himself. He always seemed wiser than his years. At this moment, he looked extraordinarily frail and young, too young to be a Rabbi and sure too young to be a dead Rabbi.

"Hey, you guys can you tell me what happened here?"

"Two men came in with guns, stood up and started shooting. They were already in the meeting when I got here." They took direct aim at the Schwartz family killing them all instantly. Brandon, you may want to speak to my Uncle, he knew the family."

"How you doing, sir? Can I get you anything? Were you hit? Is that your blood on your shirt?" Gabe started shaking uncontrollably. "Sir, would you like to go in your office so we can talk?" Ben and Joe escorted their uncle back to his office so he could answer some questions.

"I heard you knew the family?"

"They were old friends of mine."

"Do you know who could have wanted them dead?" Brandon asked passing Gabe some tissue.

"Wesley called me a couple of months ago, said that someone had threatened him and his entire family. I told him to come and stay with me for a while and bring the whole family. The temple would put them up in housing, no problem. Wesley decided to wait until the baby was older and better suited for travel. They only had arrived this morning about 9:30 and I went out for lunch with them and got them settled in the church's condo in Manhattan. They decided to come to temple tonight," Gabe gushed wiping the blood off his face with the tissue.

"Has anybody threatened you or your family, sir?" Brandon asked looking at the guys Joe and Ben for answers. They both shook their heads at the same time. "That's all the questions I have for you now," Brandon replied. "I'll give you guys a call as soon as I can find out anything," Brandon said leaving the three men hugging each other.

It seemed an eternity for the coroner to come to pick up the bodies. Nobody said a word on the long walk home.

"Gabe, are you going to be okay?"

"The God Jehovah watches over us all. Good night boys, be safe. I'll get my car tomorrow." Gabe hugged both boys and entered his home. Ben and Joe walked home in silence neither wanting to speak the obvious. It was time to leave America.

Gabe entered his home and sat in his favorite chair for a few moments collecting his thoughts. He wondered could Wesley have been right? Was there an international hit list on all Jewish Rabbis and their families? Also, was there any truth that his own family was in jeopardy and if so, who had been sending him letters warning him to leave the United States and take his family to Israel? Could it possibly be another Jewish Holocaust preparing to take place? America with all its laws and history would never allow another Holocaust to take place, would they? They had laws set in place to prevent a Holocaust and protect the people.

✡ ✡ ✡

Ben was playing with Bridgette's hair when she woke. "You okay?" Bridgette asked groggily "What's wrong, why are you looking at me that way? Is everybody alright? Is April alright? Where did that blood on your shirt come from? Did you get cut, Ben? Ben, say something," Bridgette screamed.

Joe came crashing out of his room and tripped and fell on the floor looking at Bridgette and Ben.

"Oh, you must have told her!" Joe said exciting the room.

"No, he hasn't told me, so you tell me," Bridgette snapped at Joe.

"Well there was an assassination at the temple tonight," Joe hurriedly replied.

"Not an assassination," Ben, yelled. "Joe, I'll handle this!" Ben said pushing Joe out of the room. "Friends of my Uncle Gabe were shot at temple tonight. Two gunmen killed five people."

Bridgette slid off the bed onto the floor with her head in her hands.

"Was anybody else hurt? Is your uncle okay? Who were the friends? Are they from here? Do they know who killed them and why?" Ben just grabbed Bridgette and held her close. As usual, too many questions to answer at one time.

After a few moments, Ben asked Bridgette if she wanted some breakfast? Bridgette laughed because this was Ben's way of slowing her down so he could at least answer 30 of the 50 questions she was capable of asking.

"Honestly Ben, I would like some pizza!" It was Ben's turn to laugh now.

"Pizza, I think I can manage that."

Bridgette was on her fourth piece of pizza before Ben decided to bring up the conversation again.

"Five members of the Schwartz family decided to come for a visit for my uncle to bless the new baby. In the middle of the service, two gunmen stood up shot and killed them and took off before anyone could stop or identify them. They had on yarmulkes and looked like everyone else. Brandon was one of the detectives on the scene; he questioned us. He also told me he just came back from spending the weekend with K.

"Keisha didn't tell me Brandon had come down for the weekend. Are they back together? Is he going to move down there with her? Is he going to be able to transfer his job?"

Ben looked at Bridgette and placed another slice of pizza on her plate with a laugh!

✡✡✡

"Can you believe how freakin' easy that was? I got such a rush! We got the entire family at one time it was like shooting fish in a barrel," Romero said to Zachary pretending to have a gun in his hand.

"Calm down, I saw everything on the news, and it took the coroner awhile to pick up the bodies. I'll call Rawlins and tell him that we are keeping our part of the bargain, so he had better keep his," Zachary said changing the channels on the television.

News Flash

Today the United Nations had voted unanimously that Israel was to return to its 1967 border again. This was to be implemented by the end of the year. The Israeli Prime Minister will appeal the vote. He has returned to Israel and has closed the Israeli embassies in the United Kingdom, America, and Canada.

Chapter 11

Looking out the window, Coyote poured himself another cup of coffee, scoffing at the weather. The fall wind was blowing, it was just July, and you could feel autumn. The temperatures were creeping on in, which meant there would be an early winter. Coyote knew that he needed to prepare early if he planned to do any winter runs. Winter runs were the easiest believe it or not. People usually thought it was too cold to try to escape the country. Usually, people were so preoccupied with the holidays that they didn't notice strange things at the airport or people in the woods at strange times of the night. They usually thought they were just out hunting. No biggie, but the bulk of the transfers were done in the winter time, easy to get thirty or forty people on a bus and say it was a church trip. Nobody asked questions in the winter time, it was too cold.

"Are you hungry, would you like me to fix you some breakfast?" Springlily asked eagerly.

"Nah, this cup will do. Are my heathen boys up?"

"Don't call them that!" Spring said laughing. "They're up there trying to decide is it safe for them to ask you if they can stay home from school today?"

"No, school is first."

Springlily stared at the back of Coyote's head. "I know something is wrong, I can feel it. I'm here when you decide you want to talk. You're putting very negative energy out. You may want to get a handle on that before you spend a lot of time with the boys. They can feel it too. They get confused sometimes about their feelings when it's you they're feeling. You may want to consider doing a sweat lodge," Springlily said reaching for pots to make breakfast.

"Yeah, you may be right, a session is just what I need," sighed Coyote turning around to see the boys coming down the stairs, groggy and shuffling. "Good morning my boys! You are the reason that I breathe," Coyote shouted. He was so loud he made the boys jump, especially little Juan. "You guys look like you need a cup of coffee." Both of the boys said, "Yuck!" at the same time. "It's not yucky," smiled Coyote, winking at Springlily. "It's for big strong, boys like me," Coyote said picking up both boys giving them a spin around the kitchen. Both boys gave him a big bear hug.

"Ahh daddy, are you going to take us hunting today?"

"Not today, you have school today. Tomorrow after school we will go hunting." Coyote was glad that the boys still wanted to spend time with him. Parker pulled Coyote's arm.

"Daddy, I don't want to go to school today."

"Sorry buddy, but you have to go to school. We have tomorrow after school," Coyote replied brushing Juan's hair with his hand.

"There is no school tomorrow; tomorrow is Saturday."

"Then we have all day tomorrow to hunt and play. Now eat your breakfast and off to school with you."

Coyote loved that he was able to walk his boys to school and spend that extra time with them. Springlily and the boys had changed his life. They made him appreciate life. They even taught him to respect life, and this showed him why he should continue the quest or the transfers.

In America, with all its technology, no one knew what was going on. This alone made Coyote's job as successful as it was. He smiled to himself for considering transfers for being a job. It was something that he was born to do. With his friend Matabazz, he has been able to increase his deliveries, more efficiently and safer. With Coyote, it was all about the safety, and in the direction that the country was going in, it was getting harder to keep people safe.

Coyote couldn't wait to see MelonHead do a sweat lodge. Every time Coyote thought about Melonhead's name, he had to laugh. Story had it that when MelonHead was born, his grandfather was senile, and their tribe tradition was for the grandparents to name the babies. Unfortunately, Melonhead's grandfather decided that his head looked like a melon and that was how he got his name. His mother wanted his father to change his name, but his father refused because he knew that he didn't have long with his father, so to honor him, the name would stay MelonHead. It didn't seem to bother MelonHead. He wore the name with pride. Coyote remembered that one of his sons was named MelonHead so thus started a family tradition. MelonHead was a good friend in spite of how he got his name. Sometimes when Coyote was out doing transfers, Melon looked in on his family.

On the walk to school with the boys, Coyote started to remember his childhood in Mexico. Coyote grew up with his mother and father and two brothers, Hector and Juan. Coyote loved his mother and father, but his family was very poor, and Coyote and his brothers wanted to go to America and make a better living for themselves. They would send money back to their parents in Mexico. Their plan was to bring their parents over later when they got settled.

His brother Hector was the first to escape to America working on a tomato farm as a migrant worker. Soon Coyote followed in his brother's footsteps as a migrant worker too. Juan was the youngest, so he stayed home for a while with his parents. Juan hated it because he wanted to help make life better for his parents as well.

One day while working in a tomato field, a man by the name of Salazar approached them about making a lot of money. Salazar wanted Coyote and Hector to help get other people across the border. He would pay Coyote and Hector more money in one night than they made in three months. All they had to do was help six people get across the Mexican border into Texas or New Mexico; whichever border was safer.

Without question, Coyote and Hector decided to take the job. They took their jobs very seriously because lives were at stake and they had one another to watch each other's backs. Neither one of them wanted to be responsible for the death of anyone that they helped cross. Because of how Hector and Coyote came to America, they were more than capable of getting people across the border with no problems.

Migrant work was hard, and Salazar made them an offer they could not refuse. They ended getting a contract with Salazar and quit their jobs as migrant workers. As a result, they lost their visas, so they were on the hook with Salazar. Their father fell and hurt his back in Mexico, so the family needed the money more than ever.

It was a good working arrangement before Salazar got greedy and careless. One night, Salazar showed up with ten people instead of the usual six. This caused a problem for the brothers because now they had to find a way to fit ten people where six usually fit. Coyote told the men that they weren't going to be able to make the trip, but Salazar had charged them extra to be taken that night. This meant that the men had to go, no money was ever refunded even if you got caught. Coyote and his brother had been doing transfers for almost two years and had never been caught or had anyone they transported been caught, so they were making a lot of money for Salazar, and they were good at their jobs.

God was smiling on Coyote and Hector that night because the border patrol was two men short. This made it easier to help the people over without being detected by the dogs. They refused to take women that were on their monthly cycles or babies. Babies cried when you least expected it, making it too much of a risk. Sometimes women lied about their cycles, so Hector would check them. If they were caught lying, he would leave them for the dogs and border patrol to lead them back to Mexico.

Anyone caught knew that they couldn't give up any information. Every week Salazar would add more and more people to the trip. At one point there were almost 30 people a night, making the crossings dangerous for the brothers. Border patrol did their best to stop it, but there were never enough of them to stop or even make a significant dent. The state of the crossings had deteriorated so badly for the people that were taking the trips, that Coyote and Hector considered stopping.

Meanwhile back in Mexico, Juan was doing some transporting of his own, but it wasn't human cargo. Juan had gotten into drug trafficking. He worked for a very dangerous drug cartel. Juan was making in one night what it was taking Hector and Coyote a year without the complications of being caught. Hector and Coyote started working with Juan. It became a family business, and they lived like kings in Mexico.

One day Hector, Juan, and Coyote were responsible for getting 3 truckloads of drugs across the border into California. Mercius Alvarez was the brothers' boss. He was found dead a couple of weeks later. Alvarez had doubled crossed the guys they were delivering the drugs to in California. Instead of three trucks of cocaine, the third truck was flour and baking soda. There was a bounty on the heads Coyote and his brothers.

The brothers left Mexico and tried to lay low in Haiti. It was a piece of cake. Haiti was under the stress of possible civil war under Baby Doc Duvalier, so no Americans or anyone else were going to be looking for them in Haiti. The country was torn apart by voodoo and corrupt politicians. The way the brothers stayed out of trouble was to pretend not to speak the language. But they became almost fluent with the language and were soon able to double their drug business. They moved weed instead of cocaine. All went well until the people that killed Alvarez saw Juan in Miami living it up. Because Juan was young, he loved to go out and party. Who wouldn't with all the money he was making? It was hard not to flaunt it.

Coyote warned Juan to lay low and change his lifestyle but knew he wouldn't. Juan had to have the best of everything which usually drew unwanted attention. This was what got him and his girlfriend killed in their sleep. They never knew what hit them. Their eyes were closed when their throats were slit.

Coyote told Hector about Juan. Hector started using cocaine every day to try and forget and to relieve the guilt of losing his baby brother. Hector used day and night. He had all the access he wanted to the drugs. He turned into a full-blown addict. All Coyote wanted to do was get the people that killed his brother.

Coyote left Hector because he knew how it would end for Hector and he didn't want to be around to witness it. He begged Hector one last time to give it up, but Coyote knew he wouldn't, he was too far gone.

Coyote had to kill whoever had the bounty on him and his brother if he and Hector were ever going to have a chance at life. Coyote was able to find and kill the persons that had put the bounty out on them. Coyote was dead on the inside. The drug game would do that to a person if you stayed in it too long. It was an in an out kind of business. The longer you stayed, the quicker your death certificate was signed.

One day Coyote decided to kidnap Hector and send him back to Mexico where he could get clean and sober, only to see him on the streets of Miami a couple of weeks later stoned out of his mind. This was the last blow for Coyote's already dead soul. All he knew was running drugs and people. He wanted a different way of life but had no idea how to get it. He had a sizeable fortune stacked up from running drugs back and forth out of Haiti. This was how he met Ira and Jordan–they were running weed from Miami to New York. He liked their style and the fact that they didn't ask a lot of questions and the trip to Miami was as dangerous as the trips from Haiti to Miami were getting.

One day on trip out to South Dakota, Coyote bumped into a beautiful woman. He found out that she was a Native American. Coyote knew nothing about Native American history, so he listened and learned, and it seemed it was the way of life that he wanted. He made the trips out to South Dakota for Ira and Jordan damn near free. He didn't care as long as he was able to see Springlily while he was there. He knew he would marry Springlily and take on all her Native American customs. He did all the tribal requirements necessary for him to become Native American. The elders were not easy on him just because Springlily's grandfather was a Chief. If anything, they were harder, but he was finally able to prove himself to her and her people. The change was the best thing that happened to him in his short life. He sent his parents all the money they would ever need to live in Mexico and went back to see them often. He even took the boys and Springlily to meet them.

The legalization of marijuana was the best thing that could have happened to Coyote. He was still able to make a good living and take care of his parents and his new family.

During his days in drug trafficking, he met Matabazz on his trips back and forth from Haiti to Miami. One thing about the drug business, it was an equal employment opportunity. You had people from all walks of life trying to do the same thing get rich at all cost if the lifestyle didn't get them first. You had to be very disciplined not to get caught in the game yourself; one slip could cost you your very life.

Bazz and Coyote had made over 50 trips together from Miami to Haiti. They knew each other well, so it was not strange when Coyote decided to start the transporting business, he would call his good friend Matabazz who was an ex-Rwandan refugee. It only made sense he would know the cost of life trying to get people to their destination and Coyote knew he would never be careless. It only made sense that he was the man for the job. He had seen it all, and he knew the consequences if any mistakes were made.

Back to real life, Coyote hugged his boys as he dropped them off at school that day. He went home to prepare for his next transfer. Most of the world wouldn't believe the people that were leaving the country, especially since the economic collapse. The whole world was in poverty and chaos, and people were doing whatever they could to leave the great country of America.

Chapter 12

Bridgette noticed her appetite had increased over the past couple of weeks and the other night she had begged Ben to bring a pizza home. She could not believe she was pregnant. She decided that she would not tell Ben. She knew he would want to keep the baby. Contemplating a move to Switzerland would be complicated by pregnancy and what about passport shots.

Bridgette wasn't sure she wanted a baby now, or ever for that matter. She couldn't tell Ben. They were already financially strapped, and Joe was in the guest room which would have served as the nursery. They needed his help financially. She tried to convince herself that she still needed to teach her yoga classes because they needed the money. At some point, while she was thinking things through, she stopped and glanced at herself in the mirror to see if she was showing yet. She wondered if yoga was a good idea when pregnant. She knew she didn't want to have this baby. She threw on her jacket and headed to her parents' house. Keisha was in town, and she wanted so much to see her. She had no idea she'd miss her sister so much when K moved away. Bridgette hoped K wouldn't notice anything different about her.

The walk to her parents' house was trying with all the different smells of the city. Bridgette noticed her sense of smell was especially sharp since she'd become pregnant. All the different smells of the food caused one big overpowering aroma. Bridgette could hardly breathe. She had to stop and hold back a gag. Bridgette had to get her emotions in check; she could get through this small hump.

"How are you liking Coral Springs K.?" her dad asked throwing her over his shoulder like she was a little kid again.

"Daddy!" screamed Keisha.

Bertrum placed his youngest daughter down starting to see her for the woman she had become for the first time. Both girls had grown up so fast; where had the time gone?

"Oh daddy, you're going to hurt yourself picking me up like that," Keisha laughed straightening her clothes. "Mom and dad, I'm good, and Coral Springs is great. It's a couple of miles outside of Savannah. My job is a cake walk. Not too much crime. It's a real quiet, sneaky town."

"Sneaky town?" her mother questioned.

"I just recently figured what the sneaky part means. It means everything is not what it seems. The people may look one way, but they are another. Everyone has a story and then there's the real story. Oh, I miss both of you guys. What have you guys been up to?"

"Well lately," Bertram said getting serious for a moment, "I have noticed that anti-Semitism is way up and you would not believe the attacks that are going on in Jewish temples and the Jewish people!"

"Well daddy, you always did say if the economy got really bad that it would start all over again."

"There is no way it could get as bad as it did during the Holocaust and World War II, we are in America," Mildred said.

Mildred was Keisha's mother. Mildred was a star on Broadway in the early eighties. She always talked about the racism she saw there. Having grown up in the south, you would have thought she was talking about color racism, she was not. The racism she saw and tried to prevent was the racism that was shown to the AIDS victims in the early eighties. Before the world and medical community knew that AIDS was not just a gay disease, the gay community was treated extremely bad. At one point, Mildred and Bertram opened their home to more than a few of their friends that were dying from the disease who could not afford hospitals or didn't want to be shunned because of the disease. Mildred was small but mighty. Keisha's father would often call her Mighty Mouse behind her back.

"What's that supposed to mean?" Bertram questioned. "When you know things in America have been on a downward spiral for about twenty years. Starting with the attack on Columbine High School. That was the most surprising thing to me," Bertram said shaking his head. "My Lord and the babies at Sandy Hook. I sat in front of that TV for days praying for those dear parents. It's not natural for a parent to bury a child. Now those two things shocked more than 9/11."

"More than 9/11 daddy, and we live in New York?"

"I always thought living here in New York, we as Americans knew we were targets for other nations. Mildred, I tried to prepare you and the girls for what is coming, don't roll your eyes at me, you'll know when it gets here."

"Baby, please don't start with the little black book that you supposedly have hidden in your office. Bertram, please if something does happen, you have to go all the way downtown to get it."

"When we need it, it will be there. Just remember, I have been working on some things for the girls, us, and their families if need be."

"Whatever, I have been hearing about this book for 25years. I have never seen or read this book, and I have my doubts about its existence."

"Believe me, it exists. Just hope you never need it," Bertram said rolling his eyes at Mildred.

"Bridgette must be running late. She usually beats me here when I tell her I'm coming," Keisha said trying to change the subject from the black book and the stalemate that it always caused.

"She has picked up a few more yoga classes lately. She and Ben are having a difficult time right now. Don't tell her I told you, she would have a fit," Mildred sighed. "I just hate she has to work so hard."

"Ma you know Bridgette would do yoga in her sleep if she could. Are we having dinner here or are we going out?" Keisha asked stomach starting to growl.

"Don't you know your mother doesn't cook anymore," Bertram complained.

"You are not here to cook for!" Mildred shot back. "We usually just have breakfast and a big lunch, you asked for a snack."

"That was one time I wanted a snack instead of dinner, not every night Mildred!" Bertram complained again.

"Dad, have you been at the office with the little book? Is that why you have been missing dinner?" Keisha laughed.

"Laugh all you want, that book may just save your life one day." The phone rang. "It's Bridgette. She said she would meet us at the restaurant."

"Okay, that's fine! Let's go, mom and dad. I'm starving!"

Bridgette watched her reflection in the mirror as she entered the restaurant. She patted herself on the back for coming up with the idea to meet at the restaurant. She would already be sitting in the booth when they arrived, and maybe they wouldn't notice any changes. *'I don't want to tell anyone at least not yet,'* Bridgette thought.

✡ ✡ ✡

"Hey Grandfather, how you been?" Joe asked pulling off his jacket and turning the volume down on the TV.

"How am I?" "How are you? Gabe told me about the shooting at the temple. Are you guys okay? I started to go that night, but I knew I couldn't talk David into going so I stayed at home. Have they caught the killers yet?"

"No Granddad they haven't and with the description they were given, they probably won't find them. They described them as your everyday Jewish man," Joe sighed dreading the conversation he knew he was about to have.

"There's no such thing as an everyday Jewish man anymore. You have black Jews, even native Americans have Jewish descent, Latino Jews. Jehovah said to Abraham he would make like the sands of the sea; he wasn't kidding," Heimlich said turning the TV back on.

"Granddad I need to talk you about something," Joe said hollering over the volume of the TV."

Just then David came in.

"Good, you are here too."

"Joe, you need me for something? I just came back from my walk," David exclaimed bubbly.

"Ah, yes I need to talk to you and Granddad," Joe said taking the remote from his grandfather and turning the volume down.

"Thank you for that!" David said eyeing Heimlich.

"Have you ever heard of Switzerland?"

"Of course!" David said.

"Ben and I are considering moving to Switzerland."

"What's in Switzerland all of a sudden?"

"April told me that she and Alexandra are considering moving there," Heimlich said sitting up to hear Joe better.

"There's a bank there that will pay $50,000 if you're a descendant of a Holocaust victim. They are also offering free homes if you move there. Every person in the family will get 50,000 if they move to Switzerland. Both David and Heimlich looked at each other for a few seconds without saying a word. Joe piped in, "Mom and Dad are not going because of Mom's M.S. Dad feels that the travel would be too much for her to handle. You two are healthy as horses, you could make the trip, and the entire family is going. Not sure about Uncle Gabe yet. He may want to stay behind for the temple's sake. Other than hard of hearing, you guys are in ship shape," Joe chuckled.

No one said anything for a few seconds. Nothing could be heard except the low volume of the TV in the background. Heimlich finally spoke.

"You're asking us to up and leave America, the only country we have known for over 60 years?" Heimlich hung his head in disbelief.

"What do you know about this bank? Have you checked into the people behind the bank? What corporation is running the bank? Where is it getting its funding from?" David had a lot of questions swirling in his mind, and now some of were rolling off his tongue. "I think you should start from the beginning and tell us everything you know, and we will double check the information together." Joe took a deep breath and started to explain everything to David and his grandfather.

After three hours of hard, precise questions, fact-finding, pulling up information on the internet, giving attorneys calls, the Better Business Bureau, and even one short call to Homeland Security, Joe scratched his head in wonder. He had never seen his grandfather or his great-uncle investigate anything like this before in his life. He had watched his grandfather make million-dollar deals without this much investigation. Maybe the Bernie Madoff situation had made the old man paranoid. His grandfather had never drilled him or anybody else that he knew of, in this manner.

Tears came to Heimlich and David's eyes on more than one occasion at the thought that somebody remembered the victims and set up a DNA data bank to track down the descendants of the deceased.   They both wanted to know why the Holocaust victims' museum were not the ones that did the tracking of the descendants. It seemed to the brothers that the museum would be the place with the most information and material to be able to trace the descendants, not some bank.

Was the information coming from government healthcare files and was this a breach of privacy for a bank to have this type of information? Joe had an answer for every question they came up with. He had investigated every aspect of the Bank of the Alps. As far as a banking institution, everything was legitimate. He allowed them to see and check out the brochure and the company video at the travel agent's office. Paradise Cove was given a five-star rating by its residences as well as five-star ratings for the way the Swiss government treated them.

Joe ended up leaving with David and Heimlich both saying that they needed a couple of days to think about it. Joe conceded and bid them goodnight and left. On the walk home, Joe thought about his great-uncle and grandfather; they were some tough old birds. You would have thought somebody was trying to kidnap them. Joe chuckled to himself.

Going to bed that night, David knew he had to tell Lorraine that he'd never loved a woman the way he loved her. Maybe because he had never loved a woman. He had to tell her about his gay lifestyle. He was quite sure that was his past. David knew he didn't love Barry the same way that he loved Lorraine. It had been thirty years since Barry died. David wanted to love again, he knew he could love again and if Lorraine would let him, he would die loving her and her only. He was trying to figure out a way to tell her about his past and about Barry and prayed she wouldn't turn him away.

Heimlich sat in his chair in front of the television for the first time since David moved in with him after the death of Ellen. He was alert, wide awake to life, completely coherent. Heimlich had to make a major decision about Paradise Cove. It seemed

104

everyone was in favor of leaving the country. The only reason Adam and his wife weren't going to make the trip was because of her multiple sclerosis. He didn't want to move in with them and become a burden.

Heimlich's stomach sank, something was not right, but he couldn't put his finger on it. He felt the money was adequate even with the taxing. Something about the money didn't sit well with him. Heimlich's would look into the bank of the Swiss Alps through his connections. He wanted to be sure for his family's sake. He wasn't able to take care of his mother, father and his siblings, but no one was ever going to trick his family again.

Chapter 13

"All tribes are here an accounted for Chief Mirrorlake. Let the meeting proceed."

"Have we found Native American engineers and gemologist?" Chief Mirrorlake asked.

"We have everyone in place. Sitting Bull Bank is covering the financing on the diamond digs, and we have already purchased and paid for the 18 oil rigs. The oil rigs will not be delivered until we make the announcement; really the day before the announcement. Paying cash for 18 oil rigs is cause for suspicion in the oil community. We have a big meeting with OPEC early next year Chief Wishingwell. You can cancel the meeting with OPEC–we will run our own company with no help from the outside world."

"All agree say aye, all disagree say nay," answered Chief Mirrorlake. All twenty of the Indians Chiefs agreed with a unanimous aye.

"Any more business that must be presented to the tribes?" Chief Wishingwell asked.

Coyote stepped forward.

"Greetings to the Tribal Elders and our ancestors. I come to ask for the purchase of a boat to help our brothers move from the country to escape to their motherland. This will be used later for fishing for whatever the tribes deem necessary," Coyote requested.

"How big is the boat and the price and how many of our brothers have you successfully returned to the motherland?" Chief Mirrorlake asked Coyote.

"Since 2012 I have safely return 3200 or more. Hiding them on the reservations at this time will only be tolerated in the caves. We cannot put the oil fields or the diamond mines in jeopardy to help our brothers."

"Again, if you get caught the Tribal Council will deny knowing anything about this, you or your family," Chief Mirrorlake reminded Coyote.

"It is understood that certain parts of the reservation are off-limits altogether. I take full responsibility," Coyote replied.

"You will have your boat."

Coyote let out a sigh of relief.

"Keep the dark one away until he cleanses his soul. He is in need of a soul cleansing for his sake and everyone else." That is all," Chief Mirrorlake replied. Chief Wishingwell escorted Coyote to the door, and the meeting continued.

Coyote thought it would be much harder to get the tribal community to purchase the boat. Maybe it was because the tribal community had accepted that the Jewish people were now in need of help. The Native Americans were more than glad to help.

Coyote laughed to himself at the fact that they called Bazz the dark one, not because of his skin tone but because the Chief felt he was too mysterious and had a lot of pain surrounding him. Bazz would never believe it was about his emotional state and not his skin tone. Coyote had asked Bazz several times to do a vision quest, but Bazz declined citing it was some ancient type of voodoo practice.

Bazz wouldn't have anything to do with it because he felt it was voodoo that the Rwandan Holocaust happened. Bazz was really deep, but he wouldn't let anyone in to find out how deep he really was. Then there was some mind mending that needed to take place. Bazz had decided he would never go back to Africa and he wasn't that fond of America. He felt America could have stopped the genocide if they had spoken up sooner. He had some serious issues that he wouldn't face. Asking him to face them was always an argument.

The most surprising thing about Bazz was his love of children. Not to have children of his own, Bazz had taken to Coyote's boys to the point that if something happened to Springlily or him, they decided that Bazz would be allowed to raise the boys. Bazz didn't know this yet. Coyote would let him know when the time was right.

"You need to hurry your ass up," Bazz yelled at Coyote. Bazz had been sitting outside the reservation in the truck for about 45 minutes.

"I'm coming. I'm coming. Blow your horn and pump your brakes," Coyote said laughing.

"You need to take it easy Bazz, you do know that you're not in Rwanda running again right?"

"Fuck you Coyote!! Sometimes you make me want to get a machete' at you! Leaving me out here in the sun!"

"Bazz, you could have come in. So testy!" Coyote said laughing.

"Hey, did your boys buy the boat?" Bazz questioned.

"Yeah, and the rules stay the same. If we get caught, they know nothing about it."

"Yeah, yeah, yeah they been singing that song for years, that's why they're in good standing now," Bazz said nodding his head toward the Casino.

"It's not like they didn't have trials and tribulations," Coyote stated.

"Yeah, they still had unity."

"They held it together through the rough years, and now they're a nation within a nation; that's pretty amazing. The nation paid its dues, and now it's paying off. I respect what they have done and where they had to come from," Bazz replied looking out of the window.

Another Miracle

A public school in the inner city of Chicago, K-5, had 2560 students. Due to the economic strain on most of the parents, the school feeds all the students 5 days a week. Some students even stay for dinner as no one is home to prepare a meal for them. A lot of parents were forced to work 2-3 jobs to keep a roof over their heads.

The budget was tight and the school principal, Elaine Woodson, had been borrowing from the lunch budget to feed the 1480 children who needed dinners as well. It was only halfway through the month, and the food supply had been depleted with no more funds coming until the following month; that was another 17 days.

The school pantry was down to 3 giant 32oz. cans of chicken soup and 6 loaves of French bread and two boxes of cheese. Ms. Woodson knew that was not enough to feed the children and started to cry because she could not turn any of the students away from the cafeteria.

The cafeteria staff looked to Ms. Woodson as what to do. Ms. Woodson bowed her head and gave thanks and made the soup and grilled cheese sandwiches to feed as many students as possible. The volunteer staff cooked the food and served the students. All the students ate and were full. Ms. Woodson thanked God for providing.

The next day a farmer had an overgrowth of tomatoes and mushrooms and brought them to the school. He wanted to give them to someone who could use them. The cafeteria staff thanked the farmer and sat the crates of tomatoes and mushrooms on the counter. Before preparing the food, they said grace and proceeded to make tomato soup for the students for lunch that day.

Later, a cafeteria worker went to the pantry to store the remaining vegetables and discovered 6 loaves of bread, some cans of soup and boxes of cheese. The items must have been overlooked somehow as no one had mentioned them.

That evening a vegetable vendor passed by the school. A few seconds later the vendor turned around and pulled into the school parking lot. The vegetable vendor had extra vegetables he needed to get rid of before they went bad. While they were standing in the parking lot unloading the vegetable truck, a man who was selling meat by the case noticed the refrigeration was going out on the truck. He said that by the time he could get the meat to the company on the other side of town, the meat would spoil. So, he decided to give the meat to the school. In truth, the driver didn't want to clean the mess spoiled meat would make in the back of his truck.

As usual, the staff said grace over the food. That night the students were able to have meat with soup and salad for dinner. That night the staff fed 1590 students. The number of kids increased. Word was getting out that the school was feeding students and more started coming.

Again, the staff checked the pantry and found 3 32oz cans of chicken soup, 6 loaves of bread, and 2 boxes of cheese.

Later that evening, when one of the parents came to pick up his child, he so happened to drive a vendor truck. He had a couple of cases of enchiladas whose expiration date was 2 days away. He called his boss and asked if it would be okay to give it to the school. His supervisor had just completed a freezer inventory back at the plant and found several boxes of food with expiration dates in the short future. He decided that they would take a tax write off and donated the food to the school.

After sixteen days of feeding the students on volunteer donations, Ms. Woodson noticed that the original 3 32oz. cans of chicken soup, 6 loaves of bread, and 2 boxes of cheese still sat in the pantry. She looked at the list of food and donations that people had made to the school and asked the staff had anyone donated the soup, bread or cheese; everyone said no.

In the 17 days Ms. Woodson and staff had broken bread prayed over it, the bread, soup, and cheese had multiplied. The donations had multiplied; the students had multiplied. They were feeding over 3,000 students a night. The word had passed to other schools that if they were hungry, they could go to Ms. Woodson's school and get a hot meal. They didn't have to stay home at night and be hungry, there was a place they could go where someone cared enough to make a hot meal.

God had provided the food every day and every night for 16 days. The food lasted and multiplied. One of the parents worked for the local government and was able to talk the powers that be into donating food for the night program at the school. No longer was Ms. Woodson scrounging to find food for the students. The night program was included in the school's monthly budget. Night school programs had been added for students to have nightly tutors. The program had even been extended to include summers. The miracle at PS 117 would never be forgotten.

Chapter 14

"You need to keep moving and be quiet. No sound is to be made by any of you – we talked about this earlier," Bazz whispered harshly to the family.

The family, Bazz, and Coyote had just entered the southern swamps of Georgia when alarms from the Coast Guard base sounded. Coyote and Bazz could hear approaching footsteps.

"You have got to move now, double time."

The family was at full hustle, running through the thick mud was out of the question. Coyote told the family to get down and stay down. Good thing it was dusk and whoever was leading the patrol was lazy. Bazz could see the upper lights of the truck and could tell it was military.

"Why is the Coast Guard running patrols this time of evening?" Bazz whispered. The truck shone the light another 5 minutes and drove away. Coyote called the family out of hiding and headed them to the hidden boat and loaded up.

"We may need to find another route; the military is taking Coast Guard training just a little too serious," Bazz complained. "I guessed it's because of the heightened terror alerts. We are probably at level orange today."

Bazz and Coyote got the family safely to Acapulco where their cruise ship took them to their new homeland of Israel.

"Have you ever been to Israel?" Coyote asked.

"What makes you think that I have ever been to Israel? Because I'm a big international traveler? You do know it was not by my choice that I became an international traveler."

"Bazz I still feel you should do a vision quest. You saw a lot of things while you were hiding those 21 days in Rwanda. It really could help your spirit, clear your conscience and calm your soul."

"Listen, man, for the 12th time, I don't mess with ancient Native American voodoo."

"Bazz, why do you keep calling it Native American voodoo?"

"Are you kidding me? Your ancestors put a curse on America! Every fourth president died for over two hundred years. That's some major voodoo," Bazz quipped.

"Bazz you need therapy. You need to talk to somebody and get rid of all that pain and depression."

"Please, do not ask me again. When I'm ready to talk about my past, I will!" Bazz grunted and stared out at sea.

Coyote walked away from his friend knowing that only Jesus could set Bazz free from the turmoil he suffered. *'I will pray for my friend,'* Coyote whispered to himself.

✡ ✡ ✡

David and Lorraine walked the neighborhood every evening and talked; it was the highlight of his day.

"Lorraine, I need to talk to you about something. I need to tell you about my past," David said nervously.

"David you can tell me anything. I feel like I have known you all my life!" Lorraine exclaimed joyfully.

"As a child, I had no role model. My father, as you know, was murdered in World War II. My great Aunt never married, and Heimlich and I had a lonely childhood trying to understand what happened to our family. You know everyone had horror stories about what went on over there. Having to imagine my family going through any of that was too much to bear. We never talked about what happened. All we knew was they were never coming home and that we shouldn't talk about it." David spoke in an anguished whisper. "I found out more about my family by talking to you than I have ever known and the fact that they were able to save another family makes me proud. I haven't even told Heimlich about what I know."

"You will in time, David," Lorraine said confidently.

"There are a lot of things Heimlich doesn't know or maybe doesn't want to know. When I was a very young man, I lived a life of isolation. I had no friends. I had no one I could share anything with. My life consisted of working seven days a week. When I got off, I tried to find the quickest way home to hide from the world. I just made money and stacked it. I had to wear a suit every day to work, and I only owned four not because I didn't have the money. I only wore three to work for six years, the fourth I kept in my closet. That was the suit I was to be buried in. I would try that black suit on and lie down in it sometimes, to make sure it would fit. I planned my funeral every year for five and a half years. Then one day I met a man named Barry. He acknowledged me with just a hello. That one hello saved my life. I realized there was a place I belonged, and that place was with him. Barry was a flamboyant, world renown chef who loved life and he loved me! He loved me for me. He brought air to my life. We spent almost twenty years together until he died of AIDS in the early 80's. I have been alone for 30 years. I have been alone until I found you, Lorraine. You bring a carefree joy into my life again. A joy that I didn't know I could feel after Barry died, but it's a different joy. A joy that the world can't judge like they judged Barry and me. I have to admit that Barry saved my life but it was, so I could go on and meet you, Lorraine. I lived to meet you, Lorraine," David cried. "There were times when I thought about ending it all, finally wearing that black suit. I'm so glad I met you, now my life is complete. I love you Lorraine, and I want you to be my wife. In every sense of the word."

Lorraine remained quiet for a few moments. "David give me time to think about this because you shared your life with a man for twenty years, this was not a drunken one-night stand kind of thing it was twenty years. I need time to think about this."

David stopped sobbing and watched as Lorraine turned and walked away. David's heart sank, but he prayed Lorraine could move beyond his past and knew he was able to love a woman. David knew how to love a woman he just hadn't had the opportunity to do so. He knew the needs of a woman, he even had some practice in physically learning to love a woman. He had hired a sex therapist to help him a couple of years ago. He went to her quite frequently, until the therapist knew he was falling in love with her which crossed the lines of their therapy sessions. David stood there for a while hoping Lorraine would return if only to say and kiss him good night. To go home dreading another night of Heimlich blaring the T.V. was almost unbearable.

When David got home it was quiet, the T.V. was off, and Heimlich was sitting in front of his computer.

"Good evening," David said and went to his room.

Heimlich barely acknowledged David's presence. David thought this was odd, but he would question it later, right now all he wanted was to get some sleep.

Heimlich had kept some old paperwork from his firm and decided to check some things out. He had an old list of foreign banks from the early 60's. He started there. Some of the banks had been bought out, and the names had changed, but in the old European Union, money very rarely became new, the money was old, and it changed hands. Now and then a new account was opened by a terrorist group or a new internet sensation, but overall the money was old, and it stayed that way.

Everyone in the financial institutions knew about the stolen money and that the money was hidden in accounts in Switzerland.

The money became whispers in the 60's and 70's, especially, after the hunting of former Nazi officers had slowed. The offspring of the Nazi soldiers were the ones who reaped the benefits of the money. Most of them changed their names, never to be heard from again.

Heimlich was disturbed to learn that children of former Nazi officers ran a lot of the E.U.'s major corporations. The Bank of the Alps looked good on paper. Its stocks traded high, and company investments were quite good. At one point in time, the major stockholders lived in the company owned houses in Paradise Cove.

Everything Joe told him and David, checked out. The homes and the money existed and were at the at their disposal. Theirs for the taking. The Better Business Bureau had never received a complaint. The bank seemed to be run on the up and up. The stock was considered to be Blue Chip stock.

The board of the bank had five individuals that supported the institution. The only way to get to know the true culture of a company was to investigate each member of its board and their lifestyles. This would cost money that Heimlich no longer had. It would help ease his mind about the bank and the move his family was insistent on making. "Ah ha!" Heimlich said aloud. He remembered he did know someone who could help. He had washed millions of dollars for the mob through his good friend Winthrope. The last time he saw Winthorpe was in the late 80's before a government shakedown of organized crime. It would be as difficult to find Winthorpe as it would to find the truth about the bank. He had an uneasy feeling about the situation. It was as though the past was coming back, only now the family was going back to the land where the atrocities had been committed.

Heimlich knew he wouldn't sleep well that night.

Chapter 15

There was a great buzz at Crazy Horse Cancer Research Hospital since Rabbi Dr. Elam Reuben, had arrived from Israel to continue his research there. It was reputed to be the best medical research facility in the world with the most elite staff and state of the art equipment. Dr. Reuben would continue his research in different types of medicinal herb marijuana. He'd already published a few papers eluding to the fact that he was quite close to the cure for cancer. The hospital staff was excited to have Dr. Reuben on board not only because of his wisdom and knowledge but that the cure for cancer would possibly be discovered at Crazy Horse.

Dr. Reuben felt he was so close to the cure. He couldn't sleep at night and often took long walks outside of the compound to clear his head and calm his nerves. He loved the facility and the reservation that housed it. He felt safe and felt his family was safe as well. His wife and girls were finally free of fear here. There were no suicide bombers, no anti-Jewish propaganda. The schools were outstanding, the weather was perfect, and the chaos happening around the world seemed not to affect this land at all. Dr. Reuben was seriously considering a permanent move to the reservation.

Marissa found her husband sitting on the deck of their 5-bedroom, home that the Tribal Community had gifted them.

"I knew I would find you out here," Marissa said lighting a candle and moving toward Elam to sit next to him on the deck. "It's so nice and quiet here, and the air is fresh."

"Yeah, it's nothing like home. No worries about bombs dropping on top of your head. No fear of suicide bombers sitting next to you on public transportation," Marissa added.

"America is still beautiful," Elam declared looking around. "You know, I feel I am a few days or maybe hours from finding the cure for cancer. I need to stay on here longer. It is so beautiful here that I am thinking about moving here permanently. I am torn between my homeland and the reservation. I do know the history of the Native American Indians. I understand that their heritage and our heritage go hand in hand." Elam said smiling at his wife, whose mouth was open and ready to speak.

"Yes, they have come a long way from the atrocities that were committed against them by the white man," Marissa replied.

"Look at you! You already know the term the white man."

"I just considered them men although there is a certain distinction between the paleface and the Indian. I learn as the purples learn," Marissa said smiling.

The purples, as Marissa called them, were their two girls.

"They have learned to like it here, and I don't think they want to go home. They miss their friends and family but other than that, they say they feel safe here. I would like to stay if possible. I'm not turning my back on my heritage, but it's nice not to have to worry about attacks constantly. I will always love our homeland but getting to stay here has been amazing," Marissa said.

"Remember, we're on the reservation. It's the backyard of the state," Elam said

"Well, it's a very nice and safe backyard."

Marissa laughed leaning on Elam's shoulder closing her eyes. A few moments passed, and Elam broke the silence.

"It's safe but not enough to sleep outside."

✡✡✡

Bridgette decided to make sure she was pregnant and made an appointment with the OB doc. If she was going to terminate, she had to know what the timeline was.

"Ms. Zigburgh, you are six weeks pregnant. You need to start prenatal care as well as taking the vitamins I'm going to prescribe for you, "Dr. Morris said turning his back to get pamphlets on pregnancy.

"I'm not sure if I'm going to have the baby," Bridgette said quietly.

"You have pamphlets for that also. I still feel you should get the prenatal vitamins just in case. If you are thinking about termination, then it is mandatory to see a guidance counselor," Dr. Morris said reaching for an appointment card.

"Yeah, I know," Bridgette said.

"Do you want to go today or later on in the week?"

"I'm here so might as well go now."

"Just follow the red line down the hall to the psychology department."

Bridgette started down the hall, but with so much on her mind, she forgot which color line she was supposed to be following, so she asked a nurse.

"What color line is for the counselor?"

"The red line is for the counselors pink is for breast cancer and blue is for the bunny farm mandatory testing area.

"Oh, thank you very much."

At the end of the hall, the red line and blue lines went in different directions. Bridgette was walking so fast preoccupied with about what to do next that she bumped into a young lady who also was hurriedly leaving the bunny farm department.

"Oh, I'm sorry ma'am," Bridgette said backing up to give the lady room to pass her. The two women's eyes met.

"April Hi! "said Bridgette shocked.

April ran past Bridgette as quickly as she could. Bridgette chased April down to the elevator almost knocking over two more women.

"Go away, Bridgette. I don't want to talk to anyone!"

"Wait a minute, April are you working for the Bunny Farms? You can get a job with Ben or me before you do this to yourself."

"Bridgette that's not enough money to keep my apartment or allow me to go to school and you know Joe already lives with you guys. I didn't want to live with mom and dad having to watch my mom slowly die from Multiple Sclerosis. I chose this to help me pay my bills and go back to school. Now I've decided that I am going to leave and take the 50,000 from the Bank of the Alps and live in Switzerland. Aunt Alex and I have already signed up for the program!" April scream hysterically.

"Look April you can do so much better than this. I can get you a job at my yoga studios," Bridgette said out of breath from chasing April.

"I don't know any yoga," April started to cry again

"I can teach you," Bridgette said looking into her purse to find a tissue for April. Bridgette started to cry also.

"What are you crying for?" April asked hugging Bridgette.

"I was just thinking about what kind of mother would I be when I don't carry wipes or tissues."

"A mother!" screamed April. The hospital staff told them to keep it down. "You're going to have a baby?" April laughed and cried at the same time.

"I'm not sure I'm going to have the baby. I'm scared April," Bridgette said squatting down to sit on the stairs.

"Aw Bridge, you would make a good mom."

"April we can't afford a baby. Ben's at the pizza parlor all day. I've had to let some of my yoga teachers go and start teaching most of the classes myself to make ends halfway meet."

"Bridge, all a baby needs is love," April paused for a minute and fished through her purse and gave Bridgette a tissue and the application for the Bank of the Alps. "Think about it. Bridge, it might be what you, Ben, and the baby need. To start fresh in Switzerland."

"I'll think about it, April. Don't say a word to Ben. I'll tell him when I'm ready. Plus, I have a few more weeks to teach yoga before I'm too big to move!" Both of the girls laughed and started crying again.

✡✡✡

"Hello, this Rawlins calling for Romero and Zachary."

"This is Romero."

"I see you and your brother have been busy, and you have taken out six families in 30 days in six different ways as not to cause suspicion. I just deposited 8 million dollars into your accounts and 1 million in the Brotherhood's account. I have six cruise ships full of Jewish people willing to come to Switzerland to start over. I've had to build another 26 houses in Paradise

Cove to make sure everything looks good on my part. Have to make it look profitable.

You and your and brother need to step up your game and try to deliver me fewer people that will go to Switzerland. You need to find a way to find a way to eliminate large numbers of Jews at one time. Think along the lines of striking a stadium full of people. Also, if you or your brother can't handle this, I will find someone more willing to get the job done. I will remove my money from your accounts and let Homeland Security know what you like to do for fun! Do I make myself clear?" Rawlins asked.

"Quite clear sir!" Romero answered. "I will discuss this with my brother as soon as possible sir." The line went dead. Romero hung up the phone quickly.

Romero knew that the Brotherhood needed the money, but he could not wait to get rid of Rawlins and go back to running their organization. Zachary was wracking his brain trying to find a way to get rid of more families at one time. He knew that he and Romero could not run around the country shooting entire families and not get caught. He would have to think of another way to take care of more people at one time and not get caught.

"I have already assigned some targets to higher-ranking officers in the Brotherhood that are well trained. I trained them myself. I allowed them to profile their targets and prepare to take them out. They're running surveillance as we speak. I have not given them the go-ahead not as yet," Zach said.

"Zach, I have an idea... the way we can get rid of more people at one time. Have a large Jewish gathering in a stadium and make it family oriented. We'll call it Support for Israel Night. Advertise on social media and pass out different fliers to temples. Get as many as possible and boom! That would be at least three thousand families at one time. Mission accomplished. We would make our father so proud," Romero said.

"You don't really believe that Mengele is our father and that we are test tubes? Do you?" Zach asked.

"Zach, I had another DNA test done off some skin grafts that Mengele left behind, that he wanted to use to clone himself. We were a 98.999% positive match. Zach, he is our father. I set out to disprove this crazy story too, but DNA tests don't lie. I'm so proud that his blood runs through our veins. I will make him proud." Romero was screaming at the top his voice.

"Dude calm down. You know this guy can't be our father. Our father is the same tweeker he has always been. You know he is a meth head! When I find him again, I will do a DNA test on him to prove to you we have no Nazi blood in us. Rawlins wants us to do his dirty work! If Rawlins hates the Jews so much, why doesn't he get rid of them himself? He wants somebody to take the fall when the shit keg blows up. I do my own dirty work. I do not plan on spending any more time killing a people that won't die. Do you know what these people have been through and they still thrive and live? They are really the chosen people. No other race can go through what they have and still survive and flourish. The only other race is the black race, and they're killing each other for us! Let's just take the money and start over somewhere else. Somebody else will run the Brotherhood. Let's get out while we're ahead. Romero, this is a complete and utter lost cause. You know deep in your heart that this war cannot be won. It's been going on since the beginning of time, and you know how it's going to end. You know who the winner is and it ain't us if we continue down this road! Let's quit while we're ahead and disappear before all this catches up to us. All I ever wanted was to be rich and respected. Now we are! Let's get out before it's too late!"

Zachary was begging with everything in him to get his brother to change his mind. The sad part about it, he knew his brother would never stop. He was too far gone to hear or to stop. When they were kids, all Romero wanted was to be a part of a prestigious family. He couldn't claim his mother or father as a child because they had gotten lost in drugs. Now Romero would have bragging rights to a notorious Nazi killer. He would love that more than all the money Rawlins would offer him.

✡ ✡ ✡

Dr. Reuben was working late in his lab. He couldn't put his finger on it, but things seemed different tonight. There was a spark in the air. As he went on his routine for evaluating his dosages, he decided to try something he had never tried before.

He was tired; his brain knew what his hands were supposed to do, but the hands had a mind of their own. They mixed things that his mind knew shouldn't be mixed, and then he threw it in the petri dish for safe keeping overnight. He quickly jotted down in the lab journal what he had just done with a reminder that he would review it in the morning. Honestly, he was so tired he was not quite sure what he'd done. He would unscramble it in the morning. Dr. Reuben cut the lights off, locked the door and went home to bed.

As he slept, the Lord GOD Jehovah Rapha had mercy. The concoction his hands made turned out to be the thing, the world hoped, prayed, and died for.

After yesterday's conversation with Romero, if you could call it that, Zachary knew what he had to do. He had to find their father, Marcus Dubois.

Marcus Dubois was a meth addict. He'd gone from a weed head in high school to meth. It started early it peeked, and it stayed. Last time anyone knew the whereabouts of Marcus Dubois, he was homeless and living in New Orleans, Louisiana and that was before Hurricane Katrina. Zachary didn't care where he was and what rock he had to look under to find him. All he knew was he had to get Marcus to agree to a paternal DNA test to prove he was their birth father before Rawlins could brainwash Romero even more with the Nazi crap. Who knew, before long Rawlins would have him believing that he was Hitler reincarnated himself.

That morning there was a scheduled press conference at the Crazy Horse Cancer Research Center where Dr. Reuben was to announce his discovery. The announcement was high profile and would be attended by all major television affiliates as well the Tribal Leaders and hospital administration.

"Good morning Ladies and Gentlemen. I'm here to announce to you from the Crazy Horse Cancer Research Facilities that Dr. Elam Reuben has made an incredible milestone in the history of medicine. Please allow me to introduce Rabbi Dr. Elam Reuben and his lovely family." Chief Mirrorlake began the press conference.

"To my God, I give all the glory, to my loving wife and daughters I thank you for your tolerance. To the world. I give you hope. I have found the cure for cancer…"

About the time Dr. Reuben uttered the word cancer, multiple gunshots rang out striking Dr. Reuben in the throat and chest. Bullets also hit his wife and daughters. Everyone dropped to the ground, ducked or ran for cover. The press turned their cameras toward the woods where the shots had come from a black SUV. It was also seen speeding from the scene.

Dr. Reuben and his family were placed on gurneys and wheeled into the hospital's emergency room immediately. The tribal leaders started an immediate hunt for the shooters.

The media remained to cover the shooting and monitor Dr. Reuben and his family's status. While the tribal leaders understood that it was news, they respectfully requested the media leave the reservation with a promise of hourly updates on the status of their findings. The reporters were not happy about being asked to go, and a reporter was quick to throw out that the public had a right to know, and they were infringing on freedom of the press. Chief Mirrorlake gently reminded the media that they were on Indian land and that they were not obliged to follow the laws of the United States. With that, the reporters were escorted off the grounds and kept company by armed tribal officers at the entrance.

Chapter 16

"Sir, we have the subject Marcus Dubois on the streets of New Orleans. He lives in a shelter four days a week and receives a check from the government for $682 a month which 90% is spent on meth," the private investigator reported.

"What's the name of the shelter?" Zachary asked getting a pen and paper.

"Eagles Nest," replied the private investigator.

"Okay thank you, you can pick up your check on your way out. The receptionist will see you out. Romero, I need you to take a trip with me next week. Give me a call when you get this message." Zachary left a message on Romero's phone. He was away working on the big stadium deal.

Zachary was determined to prove that Josef Mengele was not their father and that Rawlins wanted them to do his dirty work.

"Vincent Wargold is here to see you, sir," Zach's receptionist announced.

"Send him in. What is Vincent doing here in my office, he knows never to come here? What the hell is going on? Zachary was talking to himself as he spun his chair around to face the door.

"Sir, I'm sorry I'm here, but I didn't want to call and leave a message on your cell phone. We have a slight problem. The officers you sent out to do a certain job acted without consent and may have caused a security breach for the Brotherhood."

"What do you mean?" Zachary asked huffily.

"One of the candidates chosen by the officers a world renown cancer research doctor. He was staying at The Crazy Horse Cancer Research Center in the Black Hills of South Dakota."

"I must say, they were ambitious," Zachary snorted.

"Those officers chose to execute Dr. Reuben in front of the worldwide press when Reuben was announcing that he had found the cure for cancer."

"Are you serious? In front of cameras? The world saw it? This will instill fear in all Jews around the world. We have done what we set out to do–shake up the Jewish community," Zachary huffed.

"Sir you don't understand. Homeland Security and Tribal Police officers are tracking the men. If they are caught, all evidence will point back to the Brotherhood, which will put the entire organization at risk," Wargold explained. "I came to tell you what is going on. I am on my way to Buenos Aires. I suggest you and Romero prepare to make a move," Wargold said leaving the office.

Zachary got busy trying to prepare an escape for him and Romero out of the country.

"Marge, call the bank for me, let me know when you get them on the line!"

"Yes, sir."

Zachary thought to himself that now was a good time for him and Romero to leave the country and get him away from Rawlins. Romero seemed to be getting caught up in the fantasy of Rawlins.

"Sir, I have the bank on line one."

"Thank you, Marge," Zachary said, picking up the phone. "How you doing Elliot? I'm fine this is Zachary. I need you to transfer money to my account in Greece. I will give the Federal Trade Commission a call to let them know that money is transferred. I need at least a million transferred. Yes, three days will be fine, thank you," Zachary said, hanging up.

He'd let Romero know the plan once they were in New Orleans.

✡✡✡

The news was sad on the reservation. Dr. Reuben and his family had all succumbed to the gunshot wounds. Not one lived.

"The press is having a frenzy outside the reservation," said Chief Mirrorlake.

"Most important, we have the medical community coming to see if they can go through Dr. Reuben's medical files to see if he documented his findings on the cure for cancer. This is the thing the world has been waiting for–the cure for cancer, and it was discovered at the Native American Cancer Research Institute," Chief Wishingwell replied.

"I have never been so emotionally conflicted. The fact that Dr. Reuben and his family were murdered on Native American soil is an atrocity within itself but to assassinate him in the middle of a press conference announcing that he has discovered the cure for cancer. It deprives the world of the contribution this man made to help humanity," Chief Wishingwell stated voice starting to crack and tears streaming down his face.

"The Jewish people have suffered much, as much as the Native Americans," Chief Wishingwell continued. "The tribes will find the killers, and they will be brought to justice. We may need to bring Coyote and the Dark one in on the hunt or at least find out what they might know."

A knock at the door caused Chief Wishwell to wipe the tears from his eyes and clear his throat.

"Come in," Chief Mirrorlake said for his friend. It was Delaine Wishingwell looking nervous.

"Dad, Chief Mirrorlake, we have some people here from the American Cancer Society and the National Cancer Institute asking to look through Dr. Reuben's lab and his notes and files. What would you like for me to tell them?" Delaine asked.

"Please send them in," said Chief Mirrorlake standing.

"I'm so sorry sir, please accept my condolences for the family. We know that the whole tribal family is in the grieving process. I do apologize for my timing. My name is Gordon Ayers, and I'm with the National Cancer Institute. This is Elkana Slevoric from the American Cancer Society. We would like permission to go through Dr. Reuben's lab and files to see if he indeed found the cure for cancer. We would like to give him credit for his discovery." Any financial contributions will be passed on to his next of kin," Gordon Ayers said.

"We more than willing to oblige you for the sake of the cure. Delaine will show to his lab and your rooms. Let us know if we can be of any service for you."

"Thank you, sirs, for your hospitality. I wish it were under different circumstances."

"Delaine, show them to the penthouse hospitality suites."

As they left the room, an idea came to Chief Mirrorlake. "We have to make sure no one is snooping around the reservation, so no one discovers the oil or the diamond mines. Call the tribal police and tell them to tighten security in all the hot spots." He was interrupted by another knock at the door. "Come in," Chief Mirrorlake hollered. Coyote and Bazz entered into the room.

"Good evening Chief this is my friend and associate Matabazz Obassa.

"Listen up and listen well. I know what you boys do. I don't know why you do what you do, but I know it is a very successful enterprise," Chief Mirrorlake said looking directly at Coyote and Bazz. "Right now, we're in a situation where you scratch my back, I scratch yours. You guys need more equipment to do what it is you do. I know all about you hiding the families in the upper caves overnight. You are going to have to move them. It's too close to the oil."

Bazz shot Coyote a look. Coyote shot one back as to say I'll tell you later. Chief Mirrorlake continued with the conversation looking out the window.

"Son, you have a lot of hurt and pain in you. You carry it like a wet blanket. Do something about that, please. What I need from you two is to see if you can get a track on the people that killed Reuben and his family. If you find them, let us know. We'll do the rest. Thank you, that's all." Chief Mirrorlake didn't turn around.

"Thank you, Chief," Coyote said turning Bazz toward the door.

"Wet blanket son," Chief Mirrorlake said. "Wet blanket." Coyote closed the door behind him and looked at Bazz. He knew he was about to get an earful.

"What does he mean I carry a wet blanket?" Bazz questioned.

"I told you man, you were oozing pain, and those that are sensitive can feel your pain, and it doesn't feel good. You see you have worked through enough of your pain that you can function, but not enough to heal."

"I have healed. I barely have nightmares anymore. I don't hate Hutu people anymore."

"You may have let it go to the point that you can function, but not enough to settle down with a life partner and have a family. That's why I share my family with you. I have never seen you so happy except when you are playing with my boys. I want to see you happy with your own family."

"So, you're trying to tell me I'm not invited to dinner anymore?" Bazz asked smiling.

"No man, I'm saying you need to do a sweat lodge, a vision quest."

"Man, I have told you about that Indian voodoo. You want me to sit in the dark and sweat until I become dehydrated and delirious then start seeing stuff right before I have a heat stroke. And I'm supposed to believe that what I'm seeing is supposed to mean something to me; that the spirits are revealing something to me. You come out better offering me some LSD and then ask me to believe my lying eyes!" Coyote just shook his head.

"You need to let the grief go and get a girl."

"You do know that I'm not gay and that I really, really really, like girls?"

"Thou does protest just a little too much," Coyote said and started laughing. "I'm just saying   get it out of your soul before you become sick or bitter!"

"How does Springlily deal with you and the work we do?"

"She is very understanding and knows that if I die, it will be helping another human get to freedom, one way or another."

"I just don't think many women would understand the disappearing we do. I don't have to justify what I do to anyone, and that makes my life easier," Bazz said looking at the ground as he walked.

"Bazz, all I'm saying is talk to somebody even if it's only God."

"Some things I have done in this life are so bad that I can only tell God."

"If I need to talk, Springlily is there. I don't carry a heavy conscience or a wet blanket around," Coyote said getting into the passenger side of the truck.

"Is a vision quest really what I need to do?" Bazz asked after being quiet for a few moments.

"I'm just saying let that stuff out before you explode Dark one!" Coyote started laughing.

"You know if I didn't know any better, I would think you are trying to change my name to an Indian one on the sly."

"Dark One, yeah I got his Dark One." Changing subjects, Coyote said, "I'm going to give a close friend of mine a call and see if he's heard anything about the killings. Milton moves around a lot, so he might have heard something. He keeps his ear to the ground."

Chapter 17

Zachary was glad to be leaving New York. It wasn't safe. The money didn't matter anymore he just wanted to get Romero away from Rawlins. He would be okay in Argentina; he'd be able to himself again. Zachary would tell Romero about the money that he transferred to the new account as soon as they left New York. Argentina would be a fresh start for them. Who knew, they might even meet some beautiful women and settle down. Argentina was looking better than ever. When Zachary arrived at the office with his bags, he could see that Romero was already there.

"Hey glad you're already here. I have already scheduled a cruise to Barbados and then on to Argentina. We are so in need of a vacation," Zachary exhaled and inhaled to relieve stress.

"Zach, I just came to tell you I'm not going. I don't belong in Argentina. I belong here. I have a job to do. I have booked a stadium, and I have the Jewish speakers all lined up for the night. It's called "Save Israel. I'm preparing the pyrotechnic entertainment for the evening. I can't go."

"Romero now is the time to go. If we stay any longer, nothing good is going to come out of this. We are not death angels. This is not who we are! Let those people live. Nothing good can come from this. Even though I detest these people—the Jews—I have learned from their history that they are protected and that they can only be their own worst enemy. No one else can truly touch them. Nobody can destroy them. They can only be destroyed by their own hand. History shows that if you throw a rock at them, they will throw a mountain back. It may take a while to throw it, but believe when they do, it will be a mountain. They mind their business. They do not interfere with others. They are a protected people. Romero, man it's not worth it. Let's go while we can! Let Rawlins do his own dirty work! You are all that I have. It's always been just you and me."

"See, that's your problem Zach, when things get dark, you always want to leave. You want the easy way out. You have to stay and see things through! Zach, I need you to stay and help me run this financial kingdom the Jews are leaving behind after we get rid of them."

"Romero, if we stay, the only kingdom we get will be a suite in prison. I'm not going out like that. I'm not doing jail time for Rawlins. The Brotherhood is disbanded, and there's no telling who they are snitching too. We have got to go now!" Zachary finished, heading to the door.

"Wait, Zach," Romero called out. Zach turned around in front of the door and looked back at Romero.

Zachary felt a hot slice of lightning hit his upper chest. He dropped his bags to the floor. The burning pain increased. Zachary could hear his heartbeat growing louder then slower until there was no more sound. Romero walked over to Zachary, kissed him on the forehead and left the room. "Goodbye brother." He picked up his suitcases, closed the door, and threw the knife down the mail chute in the hallway before exiting the building.

Chapter 18

David came home one evening from his walk and found Heimlich unconscious on the floor. He called 911 and then the family to let them know what was going. The family waited huddle together in the e.r. waiting room, anxious to hear how Heimlich was doing. After a couple of hours, a physician came out and sat with them.

"I am so sorry. We did everything we could. He had a massive stroke and we just..." the doctor's voice trailed off.

"Can we see him?" David asked.

"Yes, of course. I'll have the nurse take you to him. Again, I am so sorry for your loss."

David went out the following night to take a walk. The house was so empty without Heimlich. He missed him terribly; even the loud television programs. David wasn't planning on seeing Lorraine, but his legs were on autopilot; they took him down her street. As with every nice New York evening, Lorraine was sitting on her stoop drinking her tea.

"Oh David, I'm so sorry to hear about Heimlich. I know you loved your brother and he will be missed."

"Thank you."

"Did he show any sign before he had the massive stroke?" Lorraine asked lovingly.

"No, he hadn't been stressed. He'd been staying up late the last couple of nights searching for something. That was a couple of nights before I found him passed out on the floor. Other than that, there was no odd or strange behavior," David answered quietly. "I know I said my brother and I didn't have any contact for twenty years, but over the last ten years, we had grown quite close. When I walk into the empty house now, I turn the TV on and turn the volume up a bit just so the house won't feel so lonely. I see the pain in the kids' faces and the grandkids'; it has affected them more than I thought it would. There is no life in April. Heimlich spoiled her and Alex. He spoiled both of the girls. It's good they have each other to share the grief. It may help that they're here together instead of two continents away." David began to sob uncontrollably.

"Oh David, I'm sorry," Lorraine said wrapping her arms around him.

"Lorraine, you know you never answered my question about marriage," David whispered.

"David, I have thought about it every day since you asked me. How do you know it's me that you love? How do you know that you now want to love a woman? I always thought that if you were gay, you would always be gay, or are you bi-sexual?"

"Lorraine, I loved a man thirty years ago. It was physical, mental, and emotional. I now have those same feelings for you. I've never had those feelings for any other woman and never any other man after Barry passed. I know this is all new for you just the same as it is for me. All I know is that I can make you happy and satisfied as any other woman is with her husband. I want to satisfy you in all the ways that a man can satisfy a woman. I live my life for you and the few weeks I have been apart from you, have been the hardest times of my life. I never want to be away from you again, Lorraine. Not one more day, not one more hour. I want you and only you! Lorraine, marry me and spend the rest of your life with me. There is no reason we should be apart. I love you with all my heart!"

"David, I have missed you, and I'm not a young woman. I am 68 years old and to start a life with you now seems crazy, but yes David, I will marry you. I will be your wife in every sense of the word." Lorraine laughed and cried at the same time. "I can't wait to be your wife," Lorraine said leaning in to meet David's kiss. The kiss lasted long enough for David to fish the engagement ring he had been carrying in his pocket for six months.

"I want you to put it on now." David placed the ring on Lorraine's finger.

The evening was getting cooler, and they went inside. They sat and talked for a while then one thing led to another. David found himself in Lorraine's bedroom laying on her bed. She reached over to turn off the bedroom light.

"No don't turn this light off. I want to see and feel all of you," David exclaimed. Lorraine smiled and left the light on and undressed for David.

"You are more beautiful than I could have dreamed. I'm so proud that you accepted me to be your husband. David pulled the sheets back on the bed and waited for Lorraine to enter then quickly undressed and popped in beside her. "I have waited all my life for you," David told Lorraine and kissed her passionately.

Chapter 19

Shea sat with a list of names in front of her. She was researching the Bank of the Alps and had created a list of names with a connection. Ironically, 19 research hospitals had come up. Too much to be a coincidence. Lapstar protected most hospital servers. She didn't know exactly what she was looking for, but she'd know it when she found it. She called the first center on the list.

"Hello, Crazy Horse Hospital. May I help you?" Delaine Wishingwell asked in her most professional voice.

"Hello, my name is Agent Maxwell. I'm with Homeland Security. I have a survey or questionnaire for your medical records department."

"I'll transfer you now."

"Hello medical records, may I help you?"

"Yes, my name is agent Maxwell. I'm with Homeland Security. I have a few questions I'd like to ask you.

"Ok," replied the records clerk.

"Are your files and database kept in separate buildings?"

"Well ma'am, we're not allowed to answer any questions about our security. Doesn't matter if you're Homeland Security or not. We are a nation within a nation, and we are not governed by the laws of the United States of America. Our manual files are kept in separate rooms, and the database is on a separate reservation altogether. That's all I can tell you, ma'am. Thank you and have a nice day."

The click was very loud in Shea's ears. "Damn, damn, damn." Shea hung up the phone looked down at her list and crossed Crazy Horse Hospital off. She picked up the Bank of the Alps brochure realizing what was happening. Shea reached for the phone again.

"Hey girl," Keisha answered the phone.

"Sit down, K. I need to talk to you."

"Shea, what's wrong?"

"I figured out how that bank knows who is Jewish and who is not. They've hacked the national healthcare medical records database. That's how they were able to get the DNA profiles. I have no idea how they got past Homeland Security, but they did," Shea said disgustedly. "Millions of dollars spent on Homeland Security cybersecurity and the company that secures the database is the culprit!" Shea said hissing and speaking in Chinese.

"Wow Shea, I know you're mad because you're speaking in Chinese. Slow down and explain what you're talking about?"

"You know a couple of months ago we were trying to figure out how a bank knew who was Jewish and who wasn't?"

"Yeah, I remember."

"We thought they went through the Holocaust Victims Memorial List and followed the descendants or closest descendants, and even then, you would have to go through the Ancestry.com to get that type of information."

"Even then that would take a whole lot of time and a lot of skip tracing to find out who had Jewish DNA. Since I work for the Dept. of Healthcare, I was able to follow a trail without Homeland Security becoming suspicious. I looked up what company was in charge of the security or the backup of files for entire healthcare databank. Lapstar is responsible."

"So!"

"What do you mean so?" Shea was screaming again.

"Calm down Shea and explain."

"Lapstar changed the spelling of laps, and you get what? You get Alps Rats! Look at the back of your brochure and the printing media of the paperwork is printed by Alps Rats."

"Shea you're reaching!"

"Reaching, my ass. I called Alps Rats of course. Bank of the Alps owns Alps Rats. Bank of the Alps also owns Lapstar! Lapstar supports all the major healthcare and hospital data banks, and they just updated all the security banks in the last eight months. The same time everyone started getting brochures from Bank of the Alps! Lapstar is headquartered in "Switzerland! I also checked all the major hospitals in America. They all have Lapstar as their database supporters."

"So maybe Lapstar does medical security backups for all medical institutions."

"Only the medical institutions in America?" Shea replied.

"Ok, Canada and Mexico don't have them?" Keisha asked concerned now. "Shea, how did you find out all of this information?"

"I pretended to be a Homeland Security agent doing a systems survey."

"A what?' Keisha asked in disbelief.

"A Homeland security agent and people gave me the information I asked for. The only ones who didn't answer questions were the Indian Reservations. They are serious about their security."

"Shea, do you know you can go to jail for that?"

"For what? Pretending to be Homeland Security?"

"Yes ma'am, that is a fraud.!"

"That's the only way that I could get the information."

"Let's not worry about jail, let's worry about what they are doing with this information and why they want it. Shea, I called my dad a couple of weeks ago, and he hasn't gotten back in touch with me yet. He was saying that the fact that this bank is offering this only to Jewish descendants is a red flag! Since I didn't know anyone willing to take the deal, I didn't push him or follow-up with him."

"The fact that someone has access to your medical records and info doesn't worry you?" Shea asked.

"I'm healthy as a horse so no it doesn't worry me," Keisha shrugged. "Shea I will phone my dad and tell him what you found and see if he has anything new on his end. Meanwhile, please stop impersonating Homeland Security. I will find out what is going on."

"Keisha, you're supposed to be the Poe Poe!"

"Hang up the phone Shea!" Keisha squealed.

Keisha thought about what Shea had told her. There was no way that all the shootings in synagogues and other Jewish specific targets was a coincidence. Somehow the bank and these killings were linked. She called her father.

"Hey daddy, I just got off the phone with Shea. She is freaking out! She just found out that the Bank of the Alps owns a company that maintains all the medical database systems in the country!" Keisha said.

"Dadblastick!!" Bertrum said. "That's how they're doing it."

"Doing what?"

"Keisha, they're hacking into the medical data banks matching the DNA up to Jewish DNA. I believe that they're targeting everyone on their Jewish list. Old and young are going to be targeted. For what purpose K, I don't know. I found out that the money used for this scheme is cursed. It has been used to finance wars and supply military equipment in wars in North Africa, Georgia, Serbia, and Albania! They haven't been able to get rid of this cursed money! This is money that was stolen from the Jewish people including the gold that was taken out of their teeth. It's blood money, Keisha. People died so this bank could have this money. This money brings death and the pain of life! Have nothing to do with this money, let Switzerland keep it! The people who run this corporation are questionable at best. Shea did a good job with her research, and now this has to be turned over to a higher authority. You're the police Keisha, let some higher authority know that the United States' infrastructure has been compromised. The intelligence agencies need to be warned, and this bank has been reported to the federal reserve. This country must be on high alert," Bertram said anxiously.

"Wow Dad, this is huge. There can't be a coincidence with the violence against the Jewish people," Keisha barely got a word in edgewise.

"I hear from others that there are death squads. They're tasked to kill Rabbis and their families in the temples. You're the police baby girl. It's up to you now to make sure the information gets to the right channels and, over and above that, it's followed up on."

"You can be sure of that Dad. It has to stop, and I will do everything in my power to get things going."

"Something else Keisha, and you're not hearing this stuff, I don't want to scare your mom, but I'm thinking about moving out of the city to the country and start doomsday prepping. I'm in

139

the process of liquidating stocks and bonds to gold and looking for places to live until this thing is over. It's getting bad Keisha."

"I'm inviting Ben and Bridgette over to tell them to prepare. It's going to get uglier. Shea may be right about this bank. If she is, this is the bank that is financing the death squads."

"K, have you seen or heard anything in the last couple of months? Is there any information from the military? Seen anything odd?"

"Daddy a few months back I saw some pictures of a family trudging through the swamps. I didn't pay a lot of attention to it at the time, but now that I think about it, they seemed to be escaping from something. I thought they were doomsday preppers. It never occurred to me they might be fleeing from something. Daddy hang on, let me look at the pictures again."

Keisha pulled the pictures up on her cell phone, loaded them onto the computer, then emailed them to her father. There was complete silence while they studied the pictures together.

"Daddy, the old guy has a Star of David necklace on in this picture.

"That may mean that they are Jewish not necessarily that they're escaping anything."

"Just that fact he's wearing a Star of David makes you wonder?"

"Baby girl, I'm going have to tell your mom what I think may be going on. I'm sure she's already suspicious. I've been at the office every day for the last two weeks trying to figure this mess out. What I believe is that they're using foreign terrorist to attack the banks and financial security systems of this country. I'm going to hate telling your mom what's going on. The fact that she is from the south is going to confirm every racist suspicion she's ever heard or seen."

"Mom's a tough bird. Being from the south prepared her for this, and worse if necessary. All the stories she told me about the south and racism and her own experiences will come in handy right about now. She grew up in the cradle of racism– Birmingham, Alabama. I don't think she'll be surprised about anything going on."

"Yeah, you're right."

"What does this mean Dad?"

"Foreign investors are trying to find a way to collapse the American dollar, the medical information being stolen from national data banks, death squads being financed by foreign banks to kill American citizens. It should be a declaration of war, but because it's this race of people, nothing will be done. Those of us who know must tell the rest of the world what is going on. Connect the dots, Keisha!"

"Thanks, Dad. I needed to run this by you. A sanity check I guess before I take it up the chain. I'll try though. I love you, dad. Talk to you later."

"Bye honey, love you too."

Keisha hung up the phone sick to her stomach. To think that someone wanted you dead because of your religion and the color of your skin was heinous. It went beyond religion and skin color–it went back to DNA. It was unreal; they were implementing a plan for a second Holocaust. Keisha wondered who "They" were, and could they be stopped. Questions were running through Keisha's head so fast, but she couldn't answer them all. Whoever "They" were, they had to be stopped at all cost. It had already happened twice; The Jewish Holocaust and the Holocaust in Rwanda. She couldn't believe it was happening. Keisha decided to call Shea back and let her know what she suspected, and that Shea was right.

"Hello Shea, this is Keisha."

"It must be pretty bad for you to be introducing yourself like I don't know who you are," Shea said quietly.

"It's pretty bad. In truth, "pretty" has no place in what I'm about to tell you."

"Tell me, I can take it!"

"The Bank of the Alps is using info from the medical data banks to find Jewish people then using death squads to kill them," Keisha said bluntly.

"Are you telling me this bank uses the fifty thousand to lure you out so they can put a hit out on you?" Shea asked.

"Pretty much," Keisha said quietly. "All the murders in the temples and the bombings, the killing of the Rabbis is about a second Holocaust. We have to notify all the intelligence agencies. This is America. They can't get away with this!"

"Ira has so much pride in the fact he has Jewish heritage and now I have to tell him that there may be a hit out on his life because of it. He was trying to figure out how he could grow his payot."

"His what?" Keisha asked.

"Payot, you know the curls the Jewish men wear on the side of their heads."

Keisha burst out laughing, "Are you serious?"

"Yeah I told you, Ira is all or nothing about everything."

"Shea, I have to go and tell a few people about this."

"A few people? K. you have to go on CNN, Fox… every news network you can. You have to tell the world! Start with the intelligence community. I got to go and tell Ira this!" Shea said.

Keisha took a deep breath and started to call Homeland Security to get an investigation started. She thought to herself during the whole process that in America you are innocent until proven guilty. It would take a while for the dots to be connected working with the government. She hoped that they would zero in on the hit squads before anyone else lost their life. It was the most critical of the whole process.

News Flash

In national news today, Israel reports it has discovered that the temple mount of Solomon is located hundreds of yards from the reported Dome of the Rock. The new temple mount can now be built next to where the temple was first thought to be. This will end the geographical war of having to share the temple with other religions. The new temple will be built in less than two months. Animal sacrifices will begin again in Jerusalem.

Chapter 20

"Coyote, I have an uneasy feeling about this trip. Something's not right."

"I know Bazz, I feel it too, but I don't know what it is. Keep your eyes open. Did you interview the family? Did you do a background check? Is the boat working?

Yes, to all of the above and all the passports accounted for. We did a walk earlier through the swamps. The casino construction crew is off. We're only moving eight members; no babies, no old people…everybody looks healthy. Don't know what it is," Bazz said looking around.

"Let's try to get them to move just a little faster. Swamps aren't safe under any circumstances," Coyote replied.

The family started moving double-time through the swamps of Georgia. Suddenly, the father of the lead family stopped mid-step causing everybody to stop. Bazz and Coyote stopped to see what was going on. The father fell face down to the ground. Bazz and Coyote could hear the silencers on the guns being fired at them. Two more hits to other members of the family and the remaining women screamed and took off running in different directions. Bazz used his night vision binoculars to locate the assailants. He saw the muzzle flash of a gun in the dark. Another shot hit one of the three women. Coyote paused, aimed, and took a shot, hitting the shooter in the chest. Bazz was chasing the women telling them to get down and take cover.

"Coyote what do you have?"

There was no answer from Coyote, but Bazz could hear twigs breaking and footsteps. He knew Coyote was moving pretty fast. Bazz was trying to calm the women down so when it was time to move, they could. Coyote gave the signature whistle letting Bazz know to stay put which meant that there were more shooters. Coyote shot two rounds into the darkness. Bazz heard a big thud hit the ground, and then footsteps running in the opposite direction. Coyote gave chase but wasn't able to catch the remaining shooters. He returned to Bazz and the hysterical women.

"What the hell is going on?" Bazz asked trying to calm the women down. We just lost six members of this family. We were ambushed. Six people were killed right in front of us man! Ma'am, can you tell us anything? Did something happen at your home or anything? Anything in the last 48hours? Ma'am, did anything happen?"

The woman sat up, and through nervous shakes and sobs, she tried to answer.

"My husband received a handwritten letter in our mailbox the day before, warning us of a hit. Ralph, my husband, thought we would be safe because we were leaving the next day, so he didn't tell you about the note."

"He didn't think we needed to know this information?! Well, your husband just got six members of your family killed!"

"Come on man, they just lost their family!" Coyote said trying to back Bazz off the grieving family.

"Say what you want, we could have been killed too!" Bazz said kicking a tree stump.

"We got to get these women out of here. We'll come back and get the bodies later," Coyote sighed heavy.

Coyote and Bazz escorted the women to the boat where they went on to Acapulco, Mexico. From there they boarded the cruise ship to Israel.

"This is the worst transfer we have ever done as a team. It was sloppy," Coyote said after dropping the women off.

"Sloppy hell! Coyote you know we should be dead right about now. The hit squads know our routines, and these people have jeopardized our operation and anybody else we try and transfer. We're going have to make some major changes, or more people will be killed!"

"It's going to take a couple of days to figure out how much the hit squads really know," Coyote commented.

"Man, they hit us right here in the swamps twenty miles before the boat, so you have to assume they know everything! It's not safe. We're going to need a new plan. I didn't make it out of Rwanda to die in the swamps of Georgia," Bazz said sickeningly. "I didn't survive a genocide to die in the second Holocaust!"

"Bazz the only difference is the words."

"The only difference is I'm not going to let this one happen! What are we going to do with the bodies?" Bazz asked.

"Unfortunately, we are in the swamps, and a gator got to eat," Coyote said. "Let's get started–it will be daylight in a few."

Chapter 21

Pulling up to the house Ira wondered why Shea was calling and texting like a crazy woman but wouldn't tell him anything until he got home. He hoped they were not having dinner guests. It wasn't her birthday or their wedding anniversary so why did she insist he come home now?

When he arrived home, Shea opened the front door and started to exit when the sound of gunfire cracked the night. The bullet shattered the side and back windshield of the car.

"Get down and back in the house!" Ira shouted in Shea's direction. Ira could not see Shea, but he could hear her screaming over the gunfire. Laying on the ground, Ira reached for his gun. He could hear and see it was more than one shooter and they had him pinned down in the driveway. All he could do was try and return fire. Suddenly the boom of a shotgun blast rang out from the front door of the house. Shea had hit one of the shooters, and Ira was able to take out the other.

"You okay?" Ira asked racing to Shea's side. "When did you learn how to shoot a shotgun?" Shea was chattering incoherently in Chinese while Ira tried to calm her. "Baby, you okay? Who were these people? Did they have the house surrounded? Is that why you were calling me? Baby, calm down and put the gun down! When did you learn to use a shotgun?"

"About five minutes ago!" Shea answered in English.

"Baby are you okay?"

"I'm okay. Who are these people?"

"I promise they are not drug people from the past. Is this why you were texting and calling? I am not in anything crooked. I promise Shea! Anybody in the house? Let me search the house," Ira said walking away from Shea.

Shea grabbed Ira by the arm.

"There's no one in the house! I believe this has something to do with something else."

"What else could there be?"

"We have to call the police."

"First tell me what you are talking about," Ira said walking Shea into the house.

✡✡✡

"Hey, it's me," Romero said to the caller. "I'm going to increase the bounties another million dollars. For whole families, another 25 grand and if it's done without police involvement, you get another 25 grand. Get the word out." Romero hung up the phone and walked out on the tarmac to the waiting chartered jet.

"The flight will land in Florida for refueling in about 3 hours. Then to the airport to catch a flight, to South America."

"I'm ready whenever you are," Romero said to the pilot.

✡✡✡

Shea had calmed down and explained to Ira what she had been told about the Bank of Switzerland and that she felt the shooters were part of a hit squad targeting Jewish people.

"Hold up, wait a minute Shea," Ira said, "you're telling me that the bank that sent the brochures out for the free housing in Switzerland is going to kill me before I get there? "Baby it makes no sense!"

"Ira, the 50 grand is to lure you and kill you because you're Jewish. They're trying to kill all the Jewish people! That's who was shooting at us."

"The police are trying to pin it all on my old drug charges from back in the day," Ira said voice cracking.

"Yep," Shea said. "I looked into the bank, and their background and I found all of this information. How would a bank know anything about DNA? It made no sense to me, so I called Keisha. She called her father to see if he knew anything about it since he is a professor of Hebrew studies. He started putting it together weeks ago, he was missing the part about the

148

medical databases and the stolen information and the DNA. Keisha called Homeland Security who started an immediate investigation. The CIA will be involved, and the Federal Reserve has been notified."

"So, it hasn't made it down to the regular beat cop," Ira said shaking his head. "Somebody shooting up my house is from my days of trafficking even though marijuana is legal! Shea, a hit squad won't stop until you're dead. We're going to have to leave here! We'll need some help disappearing. I know just who to call."

"Who, Keisha and Brandon?"

"Hell no. You know you don't call the police to solve real problems. Coyote and Milton are who you need to fix some things," Ira said taking the shotgun out of Shea's hand.

"Coyote is not his real name is it?" Shea asked.

"It's his name and his occupation at the same time. Milton was Black Ops. Did some time down in Haiti back in the day when America had the secret death squads down there doing God knows what. I met them in Miami during my runs."

"The people you know . . .. I swear!" Shea said rolling her eyes. "Well call them because I'm not staying here tonight!"

✡ ✡ ✡

"I miss Dad so much. I'm just glad I got the opportunity to tell him bye and that I loved him. It makes a difference," Alex said.

"Yeah I know I'm just glad I was there to bless and release his spirit before he died. He accepted Yeshua a long time ago. He's in the Lord's hands now," Gabe said quietly.

"It's been so long since I have been in the temple and now, you're the Rabbi over the temple. I'm so proud of you and Dad was too."

"I know, he told me several times. I'm glad I was here to hear it. I thought about transferring cities," Gabe said with pride. Do you want to go to dinner?"

"Yeah, let me check my mail. I got a letter from the New Temple Mount Society. They're working twenty-four hours a day to get the temple built. It says here that the temple will be finished in the next three weeks and they're planning a big celebration here in New York for the ones that can't make it to Israel," Gabe said excitedly.

"I'm ready, my stomach is growling Alex."

"Hey, wait a second, this is a donation envelope. Somebody must have dropped it, and there's something in it."

Gabe opened the envelope and found a letter inside. He read the letter silently. When was finished, the letter fell from his hand when he slumped back into the pew. Alex picked up the letter and read it aloud:

Dear Sir,

You don't know me, but I'm behind the hit squads that are targeting Jewish Temples and families. I have killed at least nine families totaling 69 souls. I have decided this is not what I am supposed to be doing with my life. No words can change the sorrow I have caused and the harm I have caused my soul. In a hopeful act of redemption, I am writing you this letter to let you know that your family name has reached the top of the list as I write you this letter. You and your family must take all precautions to protect yourselves from the impending assault. The death squads will not stop until your family death has been achieved. Do what you must to safeguard your family."

The letter was signed:

Sincerely,
Redeemed

Alex dropped the letter and sat on the pew next to Gabe in total silence.

Chapter 22

All media groups had assembled at the Crazy Horse Cancer Research Hospital in South Dakota for an announcement from the tribal elders of the Native American Nation. All the major networks, affiliate networks, and foreign affiliates were waiting for the announcement. The buzz was Dr. Reuban Elam had discovered the cure for cancer. Chief Mirrorlake exited the front entrance of the hospital and walked to the podium.

"Hello, my fellow citizens of this great land of ours. Today is a historic day for my people. Through the years, my people have been denied certain unalienable rights by the government of this country. Our forefathers suffered and endured much, but our pride and respect remained intact. Today we remember and honor our forefathers. There was a time when we were young warriors and could not understand why our forefathers refused to give in to the American way or lifestyles of the American people. They fought hard and suffered long to hold on to tribal traditions.

Native Americans were forced to live on reservations on the worst land the government could find to give us. We could not grow adequate food on the land and our people starved. Years went by, and our people found a way to survive and thrive. We went on to realize our unity. We created and understood the wealth from the Casinos, and as a nation, we were able to write a check to the United States Government for two trillion and bought the mineral rights to Indian Reservations.

Today I stand in front of you, a proud Native American who has learned to respect and appreciate the wisdom and the patience of our forefathers. Today their hopes and dreams have come to fruition. Today, the Tribal government of Native Americans own the mineral rights and land of the largest shale oil reserves in the world. These reserves are located on six different reservations and will be processed by Native American

Oil Companies and Refineries. The oil will be sold worldwide and locally. I'm sorry, I will not be taking any questions right at this moment, I thank you for your patience, and you all have a good day."

✡ ✡ ✡

In Switzerland, Erich Rawlins was checking the operations at Paradise Cove. "Give me an overall update."

"We're still getting cruise ships from all over the world, but American ships are rare. This means that the boys in America are doing their jobs as we paid them to do. Leave it to that great American can-do spirit," the Paradise Cove manager reported.

After receiving the report from Paradise Cove, Erich contacted Romero for an update on their plans.

"In a couple of weeks, America is going to take about 50,000 Jews and give them an old fashion barn fire in the biggest stadium in America," Romero said.

"I knew good old fashion greed would be the best incentive to get America to come through for me and moving in the right direction. All hail to the red, white and the blue." Erich ended his conversation with Romero in an upbeat mood. The Jews of the world would soon be annihilated.

✡ ✡ ✡

Bazz and Coyote resumed their hike to the boat without their passengers. Both were silent as they thought about what had just happened and how the entire family had been shot in cold blood. For Bazz, the killings brought back haunting memories of when he had to hide under dead and rotting corpses in the swamps of Rwanda as an 8-year-old child. Bazz was trembling at this point and had broken into a sweat. Coyote could sense his pain.

"Hey, hold your head up Bazz, we need to continue the transfers. We need to reconstruct our plans, and we can still get the job done," Coyote said.

"I've been doing this since late 2010, and I've never lost a soul. I never had to protect anyone because I was always careful to hide everything about the transfers. Guns were a precaution, never had to use them. Coyote, shit hit the fan and people were killed. They lost their lives because of what? Because of racism. I swore on the lives of my family that I would never be hunted again!" Bazz said exploding.

Coyote's cell phone rang interrupting Bazz's outburst.

"Hey! Hey man are you okay? "Coyote asked shaking Bazz.

"Yeah, I'm good," Bazz replied quickly.

"You know that hunting you wanted to do of the people, that just hunted us? You may get your chance!" Bazz perked up to listen. "A good friend of mine barely escaped an attack by our new good friends, right outside of his home. He wants us to come up to his home to talk a transfer and maybe a counter-attack."

"Man, what is going on out there? We're not ready for a transfer," Bazz said cautiously.

"Oh, I wouldn't worry about that. My friend is an expert in the import and export business. Let's go, I'll fill you in on the way," Coyote said slyly.

✡✡✡

"You know, it's been two weeks since our engagement, and I still feel like I'm walking on a cloud. I have never felt this way before, Lorraine," David said. "It seems like I have been going through life holding my breath waiting for something to happen. Lorraine, you are what happened to me. I am so grateful for you," David said laying his hand on Lorraine's shoulder.

"David, I can't wait to be your wife. I'm glad we're starting our new life in Switzerland. I'm sad that Heimlich won't be making the trip with us. I talked to Bridgette. She's decided to name the baby after Heimlich if it's a boy."

"Oh Lorraine, he would have loved the idea of the baby being named after him. His first great-grandchild. He would have spoiled that kid rotten," David said smiling. "Alex invited us to dinner at Heimlich's house. I moved my last bag out of the house today. I've been walking a bag over every day. Alex didn't want me to move out, but I told her we are getting married and at our age, we have no time to waste. I want to spend every waking moment with you starting now!" David said squeezing Lorraine's hand.

"David, I am so glad that God sent you to me. It took a while, but God is always on time. No matter how you try to rush, God knows what or who you need. It's crazy to even believe I am starting life at 68. I'm just glad that God remembered me," Lorraine exclaimed. "Thank you, God, thank you!"

David and Lorraine basked in the glow of the television. Everything almost seemed right with the world... almost. The moment was interrupted by the phone.

"Hello... Yes, David is here... Oh, I'm as well as can be expected... At eight o'clock, that's fine with me, we'll be there, goodnight." Lorraine hung up and turned to David. "David, Alex called a family meeting tomorrow night at 8'oclock and I'm invited," Lorraine let out a scream of joy.

All David could do was chuckle at Lorraine's excitement. "Remember, you are family now."

Chapter 23

"Hey, Keisha! So, what did Homeland have to say?" Shea asked nervously.

"I spoke to someone, but they didn't seem to get the urgency. The thing about America is that you are innocent until proven guilty, which means until you pull the trigger, nobody is going to die. You have to do the crime, and then get caught. Good old fashion suspicion is not good enough anymore."

"There's a whole lot more than suspicion there I think, don't you?"

"I'm a police officer, and I know that where there is smoke, there is an inferno. You'd think since 9/11, any hint or clue should be taken seriously," Keisha said disgustedly.

"Keisha, I have to tell you that three guys were staked out around the house and tried to ambush Ira and me!"

"Shea, you're supposed to start the conversation with this information, not hold it then politely tell me."

"These guys were trying to kill us because we're Jewish, not anything from Ira's past," Shea said.

"What, are you kidding, me? Ira doesn't play about you or his house!" Keisha said surprised "Are you alright? I'll be there in about 4 hours!"

"Good, I didn't want to ask you to come, but I need you. I'm a little scared to stay out here by myself," Shea said.

"Be careful. See you soon," Keisha said hanging up the phone. Keisha saw Brandon had called her while she was on the phone–she'd call him while she was on the road.

"My guys should be here first thing in the morning. We'll make a plan from there." Ira turned to Shea and tried to comfort her. Shea moved away and headed to their bedroom. Ira couldn't remember the last time Shea was at a loss for words. There was a thick silence the rest of the night.

"Hey, I hear we are having a family meeting," Joe said as he came in and hugged his Aunt Alex and April.

"Yeah, we're waiting on David, Lorraine, Ben, and Bridgette," April said.

"You now Bridgette takes a little longer these days, Joe," April said giggling.

"You're telling me," Joe said holding his arms out like he was carrying something big.

"That hair is getting longer and thicker. I am so jealous," April sighed.

"You just wait, your time is coming," Alex replied playfully punching her niece in the arm."

"Can I get married first?" April squealed and took one look at Gabe and stopped in her tracks. "There must be something wrong. I didn't know Uncle Gabe was in the room," April said seriously.

"Uncle Gabe are you okay?" Joe asked touching him on the shoulder. "You look like a ghost!"

"I'm sorry. I'm just in deep thought, right now. Your mom and dad will join us on the phone. They don't feel like getting out tonight. Your mom isn't feeling well," Gabe said trying to sound calm and courageous. Just then there was a tap at the door; Lorraine and David stepped in.

"Hello everyone," Lorraine spoke first.

"I heard congratulations are in order you old sly dog," Joe said giving his Uncle David a soft punch. David beamed with pride.

"For all of you who don't know, I asked Lorraine to be my wife, and she said yes!" Congratulations came from everyone in the room.

"Thank you so very much," Lorraine said a bit choked up.

"When is the big day?" April asked Lorraine.

"We haven't decided yet, but we want it to be very soon," David answered.

Ben stepped through the door.

"Sorry Aunt Alex, I still have the keys to the house."

"Oh, that's quite alright, keep them. April or I may get locked out and need that extra set."

"Where's Bridgette?" April asked. "I wanted to see if she has gotten any bigger since she gave all the yoga classes to me."

"She's getting up there . . . due in eight weeks." Ben answered all the questions at once, so April couldn't ask anymore. April opened her mouth in surprise.

"At her parents' house." Ben hadn't forgotten the first question asked by April. "They're having a family meeting too."

"I'm going to call mom and Dad, so we can get this meeting started."

All three kids spoke to their parents, and the meeting started. Gabe began to read the letter out loud. It was quiet for about 30 seconds before the questions began.

"Is this a joke? Who are these people? April asked. "They can't have death squads in the United States."

"Is that what happened a couple of months ago at the temple?" Ben asked. "Can I see the letter?"

"Where did it come from?" Joe asked looking at Gabe.

"It was left in my office. I don't know when or how it got there. I thought it was a blank sheet of paper. I read it by chance," Gabe explained.

"Maybe you should give up the temple, let someone else take over," Adam said. "You could hear Anne coughing in the background.

"Let someone else walk into this mess unaware?" Gabe asked. "That still doesn't exempt us from the death squads. I don't think that would take us off the list," Gabe spoke quietly.

"Maybe it will," Adam replied.

"That's it then–we should call the Bank of the Alps and reserve our place on the cruise ships and prepare to leave this place. America is no longer the land of the free and home of the brave," Alex said disgustedly.

"Alex, you're going to try and leave the country again?" Gabe asked.

"I didn't have this problem in Italy. I have a close friend who moved to Paradise Cove in Switzerland and sent me some pictures a couple of days ago, telling me how beautiful it was. She likes the place and told me that I should consider moving there," Alex said shaking her head. "Everyone gets fifty thousand dollars. We could start life over again. We could make it if we went as a family." Alex continued to babble to keep anyone from changing their mind and coming up with excuses to back out.

"I'm willing to take a chance if you are," Lorraine said, turning to David for his answer.

"As long as we're together, I don't care."

"Mom and Dad, what do you think?" April asked.

"We can check the medical hospitals and facilities in Switzerland, that will decide our fate," Adam answered for him and Anne

"I'm going," April declared. "There's nothing here for me." Joe and Ben looked at each other.

"Maybe after the baby's born," Ben said.

"Are you willing to take that chance with Bridgette and the baby's life?" Joe asked.

"Bridgette's already a pretty big target," Ben said trying to make a joke. "I don't think that kind of strain is a good idea right now. I'll talk to Bridgette; we'll decide together."

Ben's phone rang; it was Bridgette.

"Ben, I have something crazy to tell you. I just talked to my mom and dad they told me that the Bank of the Alps is not a real bank! It's a cover for financial terrorism, and it's supplying the hit squads or death squads to kill Jewish people," Bridgette said out of breath.

"What are you saying, Bridgette? This makes no sense. How can a bank support domestic terrorism? Listen, I'm on my way to get you. You can tell everyone when you get here," Ben said hanging up the phone.

"Listen up everybody. Bridgette's father says that the Bank of the Alps financially supports terrorist groups and death squads to kill Jewish people," Ben announced.

"Death Squads financed by a bank, you have got to be kidding? Has anyone reported them to Homeland Security or tried to freeze their accounts through the International Banking system?" Joe asked out of breath.

"We still haven't a clue as to who left the letter for Uncle Gabe."

"C'mon guys, you really can't believe this? I have a friend who just moved to Paradise Cove in Switzerland, I'll call her now," Alex said reaching for her cell phone. A couple of seconds went by, and Alex had a frown on her face. "The phone number has been changed, and the new number is private."

"Sounds kind of iffy to me Aunt Alex. We'll wait for Bridgette to get here with the information from her father, so we can get the entire story and sort this situation out. Alex, try some of your other friends and see if any of them have heard from your friend who moved to Switzerland. I'm going to fix dinner– seems we're going to be waiting awhile."

"I'll help you April," Joe said heading to the kitchen with April.

News Flash

A category four hurricane is headed for the east coast. Landfall is expected within hours. The winds are howling, and the rain pours in sheets as people hasten to batten down windows and doors. Hardware stores in the Carolinas are struggling to keep up with the demand for wood and emergency supplies. The entire east coast is preparing for the hurricane bearing down with 85-mile per hour winds. Landfall is expected in the Carolinas.

Chapter 24

A strong, warm wind was blowing in the Dominican Republic where Romero was sitting on a beach having a drink thinking to himself that placing a bomb made of fertilizer in a food truck was the best idea that he ever had. A food truck parked inside a stadium filled with explosives sat waiting for the *Christians for Israel* rally to start over the coming weekend. Romero smiled to himself knowing that all he had to do was make one phone call and boom! He would be able to kill 15,000 Jewish descendants at one time. Even though the Brotherhood of Valhalla was putting in their time, he didn't want to disappoint. As the President of the Brotherhood, Romero had to make the biggest kill to prove that he was worthy to be in charge. Since Zachery was gone, he had to ensure that he stayed at the top. Blowing up the stadium would certainly maintain his status. Romero couldn't wait until Thursday. "Boom!" Romero said out loud to himself with a smile.

✡ ✡ ✡

Coyote and Bazz made their way to South Carolina for their rendezvous with Ira and his crew. Coyote was still trying to understand what Ira had told him over the phone a couple of days before.

"Hey man, explain to me again that it is a bank behind the hit that was supposed to take you out," Coyote asked Ira. "Are you sure that it's not anyone from our past life?"

"Coyote, you know that when we got out of the game, we made sure everyone got rich."

"Maybe it's somebody that thinks that they didn't get rich enough?"

"On our lives, we squared everybody up good and fat."

"Coyote, it's the bank and can you guess why? Because I am a Jew. I just found out that I'm Jewish and now there is a hit out on me because I'm Jewish. Ya Man!"

"Dude, we walked through hell with gasoline drawers on carrying two sticks of dynamite and never had a problem out of the other playas in the drug game and now that you have discovered your religious roots, you barely make it home?" Coyote said incredulously.

"The irony right. I expected it from the street but not from the church."

"Man, this is not a church, this is the long arm of the Nazi reaching down through time to slap the Jewish people just one more time!" Coyote said staring at the floor. "And you're telling me that Annie Oakley in there, was the one who saved your sorry ass?"

"No shit Sherlock, I'm shocked too!"

"Hey, that's your boy from Africa?"

"Yeah, that's him. He's a solid dude just been through a lot."

"Was he there when the genocide happened?"

"Yeah, I think that he was about ten or so."

"Man, I can't even begin to register what he must have seen and lived through. I hope that he has insight into this mess."

"You do know that he helps me with the transfers?"

"Coyote, you still do that?"

"Yeah, and he's my righthand man. Milton helps sometimes. I think of it as a way to give back for the dirt we did in the streets."

"I hear you, man. I try to give back too. I hope that one day when I get to heaven, God says that my scale of life is balanced and that we're even. How often do you do transfers?"

"I try to move a family every six weeks."

"Dude, I work you like a mule, how do you have time to move families like that?"

"Bazz took over. He lost his entire family to the Rwandan genocide, so he takes this deadly serious. He does not play. He tells me that it's a life or death situation. You are in good hands with him. He is the only person besides you and Milton that I trust to watch my back."

"Good because Shea is really shaken up. I'm glad that Keshia is here, she will help her calm down."

Keshia and Shea came out of the restroom both red-eyed. You could tell that they had been crying.

"We're going to keep a clean transfer," Ira continued.

"What's a transfer?" Keshia asked. "Or do I want to know?"

"Not if you still plan on honoring that badge!"

"Is everybody packed and ready to go?" Bazz asked.

"I believe so," Shea sighed heavily.

"I'm ready," Keshia replied.

"Not with those high heel shoes and a dress on–go change! Bazz barked.

"I didn't bring a lot of clothes with me," Keshia replied.

"Girl, you know I have clothes. We shared everything in college, and we're still the same size," Shea reminded.

Keshia went into the room to change and rolled her eyes at Shea whispering under her breath, "Who the hell is that?"

"He is here to do a transfer, meaning he is going to help transfer our asses out of here!" Shea answered in a loud slow voice

"Girl, you make me sick," Keshia said, closing the bedroom door.

We're leaving by boat," Ira announced.

"What boat? We don't have a boat!" Shea exclaimed.

"Umm yes we do. It's one I own from back in the day when we used to do transfers."

"Do I want to know?"

"You never did before," Ira smiled slyly. "We're going to ride close to the coast all the way to New York and stay out of sight of the coast guard–you know, how we used to do it. Milton and Jordan will meet us on the Hudson," Ira said speaking to Coyote and Bazz. "With the Hurricane about to blow through, the coast guard will be busy, so we will practically be invisible and will be able to get into New York with little or no notice. While I'm there, I plan on visiting the United Nations. Sometimes it's good to be a United States Congressman even if you haven't started yet. I guess you would call it a perk, but the United Nations needs to know that an attempt at another Holocaust or Genocide is happening. I would have never

163

believed Coyote, that anyone would ever try to do this again. Holocaust 2.0–what the fuck?!" Ira ranted.

"I am never shocked at the cruelness of people especially when it is demonically motivated. Life should mean something, but when there are spirits behind the hate, there is no stopping the craziness that can happen," Bazz said quietly.

"Man, I bet you got a story to tell about how you made it out of Rwanda," Ira commented.

"Seems your stories may be a little more interesting than mine," Bazz nodded toward the trunk filled with guns and ammunition.

"I just found out I'm Jewish and now I also found out some people feel the best Jew is a dead Jew. Can you believe that?" Ira asked rhetorically.

"I know the feeling," Bazz said.

✡✡✡

It was late when Bridgette and Ben finally made it to the family meeting. "Hey everybody," Bridgette said, "I have some very bad news."

"Dad and Mom are already asleep so no need to wake them," Joe said pointing to the phone. "C'mon and tell us everything."

David woke Lorraine who had drifted off to sleep. "My you're getting big," Lorraine said to Bridgette patting her belly. "When is the baby due?"

"In about 8 weeks," Bridgette answered.

"Bridgette, go ahead and tell everybody everything your father told you. Listen up, Aunt Alex!" Ben said sternly. "Were you able to reach your friend in Switzerland?"

"No, not yet."

"My father is a professor of Hebrew studies with a heavy concentration on the Holocaust… he discovered a lot about the Bank of the Alps situation," Bridgette began explaining.

After 35 minutes of repeating verbatim what her father had told her, the family was quiet for a few moments, then the questions started.

"This cannot be true!" Alex exclaimed. "I have a friend who just moved to Switzerland. Her entire family went with her. . ." Alex trailed off, starting to cry uncontrollably.

Gabe stood and said, "These are the end times. The new temple will be completed before the baby is born. We should have suspected something. If anything is for Jewish people only, it's hard to believe anything good will come out of it. We took it for granted that we live in America and believe that bad things are not supposed to happen here–that we are somehow immune because we live under the banner of the red, the white, and blue. Hate and racism exist anywhere. You have to choose what is worth dying for. After the Holocaust ended in 1944, our people vowed it would never happen again, and we meant it. America is a racist country, but they use finances to try and cover it up. If you make enough money, they try and cover it up. Hidden racism does exist. But this is not hidden, this is an attempt at a second Holocaust–killing a people. This will not happen on my watch!" Gabe finished weeping.

Suddenly a loud boom rocked the room. The floor, windows, and walls started to shake as patches of the ceiling fell and the chandelier swayed. It felt as though the thunder had cracked right over the house. The rain from the hurricane moving up the east coast had been parked over the state of New York and had already dumped a lot of rain on the city. The subways and commuter tunnels would flood if it continued. There was also the storm surge sure to come with the hurricane. The areas right on the ocean were already beginning to flood.

"It's raining cats and dogs out there, that's why it took us so long to get here. Now the lights are starting to flicker, we're looking at a blackout," Ben warned.

"I'll get the candles and lanterns prepared," April said heading toward the kitchen.

"It's getting deserted out there," Joe said looking out of the window. "I've been watching the news, and the outer bands of rain are stalling out over New York City. They're expecting a lot more flooding."

165

Chapter 25

Keshia and the crew were well underway staying as close to the shore as was safe. The waters were choppy, and the swells were getting bigger. Ira realized they'd have to find a safe harbor to ride out the hurricane. He could see the hurricane just beyond the horizon, and it looked huge like nothing he'd ever seen. Suddenly the boat lurched as though it had hit something.

"Is everybody okay?" Ira called out.

"What the hell was that?" Bazz asked Coyote.

"I don't want to say what I thought, but I know that it's not good. If I'm right, we're going to have to get out of this boat!" Coyote replied.

"Is there a problem with the Coast Guard?" Keshia asked concerned.

"The Coast Guard is the least of our worries. That hurricane is bearing down, and we need to find a safe harbor," Coyote said looking at the nautical charts. "There's a harbor just a few miles ahead that will be good shelter. Steer the boat there and do it double time. We don't want to get in that hurricane!"

"Look, here comes the Coast Guard!" Keshia said looking out toward the water.

"Quick, somebody sit on that chest," Ira instructed.

Shea quickly sat on the chest full of ammunition as Keshia sat on the trunk full of weapons. The Coast Guard pulled up alongside with megaphones blasting. "I am Captain Molten of the United States Coast Guard–prepare to be boarded," came the voice of the officer over the megaphone.

The cutter pulled up alongside Coyote's boat as it bounced on the wake. The officer and two other crew members made their way down a rope ladder thrown over the side of the cutter. Once on board, Captain Molten advised Coyote that they needed to get off the water as soon as possible as the hurricane had picked up speed and was expected to hit land as a CAT-5. He instructed them to anchor in the next harbor, and he would radio ahead to have trucks waiting for them to offload the boat. He further told them that they would be taken inland away from the high surge. After giving them instructions, Captain Molten asked why they were on the sea given the weather.

"We have friends and family in New York. We're going up to help evacuate them before the storm hits. It gets pretty bad there," Coyoted answered.

"It's already bad there. There's a blackout, and the military is out on every corner protecting the city from any danger from inside or out. You probably won't be able to get into the city–it's locked down pretty tight."

"Hello Captain Molten, I am Congressman Ira Brown of North Carolina. I'm going to need to be able to get into the city," Ira stepped forward.

"I know you Sir. Glad to meet you. You saved the Post Office. My wife works for the Post Office and because of you, she still has her job rather than working out here with me," Captain Molten said with a chuckle. "Look sir, I just really need you guys to get off the water."

"Thank you, sir," Ira said shaking the officer's hand and leading him off the boat. The cutter untied from Coyote's boat and was off.

"Well sometimes it pays to be a government official," Ira said laughing.

"Man, you don't remember that dude? When we were making trips up and down this very same path about eight to ten years ago, this guy would always try and catch us doing something illegal," Coyote said laughing.

"You were doing something illegal," Keshia said shaking her head.

"Yeah, but he didn't know that," Coyote responded.

"Yeah he did, he just couldn't catch you in the act. You notice how he said he didn't want to know what we were doing out here in a hurricane . . . already he was suspicious," Keshia explained.

"Anyway, let's get into that harbor and off this boat. I heard him say warm and cozy and I can go for that right about now," Shea said buttoning up her jacket.

✡ ✡ ✡

After dinner, Bridgette took her time explaining to everyone what was going on with the Bank of the Alps in Switzerland. After speaking for 35 minutes, the questions started.

"How could anyone do this?" David asked disgustedly.

"The money is supposed to be cursed. I found out from my father that the money has always been with the Bank of Switzerland because no known high-ranking SS officers came to claim it. But the money has been borrowed or used by some unscrupulous characters like Idi Amin, Muammar Gaddafi, the war in Liberia and several different wars in Africa, like the Rwandan genocide," Bridgette answered.

Lorraine gasped, "So this money can cause harm to people? If it's put in the wrong hands, people have the potential to die because of some madman?"

"Aunt Alex, have you been able to get a hold of your friend yet?" Ben asked sternly.

"I probably won't hear from her ever again. These people must be stopped," Alex replied.

"We need to get the word out about this bank and this money somehow," Joe said hyped.

"The streets are flooding, and the rain from the outer bands of this hurricane is just sitting on top of us. It's only going to get worse. Getting the news out tonight is not happening," Ben said sighing. "Looks like we're going to have to stay here tonight, Bridge."

"Good. I'm too tired to go back out, and the little one is kicking up a storm."

"Have you talked to mom and dad about what you found out?" April asked.

"No, it's late. I'm sure that they're asleep, and mom wasn't doing that well, so she needs her rest. I asked dad if would hire help for her and you know him, he refused. Eventually, he's going to need some help with her," Ben said.

April spoke up.

"I already have help lined up for mom. All dad has to do is make the call. It's already paid for. Joe and I used the last of our stocks to go ahead and pay for it because we knew that with the baby coming, you guys were going to have your hands full. That was when I thought I was going to Switzerland...." April trailed off slowly.

"April, it seems that none of us are going to Switzerland. This seems like some a bad dream that I'm waiting to wake up from," Ben said.

"Life is not so bad here. It's what we make out of our lives with the baby coming. I am looking forward to living here in New York with you guys, going to David and Lorraine's wedding. I'm going to miss Granddad, but we're going to be okay. I love my wife for not making me go back out in the storm to go home," Ben started to laugh.

"Ben, it's not like we didn't live here when we first got married," Bridgette teased.

"Yeah babe, but that was seven years ago."

"Yeah, but you know this place is big enough to hold all of us comfortably. Granddad made sure it was big enough for all of us just in case something bad happened and I guess this is bad," Ben defended.

"What else did your dad tell you?" David asked curiously.

"My dad went on about end-time prophecies starting to unfold and that he needed for me to go over everything that he taught us when my sister and I were little girls. He taught us so much that I can' t remember it all. My sister might remember more, but she really didn't like it because it really scared her. She always thought the end of the world was going to happen at any moment when we were little," Bridgette answered.

"Uncle Gabe, you haven't said anything all night. What are you thinking about?" April asked.

"I was thinking that a lot more is on the crest of happening with the temple almost being finished. If you read the book of Revelations, the temple is built, and the Anti-Christ is supposed to enter the temple and declare himself God. The two witnesses are supposed to return. Some feel that the temple is rushing the return of Christ, some feel that the temple is prophesized, so it has to take place–it has to be built. All I know is that whatever is going to happen, it's going to happen fast. I mean at breakneck speed. But tonight, we're all healthy and happy and, we have to be grateful for that and these days which is no minor feat," Gabe finished, looking around at the family. "It's getting late, and the lights keep flickering, so I'm going to head in for the night. I'll see you guys in the morning," Gabe excused himself, heading to the upper floor of the brownstone.

Chapter 26

Coyote and the passengers of his boat were safely tucked into the Inn Captain Molten had told them they'd be taken to. The Inn was inland somewhere between Baltimore and New York. Outside the winds blew and the rain poured as the hurricane moved its way into the area. The tension was thick at the Inn as strangers waited out the storm together. The group tried to take their minds off the situation playing a game of UNO.

"Coyote, have you been able to get in touch with your family?" Bazz asked.

"Yeah, man, Spring said the weather is nice in the mountains and that we are to hurry home because the boys want to go camping and fishing with us!" Coyote shouted over the wind.

Keshia yelled, "UNO out," as she dropped her last card.

"Damn, I have a handful of cards, and you already won," Shea screamed. "Man, this takes me back to the old days, when life was easy and free," Shea finished, getting another soda out of the ice chest.

"Shea, nothing was free, I just paid for everything," Ira said patting his chest.

"Like I said, everything was free. I bought the Chinese food that you ate every night," Shea laughed

"That was just food you had left over from cooking in your dorm," Ira said.

"You still ate it," Shea said sticking her tongue out at Ira.

"Hell, we all ate, or we would have starved to death in the winter time. No one was going to walk across campus to go to the cafeteria in 5-7 inches of snow, no way so, Shea had to cook," Keshia said. Then to Bazz, "Bazz, can I ask you a question? Have you ever thought about going back to Rwanda?"

Bazz sighed, "Too many memories and I don't think that I can ever call it home again. I left a year after everything happened."

"What did happen there?" Keshia asked.

"What happened during the genocide is what always happens to the black race. The colonist divided them, and one tribe was told that it was more superior than another. They chose to believe this and fell into the trap of treating each other in very disrespectful ways. Hate took over, a murdering spirit entered, and the killing began. The seeds were planted hundreds of years before, but the real charge took a couple of weeks to prepare. It was a coup by the military that spilled over onto other people. It's called the Amorite or the spirit of Haman."

Ira listened carefully as Bazz spoke. Coyote listened too because he had never heard Bazz talk about Rwanda at all and was surprised that he did it now.

"Ira, can I borrow your phone? Mine is dead, and I can't charge it now," Keshia asked.

"Keshia, you know what's mine is yours. Anyway, ask my lovely wife."

"Ira, I don't happen to have boats that are just lying around that my husband doesn't know about like you do, so sure Keshia can use the stuff I have because you know everything that I have." Shea smiled sweetly at Keshia as she got up from the table to go into the hallway to use the phone. Keshia closed the door because there was a lot of chatter from the people gathered inside. Keshia decided to call Bridgette but got no answer from her home phone then decided to give Ben's cell phone a try.

"Ben, this is Keshia is everybody okay? Did Bridgette tell you what our dad said about the bank? I'm on my way to New York to go to the United Nations and stop by and see my mom and dad and you guys while I'm there. I'm not in Georgia. I'm with Shea and Ira. We're somewhere between Baltimore and New York at an Inn. We've been traveling by boat since all flights have been canceled. We needed to get out of North Carolina in a hurry. The hurricane was bearing down on us, so we had to anchor in a harbor then a Coast Guard transport truck took us here to the Inn. I'll tell you about it when we get there. Tell Bridge that I will see her soon. Yeah take care, love you.

Kiss Bridge and the baby for me." Keshia paused listening to Ben for a moment. "Oh, the Lincoln Tunnel, Holland Tunnel, and Murray Hill Tunnel are starting to flood . . . Thanks for telling me. I'm not sure how we're getting in, but we'll be there soon okay. Take care. Talk to you soon."

When Keshia re-entered the cabin, Shea and Ira were still discussing the boat. Coyote shot Keshia a look of 'help me, I don't want to get into it with a married couple.' Keshia laughed, understanding what Coyote meant. Keshia decided to call Brandon and went back in the hallway. He would know what they were getting ready to walk into when they arrived New York. "Hey Babe, I miss you."

"It's good to know that I'm still Babe, K! How are you and where the hell are you? I've been calling you for hours. Last time I spoke to you, you were on your way to Ira and Shea's."

"Yeah, I got there and found out that someone tried to assassinate Ira."

"Was it an old drug beef?" Brandon asked cautiously.

"No Brandon, it was not a drug beef, you know that Ira is out of that life."

"Sometimes just when you think that you're out of the drug game, it has ways of dragging you back in. Keshia you know this, you have seen it a hundred times."

"Brandon, when Shea begged Ira to change, he did. I saw it with my own eyes. It was hard, but he did it, and I am so proud of the both of them. I remember nights when Shea didn't know if he was alive or dead. She would cry all night and get up in the morning and go to class. Ira went to work with the Power Company and wasn't making the money he was used to, but he stayed with it for the sake of Shea. When he borrowed the money from her parents to start the medical marijuana transfers, he made sure he paid it all back and then took care of her parents when they were sick with cancer. Shea was able to stay at home and take care of them until they passed. Not many people can do that for their in-laws, or even want to for that matter."

"You have a point, K."

"When are you going to get here?"

"It's hard to say. We're in a storm shelter, and I don't think the boat is going to work with the high seas. We're going to have to figure something else out. What is it looking like in New York?"

"A lot of flooding, and the military is on high alert because of the Jewish population here and the attacks on the Synagogue and Jewish people. The city is strangely quiet. There is a tenseness in the air that New Yorkers don't usually have. Whatever it is, the city is bracing for it."

"Brandon, I should be there soon. I'll call you when I get there. Ira is going to the United Nations to speak to the ambassadors about what is going on."

"OK. Tell Ira whatever he needs, I'm there. I want to go with him to the United Nations as a security escort, that way I get to spend some more time with you guys."

"I'll tell him and thanks Brandon, I love you."

"K, I have waited months to hear you say that again. I love you too. See you soon."

"Bye"

Chapter 27

Romero was listening to the weather conditions for the east coast while relaxing in the Dominican Republic. He heard New York streets were flooding with up to three feet of water in some areas. He also heard that the Christians for Israel rally had been canceled and would be rescheduled for a later date. Romero now understood that missing the opportunity to assassinate the 15,000 Jewish people at the rally might well cost him the 12 million dollars he'd been paid by Erich Rawlins and the Swiss Bank of the Alps.

Romero decided that no one knew that he was in the Dominican Republic and since Rawlins had paid him with a cashier's check, he wasn't worried. If Rawlins pushed him to return the money, Romero had decided he would alert Homeland Security about the bank's involvement in the sudden upswing of Jewish attacks and desecration of synagogues. The rest he would blame on his brother Zachery. It wouldn't be the first time that a dead man would become the fall guy. Romero didn't care what happened in America. As far as he was concerned, out of sight, out of mind. He had a new life to plan. He only wished Zachery could have been there to share it with him. Zachery had the crazy idea that they would never be finished with the Jewish people, but he was wrong. Romero had no problem in living a good life to prove his brother wrong.

Romero had been on the island long enough to know that the Dominican Republic was a beautiful place and that this would be a good place to put down roots and start all over again. Real estate would be a good way to wash the 12 million dollars. He felt that between Haiti and the Dominican Republic, he could live in paradise, starting his life all over again never looking back.

Chapter 28

The group had spent days at the shelter and had made another plan to get to New York. They knew they wouldn't be able to go by boat. The winds had calmed down even though the rain still came down in buckets, but they had to head out. They spoke with the owner of the Inn asking if there was a car dealer in town who sold 4-wheel drive SUVs. The owner directed them to the Humvee dealer down the road. He was a friend of hers, and she would call him to be sure he was open. Grateful, Ira gave the Innkeeper an envelope full of cash for her trouble.

"Thank you for everything you've done for these people and us . You didn't have to do this at all," Ira said, handing the Innkeeper an envelope. "The guys and I are going to head out to see your friend now. We'll be back for the girls and the trunks."

"Hey, look the wind is calm enough for us head out toward New York again," Bazz said looking.

"This downtime has given me time to write my speech to the United Nations and make my plea for Israel," Ira said.

"Ira, are you prepared for this?" Shea asked.

"Babe, I don't know how you get ready to tell people that the Holocaust is happening again and only a few people have noticed," Ira answered.

"How could it be happening again and in the United States at that? This is the country that believes in the land of the free and the home of the brave. Israel is our friend. We cannot allow this to happen to her people," Keshia said. "Coyote, you're native American, right? What would you tell the United Nations to save your people if you could go back and save your people from the massacre that faced them?"

Coyote was quiet for a moment and closed his eyes then took a deep breath before answering. "I don't think there was anything that could be said that was going to save my people from the atrocities that shaped history. My people weren't even seen as people, they were considered to be savages, heathens and stood in the way of what the white man wanted. What they wanted was their land, and they were not stopping until they stole it, took or massacred to get it."

"It's what they did to the black man in the south that had anything to do with what the black man wanted. They would steal or kill to get what they wanted from the black man," Keshia explained.

"Ira, I don't envy you at all to have to go before the United Nations to let them know about the possibility of a second Holocaust or Genocide, especially since the UN does not seem to be fans of Israel lately," Bazz contributed.

"I haven't been able to reach anyone in New York for the last couple of days on the phone because of the blackouts," Keshia said.

Shea was agitated as she screamed, "What do you mean you can't reach anyone? Are they all dead? Have the death squads killed everyone!?" The group looked at Shea, stunned at her outburst for a moment until Keshia put a comforting arm around her and led her out into the hallway.

"I'm sorry K, I'm just tired of him acting like this is just one big joke or a transfer as he calls them. Doesn't he realize that we can't go home until these death squads are stopped or worse when we're dead?" Shea said sobbing hysterically. "I didn't sign up for this!"

"None of us did," Keshia said trying to calm Shea. "Just think, six months ago Ira was just an ex-drug trafficker that happened to be Jamaican. Now that he finds out that he is Jewish and that his life expectancy has just been cut in half. He hasn't had to deal with this kind of stuff since he was in the drug game. You can take the man out of the game, but you can't take the game out of the man. Good thing he still has that edge because if he didn't, we might be dead right now. Didn't you wonder all those nights exactly what he did when he said he was making transfers? Now you get to see him in one of his elements, and he always made it home to you!"

"Yes K, but I begged him to quit!"

"And he did Shea. He got out the game and became an upstanding member of society. He owns his own business . . .. 7 stores earning millions of dollars each a year in profits. He made his friends millionaires. He took care of your parents when they got sick, bought their home and hell if truth be told, bought my home too through the investment I made in your company! You see, it just got real for you. You saw the financial side, but he never allowed you to see the dark side of where the money came from. Now you have an idea of what he did. The paranoia that you have to have to stay alive in the game does not go away like that."

"K, he acts like we didn't have to kill two men in our driveway. K there's no coming back from the fact that I killed a man to protect his life."

"Shea, understand that it was not from the drug game that this happened. This happened from a situation that he has no control over. None of us know who is in our family tree and what they did to survive. I'm sure a lot of Jewish descendants hid or still hide the fact that they are Jewish because of the Holocaust. Ira didn't ask for any of this. He didn't even know he was Jewish until the bank sent him the information. Shea, what do you want from the man?"

"K, I don't want to be bouncing around on a boat in the harbor running for my life."

"Neither does he, neither do I, and we're not going back on the boat. Right now, I'm thinking my dad is Jewish, my sister married into a Jewish family who are direct descendants of Jewish Holocaust victims, tattoos and all and I'm wondering are they safe? Are they okay? Can they protect themselves while I'm sitting on a trunk load of weapons and ammunition? They also have a bounty on their heads. We have to get to the U. N. and tell them that the Jewish people in America may not be safe. We have always taken for granted that America is a safe place. Hell, America herself takes it for granted that she has always been safe. That's how 9/11 was able to happen. We haven't had war on American soil since the Civil War. But, if we continue to think that America is invincible, we will look up, and there will be war on American soil. So, our job now is to sound the alarm so others will be aware that their lives are in danger because they're Jewish." Keshia grabbed Shea by her face, looked directly in her eyes and said, "Shea, Ira is a black man in America that just found out he is also Jewish. Shea, you know that this is a double noose around his neck. Girl, I don't know how and if we'll make it out of this, but I do know that I will see it through to the end, whatever that may be! Because it's a Jewish situation, lives may be lost. I know you have to die for something, but I plan to fight with every fiber of my being, I have no choice. Neither do you or Ira. I'm just asking that you pull it together. I know this is the hardest thing you have had to go through outside of your parents' deaths. I'm here like I was then. I'm not going to leave your side. Whatever happens, we're doing this thang together." Keshia began to cry as they hugged.

"Keshia," whispered Shea, "I see Ira watching us out the corner of my eye."

"Girl, so what? He already thinks we are crazy anyway." Both women started laughing. Ira turned slowly and tiptoed back to the main salon only making the two women laugh even harder.

"Girl, that is your crazy husband."

Chapter 29

"I haven't been able to reach mom and dad by phone. I know that the power is sporadic...." April began.

"Ben and I are on our way to check on them and make sure that they're okay. We're going to try and get them to come back with us," Joe assured as he was eating a peanut butter and jelly sandwich.

"Okay, good I was starting to worry," April sighed relieved.

"Bridgette is getting worried that she has not been able to reach her mom and dad the last 48 hours. She was able to reach Keshia on Ira's cell." Joe and April shot each other a quick look.

"Yeah, but she hasn't been able to reach her mom and dad right outside of the Bronx. The radio is reporting that the Bronx area has been hit pretty hard by the flooding, so Keshia and her team are going in to check on them when they get here sometime tomorrow. She said that they're well supplied and that she's bringing Shea and her husband with her."

"Oh, wow I like Shea, she is funny," April said smiling. "Aunt Alex, what are you thinking about?"

"I'm thinking that I left Italy to come here and try to convince everyone that we should take the 50,000 and move to Switzerland. If we had gone along with the plan, we would be like my friend Laila. She's lost...The entire family missing...Just gone. To be fooled or taken advantage of because of your DNA and your beliefs . . .. our people have been preyed upon since biblical times. We are not violent people. We had to be taught how to fight . . .. to be made to fight by the Almighty. We don't want to fight just to live life in peace. I look at Israel, and I see that they want to live in peace with the land that God promised them, and they cannot because of other countries who have told them they will wipe them off the map. The rest of the world watches as pebble by pebble is thrown at Israel, and when

Israel decides to throw a mountain, then it becomes a problem. The attacks were unprovoked, and the world wants Israel to back down, to turn the other cheek, while they're fighting for lives or better yet, their very existence. We want to live in freedom," Alex almost cried.

"Alex, I grew up the child of a bi-racial couple. You would not believe the hate my mom and dad received just by being a bi-racial couple in the 80's. You can't believe some of the things that were said to my mother, by both black and white people. I felt so sorry for my mother, and I would defend my mother and father's right to fall in love and get married and have kids until my father said that we as kids didn't have to justify the love that he and my mother shared. We were just supposed to grow up and blossom from the love that our family shared and that nobody could take that from us or make us feel shame for who our family was. Because when all was said and done, we were loved and appreciated. My father said there were people in the world who were jealous of our love for each other and we must embrace the good with bad. My mother taught us that racism came from a sick and ignorant mind. God made all people to worship him, even Noah had a bi-racial family, and God loved them enough to save them. God loves everyone, so why can't we follow his lead and love everyone too?" Bridgette said holding her stomach and weeping

"Are you okay, over there?" April asked concerned looking at Bridgette's belly.

"Oh, I'm sorry must be the hormones but I'm thinking we're going to have leave New York at some point. I don't feel safe here anymore, and America is the only country that I have ever known as home."

"How can we leave New York?" April cried.

"April, you're going to have to face facts. There is a bounty on all our heads, and because America is going through hard times, we're worth more dead than alive."

"My family has already left one country to be safe, and I will do it again, in a heartbeat," Lorraine said sitting next to David listening to the conversation.

"Where she goes, I will follow," David said softly. "The only place I feel left to go is Israel," David confessed.

"How can we get to Israel without passports and New York flooded?" April asked looking out of the window.

"I don't know, but I don't feel safe here anymore. I want to bring my baby up in a safe environment or at least in a country that's willing to back me up and protect me. Keshia is on her way here. Maybe she'll know something since she is the police."

"If anybody can get here it's Keshia and the crew," laughed Bridgette. "I'll say a little prayer for them and wait."

"I'm going to go and check on the synagogue, want to go with me, David?" Gabe asked. David turned toward Lorraine as if to ask permission.

"Of course, go, go," Lorraine said, "I will be fine."

"We will take care of her Uncle David," Alex said shooing David and Gabe out the door.

✡✡✡

Out on the streets, David and Gabe noted the increasing levels of water in the city. Basements and subways were flooded, and the water kept coming. Rats scampered nervously on the streets, buildings, and wires, the homeless made shelters of plastic and waterproof scrap materials on fire escapes, balconies, or wherever they could. They were genius when it came to survival. Soup kitchens had been set up in many places. First responders were tending to the ill and injured. The hurricane still hadn't hit the city, but the rain kept coming, and the storm surge was relentless. New Yorkers came together to support each other, helping to feed the hungry, and were unrelenting at filling sandbags to try and protect the buildings.

David and Gabe were not ready to see the city at its worse. They dodged large rats and steered away from heavily flooded streets. Although they didn't see it, areas of some streets had up to four feet of water. These areas were cordoned off. David suggested turning back several times, but Gabe was insistent. He wanted to get the scrolls and Torah out of the synagogue. They arrived at the synagogue to find the lower levels flooded. Fortunately, the Torah and scrolls were kept on the second floor and were safe.

"Gabe, I'll wait outside while you go in and grab the Torah. Everything else is covered by insurance, and I'm not in the mood to fight any more rats," David grumbled knocking a rat off his shoulder.

"I'll make it quick," Gabe said sloshing through the water flooding the synagogue.

Gabe retrieved the Torah and scrolls, wrapped them into large plastic trash bags, then bound them together to carry them out. As he worked, he realized it was time to leave New York. There was nothing left for the family here, and that reality pained him. It was time to go to Israel. Israel, had its problems, he thought, but then who didn't? They believed in defending themselves against all enemies, foreign and domestic like America but America was blinded. They didn't see her enemies had penetrated her borders or already lived within them. Those enemies were the worst kind because they blended easily with the American lifestyle.

Chapter 30

In the small country of the Dominican Republic, all TV stations were reporting on the flooding, massive power outages, huge storm surge, and outrageous behavior in New York City. Hate crimes were up, there was looting, and people were going nuts. The flooding hadn't even caused that much damage yet, and the worst was yet to come. The hurricane was expected to hit the city head-on within the next 48 hours.

Romero realized that his stadium bomb plan had failed. He decided to up his stakes on the killings and sent an email to his death squads.

Exterminate all that are on the list. The money is plentiful.

Romero transferred another 2 million to the lower ranked members who remained loyal to the organization after the attempt to shut down some of the chapters of the Brotherhood. Lately, he had the feeling he was being followed. His thoughts were interrupted by a knock at the door.

"Hello, Romero. I've been trying to get in touch with you," Rawlins said coming in and closing the door. "You have been really hard to find. I want to congratulate you on your success. Your members have really been busy taking care of business. I always did like that about you. Strictly business. Where's your brother?"

"Zach is back in the states closing up shop and will be joining me shortly," Romero said gritting his teeth.

"I just came to thank you in person for the great job you and the Brotherhood are doing. I knew from the moment I met you, you'd be good at what you do! You would have made your father so proud! I'm truly sorry he's not around to see what you have become."

"Thank you, sir. I appreciate you showing me the way," Romero said uneasily.

"Here is the check I promised you. I wanted to hand it to you personally. You understand right?" Rawlins said looking around the room.

"Yes, I understand," Romero answered quickly. Rawlins' presence for some reason was making him feel uneasy, almost nauseous.

"Thank you again, son," Rawlins said shaking Romero's hand. He turned to leave and did not look back.

Romero felt relief that Rawlins was gone, and he looked down at the check; 12 million dollars. Romero decided to increase the bounty on the Jewish people. He had all the money he would ever need. Life was good. He only wished his brother had lived to see it.

Romero looked around the hotel grounds from his suite window. He still had the feeling someone was watching him. He shook it off telling himself the feeling of 12 million dollars in anyone's hand would make them paranoid.

News Flash

Today Israel is celebrating the completion of the new Temple Mount, located on the side of the old Temple Mount and the Dome of the Rock. The Temple priests performed dedications of the temple and animal sacrifices during three days of the Sabbath. The Temple was built in record time. The peace in the Middle East had been accomplished according to reports from the world media.

Chapter 31

The ride was slow as the four Humvees made their way from Baltimore to New York City. Keshia sat quietly in the back seat thinking about the entire situation. She couldn't believe the reality. A hurricane was bad enough, but there was so much more. All over the world, strange things were happening; in some places miracles and others hell had been unleashed. She remembered the stories her father had told her and Bridgette when they were little girls about the end of times. *Was this it?* she wondered. She looked at Shea sitting next to her and was grateful she hadn't lost her to the death squad that had come after Ira. Suddenly she began to panic and hyperventilated as she thought about what her sister had told her about not being able to reach their parents.

"Is she okay?" Bazz asked Shea.

"All I know is that her sister wasn't able to reach her parents. She's been quiet ever since," Shea whispered. "I'll take care of her," she said to Bazz. Turning to Keisha, "K, baby? You okay? We're almost there. Won't be long now." Shea handed K a cup of rum and coke. "Drink this, it will make you feel better."

Keisha gulped the cup down and started to gag. "Sorry, I thought it was coffee," Keisha explained choking.

"Sorry to surprise you!" Shea said wiping Keisha's face with a wet cloth. "Now tell me, what's going on?" Shea asked.

"I'm worried about my mom and dad. My mom isn't in the best health. My dad isn't exactly young either. No one has been able to reach them, and I'm just terrified something horrible has happened," Keisha whispered.

"I know it can't be easy, but we're getting there. It's slow going but faster than the boat would have been. We'll get there, and we'll check on your parents first thing," Shea reassured.

"Hit me again!" Keisha said.

Shea obliged pouring extra rum this time.

"I'll fix me one too."

The Humvee caravan arrived in New York City in the dark of night. Coyote gave Milton and Jordan a call. They'd been hiding out in an old warehouse.

"Hey man, I'm surprised it isn't flooded with the surge," Milton said letting everybody in.

"Jordan is shaken up–he's never experienced a hurricane before. Can't wait to see what he does when it makes landfall." Milton shook Bazz's hand after introductions were made. Milton winked at Coyote, "Watch this." Milton threw two pots in the room where Jordan was. When the pots hit the floor, the noise made Jordan holler out. Jordan turned around to see everyone standing in the next room. He calmed down but was a little embarrassed.

"Very funny man, very funny. Hey, good to see you guys made it. This hurricane thing is rattling my nerves just a bit," Jordan said looking out at the water.

"Man snap out of it! It isn't that big of a deal. We got work to do before that baby hits land!" Milton said.

"I heard you got attacked. Is everybody okay?" Jordan asked changing the subject.

"Yeah man, right in my driveway."

"At your, home?" Jordan asked in disbelief.

"Yeah man. Two of them; a possible third."

"What are they trying to do?"

"They're taking out Jewish people!" Ira said.

"Ira you are Jamaican," Jordan said confused.

"Apparently, I'm a Jamaican Jew," Ira said. "Don't worry man, it's all kosher!"

Shea suddenly screamed.

"Baby what's wrong?!" Ira asked running into the next room with Shea.

"I told you that if you used the word kosher one more time what I would do!" Everyone laughed. The scream broke the mood, even Keisha laughed.

"On the serious side, what are we going to do?" Milton asked.

"I need an update on the city. I could see a lot of damage as we got into the city," Ira said.

"How far into the city do we have to go?" Milton asked.

"Into Manhattan and the Bronx," Ira said. "We need to get to Keisha's parents then we need to get to Manhattan where the rest of the family is."

"Hey, you holding up okay?" Shea asked Keisha.

"I know I'm a police officer and I see death every day, but these are my parents, I'm not ready for that," Keisha said exhaling.

"Look, we'll be there soon. You don't know they're dead. We got here before the hurricane, and we'll get to them before it hits. By morning your family will be all together," Shea tried to reassure her.

News Flash

California geologist and geophysicists are concerned about increased seismic activity in the Long Valley Caldera. A long-quiet yet massive super volcano, dubbed the "Long Valley Caldera," has the potential to unleash a fiery hell across the planet, and the magma-filled mountain has a history of doing so.

The Caldera was formed 760,000 years ago after a cataclysmic eruption. The eruption blew out approximately 150 cubic miles of molten rock. Pyroclastic flows covered most of east-central California and ash fell as far as Nebraska.

While scientists are optimistic that the recent activity isn't a precursor to the "big one," they do not discount the possibility of smaller scale eruptions.

Chapter 32

"Hey, babe you okay?" Ben asked Bridgette. "You been sleep twenty-eight hours."

"Yeah, I dreamed about my dad. He was holding a baby wrapped in a pink blanket, smiling at me and saying that he was okay."

"He is okay Bridge. You have to be okay. Your mom still hasn't uttered a word, just stares out of the window," Ben said.

"I'll check on her," Bridgette said getting up.

"You're sure you want to get up now?"

"Yeah, I have an awful taste in my mouth, and I want some pizza."

"Babe the restaurant is destroyed by the water. I'll make you some homestyle pizza."

"I'm sorry Ben, I know how much you had come to love that place."

"We're insured, I can rebuild if we decide to stay."

"Are you considering staying here?"

"I was thinking of maybe moving back to California, or at least maybe west. My dad said the Ozarks would be pretty safe. He always said go the Ozarks if things in the world got crazy."

"Ben, we have to get my dad's book from his office, it will tell us what to do. He knew about end time prophecy."

"Bridge do you think it is the end of time?"

"Ben, look around you! They're trying to start a Holocaust again. Not on my watch," Bridgette said getting out of bed. "Where's my momma?"

Ben walked out the door to the kitchen and passed Joe. "She's back!' Ben said winking at Joe.

"Momma?" Bridgette said walking into the other room seeing her mother looking down at her hands. "Momma answer me?" Bridgette tried holding her mother's face in her hand.

"Momma you know daddy wouldn't let you pout or be mad. I know you are mad at God right now. Momma God needed daddy more than we did, that's why he took him!" Daddy left but God did not leave us, he is still here with us, and he can lead us better than daddy ever could. I will miss daddy so much, but we have to go on, momma we can't stop here."

Mildred started to weep silently and then louder and moaned. "We have been married 32 years through the good and the bad. When you girls came along Bert was there, and now he's not. I need him here with me!"

"I'm here with you mommy now. I'm here, and Keisha is on the way." Bridgette held her mother until the weeping stopped and she was able to go to sleep.

"Your mom okay?" Ben asked pointing to the pizza in the oven.

"She will be, we have to go get the book," Bridgette said smiling and inhaling the smell of the pizza. "Did you fix you one?" Bridgette asked.

"Bridgette that is an 18inch pizza, you can't eat all that by yourself!"

"Ben, you know I'm eating for two and I have to make up for lost time. I slept for a whole day, remember?" Ben just shook his head and took the pizza out of the oven. "I'm dreading having to tell Keisha that daddy is gone. I'm not ready, but I have to let her know that daddy had a heart attack. I can't do it over the phone, so if she calls, tell her that I'm asleep because I know that she will hear it in my voice. Sleep Ben got it?" Ben nodded his head.

✡✡✡

Keisha was awakened by the sound of gunfire around 4 in the morning "What the hell?" Keisha said reaching for her gun. Keisha came downstairs into the warehouse in time to see someone leap out of the window and two bodies lying on the floor. One of the bodies was that of Jordan, shot through the chest. It was just enough light for Keisha to see so she checked the warehouse. The second body was a man that Keisha had never seen before, but he had a gunshot wound to the head.

"Way to go Jordan, you got one on your way out!" Keisha whispered to herself.

Bazz came out from behind a door scaring Keisha because she was not expecting anyone to be that close.

"You got hit," she said to Bazz.

"Yeah, just hit in the shoulder. Not too bad. I believe this guy was with the death squads," Bazz said.

Keisha checked the dead man's pocket. "There's a list with Ira and Shea's name on it and everybody in my family and Jordan's name is on it."

"Damn, it's a hit list, for real!" Bazz said looking over Keisha's shoulder. Keisha looked up to see Coyote, Ira, Shea, and Milton coming down the stairs.

"Jordan and I had first watch. I guess he nodded out, and they entered the warehouse from his side. We exchanged gunfire and Jordan was hit in the chest, but he got one before he left this earth!"

"How many?" Coyote asked rechecking the premises.

"Three!" Bazz answered.

"They're always in sets of three," Shea said quietly.

"Yeah, I found out a week ago in the swamps of Georgia," Coyote said. "How did they know we were here?"

"They had to make the connection through Milton and Jordan!" Coyote said. "Ira, they have been watching you for a while, to even know about Milton and Jordan. Jordan just said he had some Jewish ancestry recently, he never said anything about it before now. Ira, what is your Jewish history?"

"I recently found out that my great-great-grandfather was a Jewish Rabbi who backslid a time or two while he was on the good island saving my great-great grandmother's soul. And boy, she must have had a soul that needed saving, they had six kids together," Ira said pausing waiting for someone to make the connection. "It's not the ancestry–it's who the ancestors were. They're killing descendants of priests and rabbis. They're not killing regular Jews but Jews with the priestly genes or bloodline! Bazz you're Jewish!"

"But to my knowledge, no one was a priest or rabbi," Bazz said.

"Shea the pictures of the people in the swamps, the old guy was a rabbi!"

"Yeah all the families we have been transporting are families of rabbis or priests," Coyote chimed in.

"Why is the bloodline of the priest so important?" Ira asked.

"The priests are supposed to be the only ones who carry the Cohen gene! The priests are the ones who allegedly know where the Ark of the Covenant is located. They're trying to prevent the temple from being fully operational, thinking that this will prevent Jesus from coming back. They feel that if everything is not in place, Jesus can't return and reign on earth. The money from the Swiss Bank must be given to direct descendants of the Holocaust and the easiest ones to find are the descendants of the rabbinical priests," Keisha explained.

"Keisha, you learn all this from your father?" Coyote asked in amazement.

"Yeah, my dad talked to us about this all the time. Never thought I would need to know it though. You know how you learn some stuff for a test, but you don't plan on retaining the information? That's how I treated the information."

"I want to know more," Bazz said ripping his shirt to get a better look at the bullet wound.

"Basically, more destruction and this thing call the rapture."

"I have heard of the Rapture. I can't comprehend all the people being pulled off the earth at the same time. That is going to be an amazing sight to see," Coyote interjected.

"Coyote, you don't want to be able to see it. That would mean you're being left behind to go through the tribulations. You want to be able to meet Jesus in the air. I'm not quite sure how it works, just be ready, we don't have long," Keshia warned.

"Is this what they mean when they say look up for your redemption draweth nigh?'" Shea asked.

"Pretty much, Shea."

"That's some twilight zone kind of stuff right there," Bazz said wincing from the alcohol placed on the wound.

"Native Americans describe the same occurrence but call it something different. You learn about it when you do a vision quest," Coyote said raising his voice at Bazz.

"Yeah man, right. Like I said before, do you think I am going to sit in a tent and get hot enough to hallucinate and get dehydrated and wait to see a spirit and believe that the spirit is telling me some vital information that will help me in life?" Bazz chuckled out loud. "I know what the spirit would say already, man. All that is not necessary man."

"Okay Bazz, what would the spirit say to you?" Coyote asked seriously. Everyone was quiet listening with interest.

"The spirit would say… 'You better hurry your ass up and drink some water before you die!" Everyone shook their heads and walked off. Bazz continued to wrap his wound.

"Look you guys can kill all that talk. I just lost my friend a few minutes ago, and his body is laying here. I don't give a damn if he was a Jew or priest, I only know that I lost a good friend and I'm going to get whoever killed him!" Milton said bitterly.

"We can't stay here any longer. We'll have to wrap the body because we don't have time to dig a grave. The morgues are probably full," Coyote said looking around.

"Let's leave the other body–I don't give a damn about him. I want to know how they knew we were here," Milton growled.

"Did you or Jordan check for bugs?" Bazz asked looking around the room.

"We always used this warehouse when we did transfers, it's been locked for years," Milton said looking at Shea.

"Don't worry man, she has already put things together," Ira told Milton.

"No, we assumed it was the same lock that was on there five years ago. I want everyone to check a different room and use your cell phones. If you get an echo in your cell phone, you are bugged," Milton said.

"Out of the seven rooms in the warehouse, four of the rooms were found to be bugged. They really want to get me. The DEA didn't even want me this bad," Ira said looking around.

"Let's burn it to the ground, it's no good anymore," Milton said. "We'll burn it on our way out."

"Fine by me," Ira answered. "Try and get some sleep, they won't be back tonight."

"How am I supposed to sleep with dead bodies in here?" Shea asked.

"Baby, I don't know when you will get a chance to sleep again. We're going to have to get a move on and get out of here quick. We'll have to make a couple of stops to re-up," Ira explained.

"Re-up is when you reload on merchandise," Keisha told Shea. She knew Ira's nerves were getting short with Shea. Keisha led her into the other room quickly. "Shea that means, that they have hidden money or supplies in different places along their route. They will have to get this money. I don't think that Ira still has drugs hidden, so it's probably money and supplies."

"I thought he had left this life behind him and now I find out he still has this stuff. The boat was probably just the tip of the iceberg," Shea said almost in tears.

"Shea, are you kidding? Back in the day, this whole warehouse would have been filled with weed. He has changed, it's just hard to sell stuff that used to be used for drugs, so he had to keep it. Trust me, I would know if he was still in the game. Now try and get some sleep."

Five hours later, the warehouse was on fire, and everyone was on the move. It was about 9:00 am. The fire was started inside to give the group a chance to leave without drawing too much attention.

"We need to get across the bridge, then we'll be in Manhattan," Keisha said.

"Good. I'm ready to get out of here," Shea said looking back at the warehouse. "Is it really burning? I don't see smoke or smell anything."

"You're not supposed to," Ira said grabbing Shea's hand so she would walk a little faster.

"The city looks like a bomb went off in it, caution tape is everywhere," Bazz said.

"We're going to use this to our advantage. Keep your eyes peeled, we don't know who is watching us," Milton said.

✡✡✡

"Bridgette, do you think you can go to your father's office?" Ben asked.

"No, that's why I'm sending you, Joe and David to get the book. Here's the combination to the safe."

"Your dad kept the book in a safe, what's in the book?"

"You'll see when you get back here. Be careful!"

"Will you bring a picture back? It's the one that sits on his desk and everything that's in the safe," Mildred said handing Ben a key to the office

"Lorraine, I heard you and David have decided to go ahead and get married now?" Mildred inquired.

"In a couple of days. David didn't want to wait. He feels if we're in the last days we should go ahead and make it legal before God and family," Lorraine answered.

"Are you going to have a ceremony?" Mildred asked.

"He wants to do it here at the house with everyone present. Most of my family have passed away so there won't be anyone here from my side. Would you ladies do me a favor and stand in as my bridesmaid?" Lorraine asked.

"We would be honored," Bridgette and Alex said at the same time."

"Is Uncle Gabe going to perform the ceremony?' April asked.

"Of course," Lorraine blushed.

"I never thought David would get married, that means there is hope for me," Alex said with a sigh and stars in her eyes.

"Me, too!" April chimed in.

"We'll head to the store and try and get some things and a small wedding cake."

"We'll try and have a wedding dinner if that's okay with you?" Alex was asking Lorraine with hopeful eyes.

"I have no problem with it, and I know David would be grateful!" Lorraine smiled.

Chapter 33

The beachfront of the 5-star hotel Romero was staying in looked the same as it had each day he'd been there, but it didn't feel the same. Since Rawlins visit, Romero felt something had changed. He couldn't put his finger on it, but he could tell something was amiss.

Romero decided it was time to move out of the hotel. Maybe this would change his mood. Having a home of his own and planting roots would surely be the thing he needed to change. A different environment–that's what beachfront property was there for.

Romero called the real estate agent that Rawlins had told him about. "Tracy Rhamsey please . . . Yes, I will wait. I'm looking for a home. A very nice home. My budget is in the multi-million-dollar range . . . Tomorrow would be a good day for me . . . Yes about 10'oclock okay. Thank you, goodbye." Romero could feel the dark clouds lifting–it was just a feeling that he couldn't shake.

The next day Romero met Tracy in the lobby of the hotel. "Good morning Sir! My name is Tracy Rhamsey. I represent Sea Breeze Realty. I talked to you yesterday. One question I forget to ask you was are looking for beachfront property?"

Romero looked down at Tracy. She was beautiful with dark hair and eyes. She looked Brazilian. He had never seen a woman so beautiful. Romero had to remind himself to answer her question. "Oh, yes, beachfront property . . .. Yes, that's what I'm looking for. Are you Brazilian?"

"Yes I am."

"I could tell by looking at you. You are stunning," Romero almost drooled.

"Thank you, kind sir." Tracy smiled at Romero. "Well, let's get started," Tracy blushed. "You can ride with me unless you would prefer to drive your vehicle."

"I haven't purchased a vehicle as of yet, so I would be more than glad to ride with you," Romero said opening the door for Tracy. "I do believe I will enjoy being chauffeured," Romero said in his best flirtatious voice.

"Good, I like driving," Tracy said waiting for Romero to enter the car and buckle up. Romero knew from the start he was going to enjoy his day.

The first house Tracy showed Romero said was too small. "I'm a bachelor, but I'm looking for a home that can become a family home if need be," Romero said looking deep into Tracy's big brown eyes.

"There's a house I have in mind that you would probably like, it's just ahead," Tracy said starting the car.

"Please proceed to the next destination, ma'am."

"The next house has the square footage. It has four bedrooms and 5 baths, and the master suite is one complete side of the house. It has a pool and tennis courts on the property."

"I think this could be the one," Romero said stepping through the door behind Tracy–he wanted to see her from the back. Romero liked the house and Tracy too. He could feel the chemistry between them. He was hoping she was feeling it too. "How about lunch?" Romero asked Tracy hopefully.

"I could use a little something," Tracy said rubbing her stomach.

Lunch back at the hotel was great. Romero learned a lot from Tracy in just a few hours. The lunch was more questions than eating. Romero found out that they had a lot of things in common. Tracy and her twin sister had been born in Brazil. She wanted a large family–at least four kids. She didn't care about the gender of the children as long as there were four of them. "Romero, I have one more house I would like for you to look at today, are you up to it?" Tracy asked eagerly.

"Oh, it's back to business now?" Romero asked a little disappointed.

"Unless you want to continue to live in a hotel."

"Tracy, I would like to meet your family," Romero blurted out.

"You would like to meet my what?" Tracy asked stunned.

"I know I'm going to marry you, so we might as well get this over with!"

"Um . . . I don't know what exactly to say to that," Tracy replied blushing. "That's a first for me. The third house is on the other side of the island," Tracy said changing the subject. "We can get there in about 30 minutes. This house is a 5 bed and 6 bath house with pool, tennis court, Jacuzzi and 2-bedroom guest house. All this is on 5 acres for 5.6million dollars."

"Oh, I see how this is going," Romero said pulling Tracy close to him. "Back to business. I'm a patient man. I have all my life. We can go see the house now if you would like."

"Let's go see the house; it's getting late," Tracy said, stepping away from Romero.

Pulling up to the property, Romero decided he wanted to take a walk on the beach before seeing the house. The walk took the rest of the afternoon. It was late evening before Romero and Tracy made it back the house. By the time they arrived, they were hand in hand. Romero felt he had known Tracy all his life—the chemistry was there, and he knew he would follow her anywhere.

"So, you have a twin sister, what is her name?"

"Her name is Lacy."

"Of course her name is Lacy," Romero stated. "You're twins, oh, that's cute."

"Lacy is in Brazil going to the University. My mother is a nurse, and my father is dead."

"Oh, I'm sorry to hear that."

"That's okay, I hardly knew him."

Tracy and Romero were greeted at the house by staff. The staff included 2 housekeepers, a cook and a gardener who lived in the home year-round.

"Those cars you see belong to the staff, they don't stay overnight unless asked. The purchase of the house does include their services for the first three months. If you or they choose not to continue the arrangement after three months, changing the staff is not a problem and will have no ill feelings. This gives them time to get to know you and for you to get to know them."

"I guess that's fair," Romero said looking around the home.

"Take your time and look around, you can meet the staff later on."

Romero grabbed Tracy's hand as he climbed the stairs in the palatial mansion. It took Romero an hour to take a complete look around the home and gardens. Upon reentering the house, Romero was greeted by the staff.

"Hello Sir, I am the head cook, Greg. Tonight, we have prepared a nice romantic dinner for you. Will Miss Tracy be staying for dinner, sir?"

"I didn't know that I would be having dinner here."

"Oh, I'm sorry sir. It is part of the courtesy package the real estate company set up for each potential buyer. We would like for them to have a sense of home before the purchase."

"Since Tracy is my ride back to the hotel, I believe she will be having dinner with me. Is that a problem for you Tracy?"

"No, it isn't. We have been talking about so many other things that I forgot to mention the courtesy dinner that comes with the sale."

"I couldn't have done this any better than if I had planned this myself!" Romero said rubbing his hands together.

"Shall we eat?" Tracy asked escorting Romero to the dining room.

Chapter 34

Ben, Joe, and David got a funny feeling entering Bertram Cohen's office. Nothing was disturbed. Bertram had a lot of books and artifacts.

"Uncle Gabe would love to see all this stuff. Bertram has stuff on top of stuff," Joe said looking around the room. "The safe is supposed to be under the desk. Here it is."

"You have the combination?" David asked Ben.

"Yeah, I have it right here." Ben opened the safe and retrieved the book and all the contents. "Joe, get the picture off the desk for Miss Mildred."

"Hey, let me see that book," Joe asked hand held out. "Bridgette has so much faith in this book. I have got to see what's in it."

"I don't believe her faith lies in the book. I believe she believes that it will make her father's spirit closer to her. Right about now she needs to feel that. Can I see it first"? David said putting his glasses on to see better. "It's the Holy Bible, King James version!"

Looking into the pages of the book he saw they were handwritten. Just skimming through the book, you could see the calendar of the four blood moon eclipses, directions to century-old underground railroads the slaves used to escape slavery, and a list of Native American Indian Reservations from New York to Alaska. "This book holds special locations and dates and places. I don't know what half of them would be used for. We will have to talk to Bridgette," David said taking off his glasses.

"There has to be a method to the madness," Joe said while reading the book over David's shoulders. "Bridgette's dad must have been a real conspiracy theorist because a lot of this stuff is way out there. I even saw something about aliens in there."

"Bridgette believes that we can't begin to go anywhere without first looking at this book so let's get it back to her so she can explain what's truly in the book and why we need it so badly," Ben said heading for the door.

"Where's Uncle Gabe?" April asked setting the dinner table for the wedding dinner.

"Upstairs. He's been in the attic since all this craziness started, fasting and praying. I have not fasted or prayed in years," Alex declared. "I miss doing it. It helped me clear my mind so I could settle some issues in my life. Your mom and dad used to fast once a year. Since she's been sick, I don't think they have."

"I feel fasting is a necessary part of life," Lorraine said entering the room."

"We thought you were sleeping, getting ready for your big day with David," Alex said surprised to see Lorraine.

"It's not just a big day, it will be a big life. My first husband committed suicide. I thought I would never marry again. The fact that I will be marrying David tonight is beyond anything I could have hoped for," Lorraine sighed. "Everything is so beautiful, thank you."

"Why did your first husband kill himself?" April blurted out.

"April, you are not supposed to ask that kind of question!" Alex exclaimed giving April the eye.

"I'm sorry, I just wanted to know," April said giving Alex the eye back.

"It's okay," Lorraine answered. "My first husband was a lot older than me. He was a survivor of the death camps at Auschwitz. He never really talked about what happened to him or his family. He had scars over most of his body–more like burns. He would never talk about how he got them. He was a dentist by trade. We were deeply in love. After we had our daughter, he started to open up and tell some of the things the Nazis had done to him. They would pour rubbing alcohol on him and set him on fire just so they could see a blue flame walking. They would eventually put the fire out before it got too bad. The last time they waited too long, and it scarred his body, not his face. He was a very handsome man, but he wouldn't let anyone see his body."

"Life was good after we had our daughter. Business was looking up for us and we had just moved into a new house. Anne, our daughter was about six years old and was the light of his life. She followed him wherever he went. One day the phone rang, and he ran downstairs to answer it. Like always, Ann followed him. Running down the stairs, she tripped and fell, breaking her neck. She died. Earnest was never the same again. I went to the store one day in the Spring of '67 to come home to find he had hung himself on the same stairwell where our daughter had died. He left a note stating that he would finish what the Nazis had started. He had planned to burn the house down around him, but the match went out before it contacted the gasoline."

"Oh Lorraine, I am so sorry!" April exclaimed.

"It's okay. I have not told anybody that story in 30 years. Earnest was twenty-seven years older than me. I married him when I was sixteen years old. We were very happy for 8 years. After Anne's death, I knew I didn't have long with Ernest, so I tried to cherish every day. He never wanted more children, and because of the love he had for Anne, I knew I wouldn't have him long. Every time I would leave home, I wouldn't know if he would be home when I got there. I knew deep down in my heart there was nothing here to keep him alive after Anne died. He died with a smile on his face. I pray that somehow he truly found happiness in the end."

April continued to set the table in silence.

"I know this will be the happiest day of my life next to the birth of my daughter. I can't wait to be David's wife, and he can't wait to be my husband."

Alex and April shot each other a look. Lorraine saw the look and added, "Yes, he told me all about his past, and it's just that, his past. He has proven he will be my husband in every sense of the word." Alex and April looked relieved.

"I just know you two will be a very happy couple and I wish you all the best," Alex said arranging flowers on the table.

"Is Gabe okay? I haven't seen him in a couple of days. He is still going to perform the ceremony?" Lorraine asked.

"Oh yes he's just fasting and praying, I know he wouldn't miss it for the world," Alex answered.

"Do you think they're okay out there? They've been gone awhile," Lorraine asked concerned at the length of time the boys had been gone.

"Nothing will keep David from being here with you tonight," Alex assured Lorraine.

"I can't wait!" Lorraine smiled.

✡✡✡

"Hey, this book tells you about the blood moons. It has a list of old underground railroad stations that led slaves out of the south to the north. Maps of Indian reservations and maps of underground caves in the Ozark Mountains. Maps with just coordinates on them or maybe these are just numbers for something else. What do you think all of this mean?" Ben asked.

"Probably nothing. Maybe he was just a man who collected data–maybe he just wrote notes down like a real scatterbrained professor," David said with a smile.

"Don't let Bridgette hear you say that!" Ben warned. "The only other book she holds in higher esteem than this book is the Holy Bible."

"I hope she can make sense of it. If not, this was a wasted trip," David sighed.

"Are you okay, Uncle David?" Ben asked.

"Yeah, I'm in good shape. I've walked at least a mile a day for the last twenty years. I just don't want to stay away from Lorraine too long."

"Calm down stud, we're going to get you home to wifey, in time for the dinner and the ceremony," Joe said teasing David.

"I've never loved a person so much. I can't stand to be away from her any length of time."

"We'll be home soon, Romeo," Ben chimed in.

Later that evening after everyone was dressed, Gabe performed the wedding ceremony. David and Lorraine exchanged vows and cut the cake. Dinner was being served when there was a knock at the door.

"Hello everyone!" Keisha exclaimed. Everyone returned hellos.

Bridgette?"

"Hey sis!" Bridgette struggled to get up.

"You are huge! When is the baby due date again?"

"In about 8 weeks!"

"Bridge you don't look like you're going to make it! I missed you. Have you heard from mom and dad?" Keisha asked worriedly.

"Keisha, I'm sorry to have to tell you this, but we lost dad—he had a heart attack." Bridgette moved swiftly to catch her sister as she collapsed into tears.

"Where's mama?" Keisha asked in between sobs.

"She's in here—she'll be glad to see you." Keisha entered the room quietly and approached her mom.

"Baby you're here!"

"I'm here mama!" Keisha fell into her mam's arms and sobbed.

"Everyone, this is Shea and her husband, Ira. Shea is Keisha's best friend from college," Bridgette announced making the introductions.

"These are friends of my husband," Shea said taking the floor from Bridgette finishing the introductions. "This is Bazz, Coyote, and Milton. We have come all the way from Savannah, Georgia to get here . . . with a lot of trouble along the way. Is there someplace we can clean up and rest?"

"I'm so glad you made it! Momma wasn't doing too good for a while, there. She'll be okay now that you're here," Bridgette said to Keisha when she and Mildred rejoined the group.

"Congratulations to the happy couple," Keisha said to David and Lorraine. "How are you and the baby doing?"

"Eating a lot, missing daddy!" Bridgette said rubbing her stomach. "The baby just kicked, you want to feel her?"

"It's a her? So, you know that it's a girl?" Keisha asked surprised.

"No. I was supposed to go to the doctor in a couple of days and find out, but with the hurricane and everything, I haven't been able to go. The hospitals are full of the injured. It seems a shame to go to the doctor to find out the sex of the baby. I've waited this long, I can wait a few more weeks."

"Well, I think it's a boy!" Ben said interrupting with a big grin.

"It would be a shame to have a boy with all that hair, just to cut it off," April sighed pulling a lock of Bridgette's hair.

"Believe it or not, it has gotten longer and thicker," Bridgette laughed.

"Glad you were cursed and not me!" Keisha said laughing and pulling Bridgette's ponytail.

"What are we going to do Bridge? Things can't stay like this, and we can't stay here. You know they have death squads tracking an attempting to kill Rabbis and their families."

"You know dad said this day would come, but I never believed him . . . not for one second, K!"

"Who would believe Bridge, that anyone would attempt a second Holocaust. Just the thought is crazy. I can't believe that America has allowed this to happen in this country. I can't believe people would attempt to try this again. All I know is that it will take cooperation from all races to stop racism. All races also cause it–all races dislike one race for one reason or another."

Chapter 35

Ben sat reading the little black book when Ira came into the room. "Hey man, what are you reading?"

"Oh, it's a book that my wife and K's father wrote many years ago. It's pretty deep."

"Oh yeah, I heard about this book. May I see it?" Ira asked reaching for the book.

"Sure. Some of it you can't make a lot of sense of," Ben said handing the book to Ira. Coyote and Bazz entered the room. "How's your shoulder?" Ira asked.

"I'll live," Bazz answered.

"How long are we planning to stay here?" Coyote asked. "I do have family that needs me out west."

"Another day or two until we can get a path or direct flight into Texas," Ira said.

"Scratch that!' Bazz said turning up the volume on the television. "The FAA and Homeland Security have grounded all flights in and out of New York and New Jersey. The FAA has grounded all flights until the hurricane has passed. Man, this is worse than 9/11! At least then we were not dealing with death squads. The only good thing is, we know what we are dealing with and at the beginning of 9/11, we didn't."

"Whoa! I can't believe this..." Ben said as he turned the volume up on the T.V. "Channel 68 television just announced that all flights have been canceled in and out of New York because a 787-passenger flight bound for Israel, just exploded over New York City.

"...the FAA, Homeland Security, and other intelligence agencies are gathering to investigate the bombing of the airplane. We now have eyewitness accounts of a what might have been shoulder-fired missiles at this plane..." the newscaster said.

Bazz slowly turned down the volume on the TV. "Man, you'd think these clowns would stop with this weather. That hurricane is going to hit within the next hours, and they're still blowing things up. We can't stay here, it's not safe. If you guys have a plan, you need to spill it."

"Is everybody in travel mode? I mean is everyone physically capable of travel?" Coyote asked Ben.

"My wife is 5 months pregnant–the baby is not due for another 8weeks, but I'm not leaving here without her!"

"That's why we came all this way in the first place–to retrieve you guys and go west where it is safe," Ira said.

Ira's phone rang. "Hey man, it's me, Brandon. Have you guys made it here yet?"

"Yeah, we are here. It looks like a war zone here. K is with us. We're here at Bridgette's grandfather's apartment."

"Tell K I'm on my way. It's getting ugly out here, and a lot of people are leaving the city. I just quit my job. There is no order out here since those planes crashed. It's like post-Katrina, and the hurricane hasn't even hit yet. Every man for himself and God for us all! People are starting to use their 2012 bug out apocalyptic gear to get out of the city. I suspect we should do --" Click.

"Damn phone went dead!" Brandon is on his way; he just quit the police force, said it's like post-Katrina outside. It must be pretty bad for a New York City detective to walk off the job. You know they bleed blue!"

The door swung open and Milton stepped in. "You guys have got to come and see this!" Milton waved all the men to the windows of the apartment. People were gathering in masses with backpacks and just about anything they could carry, exiting the city. They walked through the pouring rain avoiding flooded areas. Shea and Lorraine were already standing at the windows.

"It's worse than 9/11," Lorraine whispered. "People are starting to loot grocery stores and restaurants; the cops can't keep the order."

"They can't restrain all the people," Keisha advised.

"Cops are walking off to go home and protect their own families," Ira said.

"It's Katrina all over again," April said, "except on a bigger scale!"

Shots rang out from the street below. From their vantage point, they could see two gunmen open fire on the crowds of people trying to leave the city.

"Get down! Get away from the windows!!" Keisha yelled coming up behind Lorraine and Shea pushing them to the floor. A bullet hit the window sill and ricocheted somewhere in the apartment. Everyone hit the floor taking cover from the barrage of flying bullets. All of a sudden, the shooting stopped, and all you could hear were people screaming.

"Get them! Don't let them get away!" Someone yelled. You could hear people screaming and running for their lives. Mass hysteria had broken out. People were running in all directions, people were being trampled. There were dead and dying laying on the ground.

Joe got up, peered out a window and started heading for the door.

"Where the hell, do you think you are going?" Coyote questioned.

"People need help!" Joe yelled.

"Hey if you go out there, you could get hit too!" Ben yelled back. You don't know–the gunmen could be still out there waiting to ambush more people!"

"We have to help!" Joe opened the door, but Milton slammed it with the weight of his body.

"Nobody is leaving this apartment. I just lost a good friend. These death squads are not playing, they are killing at random. I don't think it's just Jewish people anymore! Look, the weather should have stopped this even if for a little while."

"How do you know it is the death squads?" Joe asked.

"This is a predominantly Jewish neighborhood. You have four temples in a two-mile radius! They're trying to take out as many as possible," Milton explained. Joe backed away from the door.

By this time everyone was in the dining room. "We have to leave New York, it's no longer safe for us," David said looking around the room. "The second Holocaust has started!" he said holding Lorraine very tight.

Later that night everyone was sitting around trying to figure out the best exit out of New York. "Well you know if we have to leave, my best guess is to take the trains out of New York!" April declared.

"You can't take the trains or subways out because of flooding and tremors," Bazz reminded.

We're going to have to walk out of New York!" Ben said.

"If we leave in two groups, it won't be suspicious, and we won't draw that much attention," Milton said. "We'll just look like people going to loot. We can't look like we belong in this neighborhood. If we do, they will see us as Jewish and kill us all."

"When are we trying to leave?" Ira asked.

"Before sunrise, tomorrow," Coyote answered. "That's a good idea except the hurricane will be on us then. What if we leave right after the hurricane while it's still raining? No one will be out then, but we'll have to move quickly," Shea volunteered.

"Everyone be ready to move as soon as the hurricane starts to pass. We sleep in shifts, but we have to be out of here as soon as possible, flooding or not," Coyote announced.

Milton nodded his head in agreement.

"I'll see if I can get in touch with Brandon," Ira said. Milton and Coyote were headed for the door. "Where do you two think you're going?"

"We have some shopping to do–we need to find something," Coyote said winking at Ira.

"Yeah, I know all about it." Ira winked back. "Don't be long."

In spite of the weather, sporadic gunfire could still be heard throughout the day and into the evening. The police who stayed were struggling to regain some sense of order, and martial law had been activated. National Guard troops were being deployed, but few had arrived. No flights meant they had to come in by land. Despite the attempts at restoring order, the mayhem continued.

Ben and Joe were on the phone talking to their parents when there was knock at the door. Bridgette opened the door and was backed up by guns. Ira, Bazz, and David had guns pointed at the door. Bridgette cracked the door, and Bazz snatched the door open by the knocker.

"Damn man, it's me, Brandon. Ever thought about looking through the peephole?"

"You were supposed to be here hours ago," Ira said.

"I had to clean out my bank accounts and talk to my folks and let them know I was leaving the city. They're choosing to go to my brother's in Pennsylvania after the storm. I have four brothers in the city who are staying with them, so my parents will be okay."

"Sorry man, can't be too careful right now," Ira said.

Ben and Joe leaped from the phone to see what all the ruckus was about. "Bridge you okay?" Ben asked.

"Yeah, I'm okay."

"Could you let a more able-bodied person answer the door next time, please?" Ben snarled.

"Are your parents going to try to make it out of the city?" she asked Ben and Joe.

"No, my dad will not try to move my mom, he will not leave her side. I promised them that as soon as we got settled wherever we're going, we would come back and get them. Remember my dad was heavy into doomsday prepping, so he has enough supplies to take care of them for a few years if necessary," Ben stated. "That was one of the good qualities of my dad, his paranoia."

"Man, you are getting big!" Brandon said to Bridgette as he stepped by her to Keisha.

"If one more person says that to me, I will scream!" Bridgette pushed Brandon.

"No, Bridge if I fall into this room I'm going to scream," Brandon said trying to keep his footing while slipping on the kitchen tile floor. "Hello ladies!" Brandon announced with a grin reaching out for Keisha.

"Hey babe, I missed you so much!" Keisha started to cry burying her head into Brandon's chest. All the ladies spoke to Brandon, and after a few minutes Keisha came up for air.

"Hey, are you okay?" Brandon asked.

"I'm just trying to keep it together. So much has happened. You know my father died?"

"Yeah, I know, I'm so sorry. Are you and your mom okay? Bridgette seems to be handling it well."

"She knows she can't break down with the baby on the way."

"On the way? It's almost here," Brandon chuckled. "I'm sorry about your dad. He was a good man. Ms. Williams, you have my condolence."

"Thank you, Brandon."

"Hey, I'm going to check in with the guys, I'll be right back okay K?"

"I'm coming with you, no more time apart. I'm glad Brandon," Keisha smiled. "I'm going to see what the guys are up too."

"Me, too!" Shea said leaving the kitchen. "I need to know what Ira is up to."

"Ira is a grown man he needs no help from you, Miss Lady," Brandon said teasing Shea.

"Ira, he stay in trouble with me," Shea huffed and left the room.

When they entered the dining room, Ben had just set a large pizza with the works in front of Bridgette.

"Dag that looks good!" Brandon said reaching for a slice.

"Touch it and die!" Bridgette warned, taking a bite out of a slice. Brandon froze in his tracks.

"Don't worry man. I have two more in the oven for the rest of us. Miss Greedy does not like sharing."

"Remember, I am eating for two."

"More like three," Joe said under his breath. Everybody laughed and waited for the next two pizzas to come out, and everyone ate until they were full.

The girls started to clear the table when Coyote and Bazz returned with several shopping carts.

"I'm not even going to ask," Shea said.

"You may not want to ask, but you will want to know," Coyote answered.

"Know what?" Shea asked for everybody.

"I got all us heavy duty snowsuits and boots, and ammunition and more guns. Even managed to get some C4, a better grade than you have."

"C4, as in plastic explosives?" Shea asked.

"The one and only," Bazz winked at Ira. Ira popped Bazz upside his head.

"Ira my bad, I'm sorry," Bazz apologized.

Shea started to rant and rave in Chinese, so everyone knew she was mad.

"Thanks a lot man, now she is never going to stop." Ira escorted Shea out of the room as she continued raging in Chinese. Everyone laughed; even after the door was closed you could still hear Shea.

The women tried their snowsuits and did what they could to try and make them fit better. Most of the boots were a good fit.

"You guys did good," April exclaimed lacing up her boots.

"We're going to have travel lighter than we did when we left Georgia. We need food, ammunition and batteries, money and satellite phones. Maybe a couple of changes of clothes and ladies only personal hygiene stuff." Keisha started to laugh. "What's so funny?" Coyote asked.

"You might as well go ahead and tell Shea now. She is already cussing Ira out in Chinese, that way you won't take it personally when she starts on you!" Everyone laughed again.

It was good to laugh and share a hot meal under the circumstances. No one knew what the future held for any of them. Everyone basked in the lightheartedness of the moment. No one dared ask about the future. The uncertainty of everything hung in the air. It made the room feel heavy and anxious.

"I'm going to go ahead and crash, I'm a little tired," Bridgette said.

"You should be tired, you were getting ready to wrestle people over pizza," Brandon said winking at Bridgette. Bridgette shot him a bird with her middle finger.

"Are we?" Keisha laughed, kissing her sister, good night on the forehead.

Lorraine and David had the upper floor of the Brownstone as their honeymoon suite, not to be disturbed by anyone. Lorraine had candles lit all the way around the room. "Are you ready for our future?"

"My dear wife, whatever God chooses to provide us with, I'm truly blessed to have you by my side. Whatever will come, as long as we're together. I know that God will make a way."

Chapter 36

The eye of the hurricane hit at about 3:00 am surprising everyone. The storm had been slow passing everywhere else, the weathercasters hadn't predicted it would be any different. Maybe there was hope. Everyone was ready and prepared to leave New York. Coyote and Bazz had commandeered a party bus full of supplies and gas. Everyone was in a somber mood. Milton, Coyote, and Bazz provided armed escorts to the van. There were a few stragglers but not a lot of people for New York City at 3 a.m. It was still New York but a different New York. The Big Apple would never be the same.

"I can't believe we're leaving New York," April said peering out the tinted windows of the bus into the dark rainy, cold night. "We don't have a choice. Stay, and we will be killed. It's frightening, a second Holocaust. We live a decent and honest life, we never hurt anybody, we try to live the American dream like everyone else, and this is what we have to show for it . . . sneaking out of New York like we're common criminals."

"It's better to sneak out like a criminal than stay and look like an honest dead citizen," Keisha chimed in looking around the perimeter of the bus.

Everybody was in the bus except Bridgette and Gabe, who had just remembered something when he had Bridgette unlock the door for him.

"Man, this is a tight squeeze," Bridgette said getting into the bus.

"Anything you get in right about now will be a tight squeeze, Babe," Ben teased. Bridgette held her middle finger up at Ben.

"Oooh! I'm going to tell your mama!" Ben said looking in Mama Williams' direction.

"I saw her, and I didn't raise her like that!" Mama Williams replied.

"Get her Mama–she is getting so mean!" Keisha shouted across the bus from the rear seat. Bridgette turned and shot Keisha the finger. Everyone chuckled together.

Gabe emerged from the apartment with the Torah all rolled up and prepared for the trip. Gabe held onto the Torah extra tight not wanting to lay it in the back with the packed equipment. He held onto it like it was a child not strapped into a car seat going on a trip.

The only tunnel miraculously passable was the old faithful Lincoln Tunnel. People could be seen bugging out of New York with their apocalyptic gear on their backs and their children in tow. It was 3 am, and people were leaving New York in droves, taking advantage of the eye of the hurricane. Those that could leave, were leaving or preparing to leave. Others were hunkering down in New York. Looting food and other necessities was being permitted. So far, there was no one to stop them. Electronics, Jewels, and banks would be next.

New Yorkers are survivors, and this hurricane proved to be no different. The bus roared down the highway with Milton at the wheel. Coyote and Bazz were riding shotgun. Everyone else was asleep when the sun came up at 6:00. They had made remarkably good time and were now out of the path of the storm.

"Everything seems different now," Milton said quietly.

"Everything is different now. The media knows about the death squads and the killing of Jewish people," Coyote replied.

"You would think there would be more of an outcry from the American public," Bazz said quietly without looking up.

"The American public has become complacent with racism and terrorist attacks. They have suffered through them too often," Coyote said.

"The American public is in the mode of 'Every man for himself and God for us all!'" Milton said looking into the rearview mirror at his passengers. "This family is going to suffer just because of their Jewish heritage. They didn't choose to be Jewish. Look at Ira, he had no clue he was Jewish."

"It was God who decided," Gabe answered. "He knew you before you entered into your mother's womb. You were predestined to be who you are. You choose your friends, not your family. Both relationships should be cherished and presented to God for his blessings and grace."

"We are all connected now for sure," Bazz replied.

✡✡✡

"I really, really like the house and I think I would like to make an offer. I met the staff, they are exceptional, and they keep the house immaculate," Romero said looking out on the front lawn from the balcony.

"I'll draw up the paperwork tonight and bring them to you tomorrow to sign. When would you like to move in?" Tracy asked.

"As soon as possible–the hotel is starting to give me the creeps." Romero went back into the house to take one last look around. "I have an idea," he said turning to Tracy. "Why don't you bring the paperwork with you tonight and meet me for dinner so that way I can sign the contracts?"

"I don't usually go to dinner with my clients," Tracy smiled shyly.

"If you would like to make double commission, you may want to consider dinner tonight and bring the paperwork."

"Double commission?" Tracy asked wide-eyed. "I could use the extra money. I'll tell you what, let's have dinner here at the mansion so you can get a taste of the fine cuisine you'll be having every night."

"Okay, yeah that would work for me! I don't know why I didn't think of that. A quiet dinner at my mansion . . . This is a dream come true, and now I have someone to share it with," Romero said looking at Tracy hopeful.

"Slow down big boy, we're just having dinner tonight. We'll see what the future brings. About nine o'clock, that will give me time to draw up the paperwork."

"Okay cool wear something sexy. I'll ask the staff to make a candlelight dinner. I am ready when you are," Romero said exiting the mansion. "Hey, can I have the keys? I want to drive."

Tracy tossed Romero the keys and entered the passenger side and slid close to Romero.

All was right with the world and all the headaches and strains of the last year were behind him. Romero knew his future was bright. Romero knew Tracy was the girl for him. A complete life and all the inconveniences along the way were well worth it. Romero could not wait for tonight to begin. Not just tonight, but his new life.

The rental car picked up Romero from the hotel with all his bags already inside. "I took the liberty of getting hotel staff to pack your bags so you can at least sleep in your new home tonight," Tracy said sliding over in the back seat of the car. Romero entered the car and kissed Tracy on the cheek. "What's that for?" she asked surprised.

"I believe that you're about to make all my dreams come true." Tracy blushed looking into Romero's handsome face.

Romero could smell Tracy's intoxicating perfume–it filled the warm night air and car with a seductive aroma. Romero sat back, closed his eyes and planned out his new life.

Once at the mansion, the house looked different. There were candles lit in every room. Tracy stepped out of the car in a long strapless black dress. Romero eyes almost popped out of his head. Tracy was the most beautiful woman he had ever seen. He could not take his eyes off her the entire night. The dinner was superb. The staff was very professional and friendly. The dinner conversation was great. Romero learned that Tracy was a lot like him. Their lives had many parallels including being a twin.

Tracy explained that even though she and Lacy were identical, they were very different people. Tracy was more aggressive than Lacy. Lacy was quiet and laid back–like his dead brother Zachary, Romero thought to himself. The hours passed by and it was well after midnight when Tracy suggested they sit out on the balcony and enjoy an after-dinner drink. On the balcony, Romero and Tracy enjoyed the warm trade winds blowing off the ocean. Romero and Tracy celebrated their future together. He was glad that Tracy admitted that there might be a future for her here. One of the staff members brought out two glasses of wine. As they sipped the wine, a car pulled up out front. "Are you expecting anyone?" Tracy asked.

"Nobody knows I'm here."

"You're the owner of the house now–go out and greet your guest," Tracy said smiling.

Romero quickly swallowed his wine and approached the door. He greeted the young lady the staff had let in. Lacy was a replica of Tracy. It was amazing. He looked for slight differences, but aside from the way they wore their hair, he couldn't find any.

"Hello, how are you? I'm Romero, welcome," he greeted Tracy.

"I know who you are!" Lacy said coldly not bothering to look at Romero. "Do you know who I am?"

"Yes, you're Tracy's twin sister."

"Oh, I thought I was your sister too?"

"What?" Romero asked confused.

"Yeah, I thought I was your sister too?" Lacy repeated. "I thought we had the same father…Joseph Mengele!"

By this time Tracy had come in from the balcony and stood beside her sister. "Yes, Romero I thought we all had the same father?"

Romero could feel his face turning red and his body sobering up from the wine.

"We were sent by Rawlins to inform you who your real father is. Your real father was a drug addict Jew, who was homeless on the streets of New Orleans. He killed your drug addict mother with a hot dose of drugs and left her to suffocate on her vomit. How long did you think you could fool anyone that you are more than you are? We're here to take care of you."

"Do you two believe you are capable of taking care of me? Who do you think you are?" Romero asked raging. "Who do you think I am?" Romero shouted in disgust. All of a sudden Romero's head began to swim. He couldn't figure out was going on but suspected it must have been from the wine he had just drunk. His heartbeat increased, racing so rapidly in his chest he could hear it pounding. As Romero started to choke, Tracy leaned down and whispered in his ear ever so softly, "We are the daughters of Joseph Mengele."

Romero could feel the blood starting to drain as he felt the knife pierce his chest. His breathing began to slow, and his eyes rolled back into his head. He understood the whole thing now…his brother Zachary had tried to tell him. Jews were everywhere, and they could not be stopped. With his dying breath, he now understood. He was Jewish himself!

News Flash

There has been a run on American banks that are insured by FDIC. Customers are trying to collect and close accounts. Banks are trying to slow the bleed by allowing only one customer at a time. This panic has not been seen the crash in the Great Depression.

The stock market crash is causing mass hysteria. Gunmen are going into banks not to rob them but to pull money out of their bank accounts After several deadly altercations at banks across the country, National Guard Military forces are accompanying security guards. Credit Unions and Savings and Loans worldwide are experiencing the same upheaval. The collapse of the banking system has caused the freezing of the internet due to the high volume of online banking.

Certain countries have frozen some overseas and off-shore bank accounts. This includes Swiss and European Banks, as well as the Cayman Island and Netherland.

American citizens are resorting to drastic measures. Some people are choosing to commit suicide to try to ensure their families are not left destitute, to collect on insurance policies. Some are going so far as using murder for hire to try and throw the insurance companies off track.

Chapter 37

Coyote turned off the radio. Everyone was gasping at the news they'd just heard.

"I knew one day that the stock market would crash again, especially after the 2008 crash. I didn't think that it would crash the world economy," Shea said quietly changing the subject. "So where does that leave the country?" Shea turned to Ben.

"I don't know, it's the collapse of the American dollar versus the Chinese Yen. If you have a lot of the stuff hidden like those who have chosen to hide their money, they may as well burn it to keep warm. Pesos have more value than the American dollar," Ben explained.

"Ben you're an accountant…if I have Pesos hidden in an account in Mexico, then I'm a rich man, right?" Coyote asked hesitantly.

"Pretty much," Ben answered.

"How do you happen to have an account in Mexico full of Pesos?" Joe asked suspiciously.

"Well if you must know, I am of Mexican descent. I am not full-blooded Native American. I am married to a Native American and chose to assume the Native American way of life and spirit," Coyote replied proudly.

"If that's the case," Ira said slyly, "then we're all rich!" That is everyone who works for me. We all have accounts in Mexico. Milton, Coyote and me. We have had accounts in Mexico City since 1994."

"We need to make sure that Jordan's family gets his money," Milton said wearily. "I know he would have wanted it that way."

"No problem, we just have to get to Mexico," Ira said.

"Right now, we need to get some gas before we're walking and fighting the elements," Milton complained.

"Hey, there's a gas station over there, but the line is really long. There's a diner across the street where we can wait," Ira said.

"I'll get the gas," Bazz announced exiting the bus first. Everyone exited the bus and headed toward the diner.

Bazz came back a few moments later. "They're not accepting cash, do you have any Pesos on you?" he asked laughing, turning toward Coyote.

"I have a black American Express and some gold coins," Coyote said.

"I'm not sure if the American Express will work now," Bazz said concerned.

"Try these gold coins," Coyote said handing the coins to Bazz.

"That should get it," Bazz said heading back toward the bus.

Everyone else looked road weary. Bridgette knew the trip would be long, especially for her. She was starting to have small pains in her back from sitting on the bus seats for so long. She silently prayed the pains would subside. Everyone placed their breakfast order and ate, paying with a few gold coins that Ira had. Bazz returned a few minutes before breakfast ended.

"We have gas, but money isn't good anymore. Gold jewelry or expensive electronics only."

"The government just announced that they would be issuing junk bonds," Ben offered.

"Bridgette, Joe, and April, Granddad hid some gold for us. I have it packed so, we're okay for right now."

"We also have the gold Bertram saved. He made sure there was enough saved for us and the girls," Mama Williams said. "He even made some chess pieces out of gold. I have them here with me. He told me one day we would need them; that gold would take the place of money. I was so distraught when he passed, I almost forgot the chess pieces."

"Can I see?" Shea asked.

"Sure you can." Mama Williams passed Shea the box that held the chess pieces.

Shea opened the box. "It looks like a box of chess pieces."

"That's what they're supposed to look like, except they're solid gold."

224

Keisha sat up to look in the box. "Daddy was so smart. He knew this was going to happen and we never really believed him. I feel so bad about all the ribbing we gave him about being paranoid. I wish we had paid more attention to him." Keisha started to cry.

"Don't cry K. We all wished we had listened more," Mama Williams said holding back tears and brushing Keisha's hair.

"We are gassed up and ready to go," Bazz announced. "It's starting to get crazy out there because people have money and they're only taking gold and electronics."

"I believe a riot is about to break out. We need to get out of here fast," Ira said closing the bus door behind him.

Back on the road, looting of electronics and food had started. The Great American Dollar Bill had no more value. The eagle soared no more!

Bridgette had her father's book laying on her lap as she slept. Joe took the book and started to read it aloud. "It states in this book that secure places to stay are Indian Reservations and old, unused historical underground railroad passages and camps."

"That makes sense," Milton said. "The government does not run Indian Reservations. They have no jurisdiction, and because of the economy, the government has not funded historical sites. There are no cameras and you can get in and lie low for a couple of days to get some rest and refuel."

"When we get to that point," Shea said, "then we will consider hiding out. Until then, I would like to stay in a 4-star hotel."

"Baby be for real? A 4-star hotel? We're hiding not vacationing," Ira said in a muffled sleepy voice. "We're going need to be gassing up again in about another 50 miles or so. We'll need food and more supplies. We don't know where we're heading into in this new America."

Fifty miles down the road, the bus pulled over in a little country gas station. Everyone got out to stretch their legs and get some fresh air.

"Let me do the talking," Milton said. "We're going to have to barter for the gas and the supplies because money is useless and credit cards are worse. Even though we have gold, we would like to be able to keep most of it for other uses."

"Where are we?" Keisha asked.

"Somewhere in Michigan," Coyote answered.

Milton came back out to the bus. "I'm gonna need one of those statues Ms. Williams."

"No problem, that's what they are for," Ma Williams said handing one of the chess pieces to Milton. Milton took the chess piece to the back of the bus and started to cut it in pieces with the tools that were packed under the bus. As Bazz and Coyote shadowed Milton looking through the compartment side of the bus, a strange black suburban with tinted windows slowly pulled up on the opposite side of the street.

Everyone started to exit the bus just as the suburban slowly pulled up. Everyone was laughing and stretching their legs preparing to go into the gas station. Suddenly the windows rolled down on the black suburban. Coyote and Bazz yelled, "Get down!" at the same time. Bullets rang out from the black truck piercing the side of the bus. Glass shattered just above Mama Williams' head, and she screamed. Bazz, Milton, Keisha, and Brandon returned gunfire as Coyote ran onto the bus for cover and checked Mama Williams. A loud scream came from the black truck, "I'm hit! Drive off!" The wheels squealed as the black truck peeled off leaving the burning smell of rubber behind, letting gravel fly as it sped away. Ms. Williams' and Lorraine's screams were muffled by Coyote and Brandon laying on top on them returning fire.

Alex started to scream as the black truck pulled off. April's body lie on the ground just steps from the bus. Joe ran over to her and rolled her over to check to see if she was hurt. As Alex continued to scream, the blood spilled from a wound in April's chest as she struggled to breath. With every gasp of air, blood poured from her chest. The wound was a large gaping hole that Joe was trying to apply pressure to.

"Apply pressure on the wound, it will help slow down the bleeding," someone said.

"Don't apply pressure, she is hit in the lungs!" Bazz screamed back to Joe. Blood spurted from April's.

"April is hit!" Joe screamed. "Get some help!"

Alex crawled over to Joe and April and placed April's head on her lap. She cried as she softly told April that she would be okay, to just hang on. April gasped her last breath and the blood of life poured from her mouth onto Alex's lap. Joe dug up a fist full of gravel as he sat there wailing over April. Ben said nothing as he sat next to Joe with a face full of tears, crying for his sister. Alex stroked April's hair as she wept in grief.

Bridgette let out a loud gasp and looked down at her feet. Her feet and shoes were wet, her water had broken, and she bent over in pain. The contractions had started and increased. She had thought the back pains she'd felt all day were just that–instead they were contractions. Bridgette let out another gut-rattling grunt. Ben looked back at Bridgette as she dropped to her knees wailing in pain.

"Oh Bridge! Please not now! "The baby is too early!"

"Ben, help me!" Bridgette said, then asked, "Is April okay?"

"Are you sure you didn't get hit Bridge?" Ben asked breathlessly looking Bridgette over carefully.

Shea ran over to April to see if she could help assist with the gunshot wound. April had already succumbed. Shea shook her head at Keisha and Ben. "April is gone, Ben!" Bridgette winced between pain and tears.

Lorraine and Mama Williams made their way off the bus to check on April and Bridgette. David hugged Lorraine as Gabe performed the death Rites and prayers over April. Gabe and Joe broke down clinging to each other for comfort. Alex ever so tenderly leaned over and closed April's eyes. "Rest in Peace. I love you April," Alex said as she slumped next to April's body.

"Bridgette, I'm here. I'm going to need you to breathe, baby."

"Momma it's too soon. The baby isn't due for another 6 to 8 weeks!"

"No such thing, as too soon. God time is not ours, and if she wants to come now, she is coming," Mama Williams soothed.

David and Lorraine cried together. Joe pulled his jacket off and laid it over the body. Gabe repeated the 23rd Psalm over and over.

Shea and Mama Williams were coaching Bridgette with the birth as Ben held her hand. "Babe we're going to have to cut these pants off of you!" Shea said reaching for scissors.

Coyote, Milton, and Bazz decided to try and secure the perimeter since everyone was out in the open. The gas station owner told Ira that they called the ambulance earlier for the incident and didn't get a reply. Nor did an ambulance come. Ira relayed the message to Keisha who relayed the message to Shea.

"Bridgette, don't you worry about a thing. We are going to deliver this baby. I need you to listen to everything I tell you to do. Ben, I need you to hang in there for me. Bridgette is doing good, and the baby is okay."

"Shea don't bullshit me. What are we looking at as far as the baby is concerned?"

Shea gave Ben a quick look. "As long as the baby's lungs are developed, we're okay. If not, we have to get to a hospital as soon as possible."

The owner of the gas station came out and told them the police would be there as soon as humanly possible.

"That means they're not coming," Bazz whispered. "I'm going to check the other side of the gas station," Bazz whispered again.

Twenty minutes had passed, and no one said a word except Bridgette, Shea, and Mama Williams. Bridgette's screams intensified as the pain increased. Ben started to coach Bridgette through the breathing techniques they had learned in the maternity classes. Shea coached Bridgette through the breaths and prepared her to push. Twenty minutes after she started the push, the cry of a new baby pierced the air. Baby took her first breath. Shea watched the baby's breathing closely before she handed the baby to Bridgette. Shea checked the baby very carefully and saw that the baby was breathing on her own. She even spanked her twice to make sure she could breathe well.

Ben sat motionless in shock. He'd just lost his sister twenty-five minutes earlier and now had seen the arrival of his newborn baby daughter. It was a lot to comprehend and appreciate. Mama Williams took the baby while Shea helped clean Bridgette up. No one said a word; all weeping from joy and pain in the same span of time.

"What's the baby's name?" Mama. Williams asked Ben.

"April," Ben replied touching her cheek.

Bridgette chimed in, "April Serenity. Serenity will be her middle name. Ben, I'm, so sorry. What are we going to do?" Bridgette started to cry. Everyone was in tears.

"How did they find us?" Coyote asked breaking the sound of weeping. Joe was still holding April's body. Milton took the body from Joe placing it in a sleeping bag. Bazz helped Milton move the body to the back of the bus.

Brandon stated, "They have to have a tracking device or are listening to us in some way. We have to go through everything on the bus to search and see what we come up with."

"Thank you, Shea, for helping my sister and my baby niece," Keisha gushed.

"Didn't think I had it in me?" Shea smirked.

"Baby, I knew you had it in you," Ira replied kissing Shea on the forehead. "Let's empty the bus," Ira said motioning to the bus.

"I'll help Bridgette and the baby inside the gas station if that's okay?" Ben asked looking at Joe and Alex. "I don't think I can help with that," he said nodding toward April.

"Come on inside the store," the clerk nodded.

The store clerk tried to make room for everybody. "I'm going to give you the gas for free. I hope the deputy comes. The sheriff was killed a couple of days ago. Ambushed right on this same road. Looks like by the same people driving the same black truck."

"People are crazy now with the collapse of the economy, it's only going to get worse," Ben said.

"I think I am going to close up shop for a couple of days. It's just not safe right now," the store clerk replied shaking his head.

"Excuse me sir, what was your sheriff's name?" Ben asked.

"Ben was his name. Benjamin Levi," the store clerk answered.

Everyone exchanged looks, but no one said a word.

✡✡✡

Coyote, Milton, and Ira had spent two hours going through everything on the bus. They did not find any device that could have given their position away.

"I don't know how they found us. It has to be a tracking device or a listening device," Milton said exhausted. "Hey, I'll pack everything back into the bus. I hate to bring this up but what are we going to do with the body?"

"We'll have to bury her here if they will let us," Coyote said.

Milton tossed the Torah to Bazz. Bazz didn't see the Torah being tossed and it hit the bumper of the bus. A small piece of plastic fell from the Torah onto the gravel.

"What the Hell?" Bazz said bending down over the Torah to get a better look at what had just popped out of the case.

"Is that what I think it is?" Coyote asked approaching Bazz side.

"Damn skippy! A tracking device. I would have never looked for it in the Torah," Bazz said shaking his head.

"Sneaky, low down, dirty bastards," Milton said. "I hope that's the only one. Things have been turned up just another notch."

"We have to rethink our plan and get off this main road. Backwoods, haunts, and hollows…you know how we do it," Coyote said.

"First we have to get approval from the family to bury the body. We'll come back for it and give it a proper burial later, but right now we have to get out of here as soon as possible," Bazz said.

"We're sitting ducks! We have to leave before the death squads return," Coyote said as he stormed off.

Coyote went and whispered a few words to Ira who reported them to Keisha, who in turn had to plead with the family to allow April to buried there. The family conceded, and the store clerk allowed them to bury the body in a nearby field adjacent to the gas station with a makeshift headstone.

The family found it extremely difficult to leave a loved one behind. Joe and Alex cried continuously. Ben grieved, but the continuous care of the baby kept his mood a shade above grief.

"Hey Bridge, are you okay?" Ben asked protectively.

"Believe it or not, I'm okay. I can't believe April's gone and we are left with little April. All in one moment that doesn't prepare you to understand how precious life is," Bridgette said fighting back the tears. "Luckily, Shea decided to go ahead and prepare for worse–the baby early. So, we packed everything we hoped we'd need."

"I'm just glad that she was born healthy," Shea replied.

"This thing is getting unreal for me. First dad and now April," Bridgette said looking at her mom. "I couldn't stand to lose anyone else."

"We have to do something. I'm not letting anyone else I love die," Alex said looking grief stricken.

"There's a historical underground railroad station not too far from here. It will have everything we need except food, and we would be safe. Remember Keisha, daddy took us there."

"I think so," Keisha answered nodding her head. "I don't think the people that are hunting us would know anything about it."

"No, I don't think they would," David said holding Lorraine close.

"It's an old plantation that has a couple of cabins that will be able to sleep all of us. This will give us time to regroup and stay off the radar from the death squads," Bridgette explained.

"Let's take a vote from everyone," Ben announced. "Hey everyone, there's a piece of historical land not too far from here where we can lay low for a couple of days," Ben yelled out so the guys guarding the back of the property could hear.

"Bridgette, is it going be safe for you and the baby?' Mama Williams asked.

"Yeah Ma, I'll be able to get some rest and get what I need for the baby."

"I'm game if everyone is," Gabe replied.

All agreed, and the bus moved in the direction of the underground railroad.

Arriving at the underground railroad in Ohio, the bus pulled onto the well-manicured grounds in the dark of night. Everyone was solemn; the only sounds heard were the coos of newborn baby Serenity sucking at her mother's breast.

"It's just an old plantation," Lorraine commented as they disembarked the bus.

"Yes, it's an old plantation, but there are underground caves and springs that were used to hide runaway slaves," Keisha explained. "I remember coming here with Daddy as a little girl," Keisha exclaimed reaching for her niece.

"Thanks, K," Bridgette said stretching.

"Is it safe? Is there a way we can secure?" Milton asked, "so everyone can get some rest."

"Yes. That's a bell tower that can be used to see the entire valley for at least two miles. I'll show you," Keisha said handing Ben the baby. "All men follow me. We can stay here at least a week if we choose to," Keisha said looking around.

"There's fresh water and herbs," Bridgette said pointing to the back of the house.

"Bridgette, you need to try and get your rest," Mama Williams said taking the baby from Ben.

"Is there running water?" Shea asked.

"Yeah, there are restrooms with showers because of the cave tours. I believe they still work. The caves have been closed for years because of lack of funding from the government. We can go take a look in the morning."

"Okay, anyone ready to eat?" Everyone agreed that Shea could start cooking and the ladies would help.

The house proved to be in better condition than expected. There was a bit of dust and smelled a little musty, but overall, it was in great form. There were enough rooms in the main house that everyone would be able to stay together. The cabins would not need to be used.

After setting up motion sensors around the house, everyone came in to eat and discuss plans for that leg of the journey.

"So, Keisha, tell us about this house or plantation," Joe requested.

"This house leads to another house in Toronto, Canada. This house is just one in a line of houses that lead from the deep south to the north and on to Canada. If you crossed the Ohio River, you were safe. You were free until a law passed that changed that. Even though you made it to the north, you were still not free. You had to go into Canada to be free. If a slaveholder sent trackers to find you in the north, after the law was passed, you could be returned to your master. This was done quite often to discourage other slaves from trying to run. If you were caught helping slaves escape, you could be jailed. If you were a black person found to be helping slaves escape, you were killed on the spot; more than likely hung from a tree. This, unfortunately, was considered an easy death compared to what they really did to black people. Eventually, the Emancipation happened, and the slaves were freed. Some of them didn't know they were free until years later.

The homeowners sold some of the land and the houses to the government. Some were sold to the government for taxes. The land and the houses were maintained as a historical site. Lucky for us because of the government shutdowns, the property has not been used for a while, so no one will know we're here." Keisha sighed.

"Where do we go from here?" Alex asked somberly. "Are we going be safe? I can't stand to think that we could lose anyone else, I just can't. April was enough." Alex started to weep. Lorraine tried to console Alex.

"April will be sorely missed. I will never let her be forgotten," Joe said.

"Honestly, where do we go from here?" Ben questioned holding the baby.

"Well, there is a community in Kansas where the government has foreclosed on all 61 houses. I think the security they had watching the homes to prevent looters from ripping out the pipes and what not, are probably long gone for now," Brandon said.

"We have to get there first," Ira spoke up. "Coyote, I know you have to get home to look after your family on the reservation."

"Yeah, I do. If you guys would like, you know you are more than welcome guests on the reservation. You do business there all the time, so I know they would welcome you," Coyote said looking around the room at everyone.

"If things get any worse out here, we may have to take you up on that offer," Milton said coming in from outside. "All perimeter stands are hooked to trap cameras and perimeter cameras. I need to hook everything up in here. We'll know if anything the size of a baby goat or larger crosses the perimeter. That will give us at least 6 minutes to prepare for whatever! Ira, you had all this equipment for transfers? No wonder you never got caught!"

233

"I had a wife I made a promise to that I would be home, and I'd rather flee then not come home to her. No bars were going to keep me from coming home to her! Plus, when my wife is mad, it's like I'm already doing time! Don't think that I'm going to do time with Shea as the jailer. And then go to real jail! No, way, Jose! I'm sorry Coyote!"

"No problem!" Coyote said with a grin. "I'll just turn you into Warden Shea!" Everyone laughed. Mama Williams helped Shea in the kitchen to show her appreciation to everyone.

It was a pretty warm night for October, so Brandon and Keisha decided to take a walk around the property. The property had been well maintained even though it had been closed for a couple of years. Some states were able to keep historical landmark maintenance in the budgets, for those that couldn't, sites went into disarray. Places like the Statue of Liberty had been closed down for more than four years. Yellowstone National Park, Niagara Falls closed, Washington Monument closed, Library of Congress, closed, Empire state Building closed. America the beautiful was no longer beautiful. America had almost become a derelict society with no one to blame but herself.

Good old-fashioned American greed had torn the country apart state by state, city by city, block by block, farm by farm. There was no way that the country could have continued on the path it was on and expect God to continue to Bless America.

The next five days went by quickly. Everyone had been sleep-deprived and exhausted. So much had happened in a short amount of time. Everyone had their own ideas about what to do next; how the country should try to get back to his greatness. Every politician in the world was on TV or radio, trying to explain their policy to get the country back on its feet. It seemed no one had money to pay taxes. Now the politicians wanted to work harder to get things back in natural working order. To get the government's money started up. There would be no do-overs this time.

Everyone in the group took a vote to move on to the Gulf of Mexico where they would catch a cruise ship to Israel. There was nothing left in America. The police forces had been brought to their knees. They had no power to stop the death squads as much as they tried. It would be safer to leave America and maybe come back in five years' time. Hopefully, America would somehow find the strength to return to some symbolism of its former self.

News Flash

"In national news today, the body of the reputed leader of the Brotherhood of the Valkyrie was found stabbed to death in his home in Brazil. Romero McEvans is believed to be involved with the Paradise Cove scheme in Switzerland where many Jewish people were killed. McEvans had close ties with Erich Rawlins, Chairman of the Board of Bank of the Alps who funded the project. Rawlins comes from a family long believed to be staunch supporters of the Aryan Nation, and is suspected in financing the killing squads here in the U.S. He is also the mastermind of Paradise Cove according to the other four members of the board. They stand by their stories that Paradise Cove was presented to them as it was to the Jewish people–a paradise to make restitution for the heinous crimes committed against them in Hitler's Germany.

Paradise Cove earned the moniker of The Killing City after its exposure by a group of young protestors who'd discovered the real purpose of the city. The scheme was exposed on social media with images of the homes with incineration chambers beneath them. The protestors showed the world that anti-Semitism was not only alive and well in the world but had reverted to genocide. In a secret interview with protestors, their leader stated, "…it was horrible. I'd only heard the stories from my Grandparents and other family members, of the horrors of Auschwitz. Each day people would disappear, and we became suspicious. One Holocaust should never have happened and a second was heinous. We will not allow this to happen again. Every person has a right to live a life free of hatred and disrespect. Every life means something.

Paradise Cove burned to the ground in a suspicious fire. Swiss authorities are not investigating the nature of the fire given the killings. The government has further decided to build a memorial to those killed so that none forget the horrors of prejudism and specifically, anti-Semitism.

To date, the killing squads have stopped, and some of the participants have been apprehended. Nationwide law enforcement officials say it will take time to catch all remaining members of the Brotherhood of Valkyrie. It is believed McEvans transferred large sums of money to his lieutenants to aid in their escape. The investigation is a massive joint effort including, DHS, FBI, Interpol, Scotland Yard, CIA, NSA, MI5, and the Israeli Mossad. All agencies vow to work together and bring an end to Anti-Semitism once and for all.

Chapter 38

The five days that the group spent at the underground rail station had taught them a lot about society. Freedom was not free.

During the years of slavery, it was racism about the color of your skin, the right for a man to be treated with common dignity and respect. The color of your skin made the difference.

Now it was not about the color of your skin. It was about the DNA and the blood that ran through your veins. A group of different ethnicities: Black, White, Asian, Latino and Native American. If you cut any of them, their blood bled red. The DNA made the difference. Something you could have not chosen, just like the color of your skin. The color of your skin could get you killed, and now your DNA could cost you your life. Just like people couldn't change the color of their skin, they could not change their DNA.

The days spent at the railroad station were peaceful–almost too peaceful. No one was ready to leave, but they knew they could not stay. Everyone wanted to live to fight another day.

The decision was made to head to the Gulf of Mexico and catch a ship to Israel. Coyote and Milton would go back to the reservation. The few days of peace gave Keisha and Brandon a renewed look on their love, and they decided to tie the knot in front of their friends and family.

The bus was packed to the hilt, and everyone was prepared to leave. The violence in America had reached a frenzied state. Martial Law was doing no good.

"The best route for us to the Gulf is through Kentucky, Tennessee, Arkansas, and then down through Texas," Milton said handing the map to Ira.

"My only concern is the mountain men from the backwoods of Kentucky and Tennessee," Ira said as he studied the map.

"Right about now the backwoods people will do you less harm than the death squads," Joe said looking out over the plantation.

"Yeah, you got a point," Ira declared.

"Hey bro," Bridgette said tapping Joe on the shoulder. "We' going to make it. April would have wanted it that way. Your mom and dad are having round the clock prayer vigils for all of us. We're going to make it."

"Before we go, I want to say a little prayer for all of us," Gabriel said. "All bow your heads and hold hands. Jehovah, we come to ask that you send your angels to watch over and prepare the way before us and that you place a blood ring around us and protect us from all hurt, harm, and danger. Lord, we pray for enemies and ask that you touch their hearts and that you help us forgive those who took our April from us. Until we meet you in heaven, Lord, we say thank you and amen."

The bus pulled out with Bazz driving. Ira, Milton, and Ben were riding shotgun. The second shift would be David, Joe, Coyote, and Brandon with Keisha driving. They rode in stunned silence listening to the news about Romero, Erich, and Paradise Cove.

"I can't believe it's true," Alex said. "All those families went to their deaths believing it was the beginning of a dream. Paradise Cove was worse than the Holocaust on some level. People who went to the concentration camps had no delusions about what might happen. These people didn't have any idea."

"It doesn't matter what the circumstances were," David said, "the reasons and outcome were still the same–massive genocide."

"God bless those who lost their lives and keep us safe from all danger as we travel," Gabe prayed softly.

"Amen," resounded through the bus.

"Ms. Williams, can I ask you something?" David asked turning around in the seat to face her. "You're Jewish right?"

"By marriage," she replied

"So, how is it your last name is Williams? I'm just a little confused." Bridgette and Keisha giggled at the same time.

"My husband's last name is Cohen. We dated a couple of years in the sixties, and I demanded that he let me keep my last name in case I made it big on Broadway and in case the marriage didn't work out. You know, women's lib and all. He allowed me to keep it. Hell, he even took it for a while himself. He didn't care as long as I agreed to marry him."

"Aww, that's so sweet," Alex sighed. "He proved he really loved you."

"Interracial couples had it really hard back then. We had some trying days, but we managed to stay together. We agreed that there would be no quitting; we would stay together through thick or thin. Some days we didn't like each other much, but we stayed. When the girls finally came along, we were an old married couple. We spent every day together for 27 years. We took the girls on trips, went to Israel and different places. Family became an important part of life for us. I will cherish every day I spent with my husband. I just never thought in a million years that the things he taught us would ever come true. Never thought…" Ma Williams said as her voice trailed off. She stared out of the window and a tear ran down her face.

Everyone rode along in a thick silence. The strain of the events had deeply affected everyone. No one could imagine having to leave their homeland–not even Lorraine who had left Germany when she was a baby. David had left Germany when he was young as well but too young to remember much. Bazz was the only one who could comprehend what was really happening.

America, your homeland, watching her crumble would be difficult for all to bare. There was no choice; they had to leave.

"Bazz, was it hard to leave your homeland?" Alex asked.

"I didn't leave my homeland, my homeland left me. People that I had grown up with decided my life was worth less than a cockroach. I had to flee my country for my very life. Most of my family didn't make it out. I plan to go back, but deep in my heart I know I'm not ready to relive the memories or the nightmares! Because of that, I will never stop helping people escape to freedom. To give them a second chance, this is the reason I exist. Somebody gave me another chance. I feel that God chose me to do this. I might have nightmares about what I have seen and done to survive and escape. I am not proud of some of the things I had to do to survive, but I'm here trying to help someone else."

✡ ✡ ✡

Coyote pulled his hood up over his head and tried to forget his past. Helping people escape poverty and racism was his first thought, but he knew the people he used to work for used people as drug mules. They would be made to swallow the drugs and carry them across the border inside their bodies to be retrieved later at all cost. People died every day. Coyote was glad that he was able to live to get out. The legalization of Marijuana had saved his life and the lives of friends; of that he was sure. It had saved a lot of lives.

Ira thought to himself as the bus drove along about the life he left behind in Jamaica. He had worked two or three jobs, 19-hour days. He worked until his hands split and bled. Even with three jobs and working as many hours as he could, he was still not able to provide for his two children and his wife. Not enough money to fill their bellies, telling them to sleep on their bellies so their stomachs wouldn't hurt or growl so loud as to wake them from a sound sleep. It was more than Ira could bear, so when the opportunity presented itself to track marijuana and to make enough money in one night, than 2 years of working 3 jobs could not do, of course, he took the job. He needed to take care of his family. When the opportunity to live in Miami came, Ira jumped at the chance. The only catch was that he would have to walk away from his family. He'd never be able to return to Jamaica and see his wife and kids.

Ira made sure he sent his family enough money to live a good life in Jamaica. He often wondered how his family had made it without him. He was sure that money didn't cure all evils, especially on a small island in Jamaica. Ira also wondered if Shea would understand if he ever told her about his secret family.

✡ ✡ ✡

Joe woke to the stifling heat as the bus sped along the back roads. He glanced over at David and Lorraine holding hands in their sleep and smiled to himself. Joe always wondered how older people could sleep in the heat without a problem. They weren't even breaking a sweat. "I guess it comes from growing up without air conditioning," Joe thought. He struggled to open a window to get some fresh air, still smiling at David and Lorraine.

Joe thought about David being gay and now married to a woman. David looked 15 years younger since he'd been involved with Lorraine. Joe realized in that moment that love game from the heart for whoever it was, male or female. That David and Lorraine had found each other in the midst of a Holocaust gave Joe hope for his future.

He wished April could have lived long enough to have loved. She'd had so many bad experiences. Love would have made such a difference for her. Someone who was gentle and kind, someone who took the time to be in a relationship. These thoughts made Joe decide that he would change the way he lived his life. April's death had taught him that life was not to be taken for granted. He would work to live not live to work. Who knew, perhaps there was someone out there for him. Joe would live his life to honor April.

✡✡✡

Milton was trying to figure the easiest route through Arkansas to keep the van and its passengers safe. Milton passed a nice, well-manicured park that caused him to reminisce of his days with Desiree. She had been Milton's high school sweetheart, stuck by him through thick and thin. She was the love of his life. When her family put him down and said he was a bum because he had lost several jobs back to back and was not taking care of their daughter in the way that she was accustomed to. Desiree's family owned a couple of jewelry stores. No one in her family could understand what she saw in him, but he knew she loved him, and he loved her. Milton decided to move to America to better himself. He felt that drug dealing was his future. Surprising himself, Milton was able to financially profit from his decision. The only thing was that he had to leave Desiree for weeks at a time. Desiree didn't mind. She enrolled in nursing school. After 2 years she was diagnosed with stage 3 ovarian cancer.

Milton was doing great in the transfer business and was able to pay for Desiree's cancer treatments. At first, she seemed to be getting better, then the cancer took a turn for the worse. Desiree became weak and pale and losing her hair. She was so weak, she couldn't get out the bed to go to the bathroom, she needed a home care nurse to help her.

Within a couple of weeks, she was downgraded to stage four with only months to live. Milton was heartbroken. He could not believe he would lose the love of his life just when he started doing well. He was able to pay the cancer treatments in cash and still had money left over for anything they needed. Desiree's dream was to take a trip to the South Pacific for about 4 months as soon as she got well.

One day Milton came home and there was a new nurse in the home. She introduced herself as Anna and was from hospice. The hospital had sent her over to make sure that they kept Desiree comfortable. Milton had noticed that Desiree started to sleep more, but he thought it was a side effect of the medication. He was not ready to lose Desiree; she was his life the future mother of his children.

Milton would come home day after day and notice Desiree was losing color and weight and had dark circles under her eyes. The nurse told him it would not be long, possibly four weeks, maybe more. Milton asked if he could have some alone time with his wife before the end came. The nurses trained him on what he needed to do for her. The nursing staff left for the night after giving Desiree her nightly medication. That night Milton played all their favorite songs and had prepared and served a candlelight dinner in the bedroom with Desiree. Milton talked to Desiree and reminded her of their lifelong goals, their trip to the South Pacific. The two gorgeous girls they wanted to have together. He wanted them to look just like Desiree.

In five years, they would buy a ranch in Montana. Milton talked all night to Desiree. He reminded her of all their dreams. Desiree slowly slipped off into a coma while Milton was there. Milton thought she had died. He lifted her comatose body from the bed and sang to her. Milton begged Desiree to come back to him. When she did not respond, Milton called the nurse shift back and left as soon as they pulled up to the home. All his bags were packed to leave not knowing that Desiree was only in a coma, not dead.

Milton threw the phone from the truck as he drove off never to return again. The nursing staff tried to call Milton several times to let him know that Desiree had only slipped into a coma, that she was not dead. They thought he deserted her at the end to keep the pain away from being there to the end. Milton was out of the country in twenty minutes. A lifetime away. Milton left two million dollars in their account to handle any financial situations that would arise in the death of his wife and to pay the nursing staff and doctors. Milton knew the money would outlast Desiree.

Ten years had passed before Milton allowed himself to feel anything concerning Desiree. Milton had filled his life with death. Any dangerous assignment, he asked if he could take the lead on the projects nobody asked to go. Milton' life was about running up and down the east coast from Miami to New York. Living like he could not be killed or injured.

One day a creepy dealer from Connecticut wanted to do a meeting in a park. Milton hesitated, parks meant kids, kids meant jail, but the guy was offering too much to turn him down. Milton still had his eye on a ranch in Montana, so agreed to the meeting. Milton decided to scout the park out early to see if he saw anything strange. The meeting was going great, nothing looked suspicious. There were only a couple of kids and parents in the park. The bagman made his drop. Milton handed over his bag and picked up the bag money from the garbage can by the swing set. The weight felt right, there was no way he was going to check the money in an open park. If it wasn't all there, there would be consequences later. For now, it was time to get out of the park. Milton asked himself what kind of sicko wanted to do deals in parks where little kids played?

Milton turned around to walk hurriedly back to his truck when he was hit in the leg with a kid's blue ball. A little girl reached down to pick up the ball. The little girl had the most familiar green eyes Milton had ever seen. Milton tossed the little girl the ball and started to walk off. The little girl was met by her twin sister, who also had the same haunting green eyes.

Milton started a slow jog to his truck when it hit him. He knew those green eyes. Desiree had those same green eyes. It hit him like a ton of bricks–Desiree!

Milton dropped the money bag and turned around to see Desiree healthy and happy approaching the twin girls. Milton could not move; he froze in his spot. The twin girls screamed, "Daddy!" as a tall blonde man came around the corner and swooped up both girls at one time. Desiree picked up the ball and followed closely behind the three of them.

Milton could not believe the pain in his chest and the hole in the pit of his stomach. The knot in his throat was too big to swallow. Milton dropped to his knees as the reality hit him like a ton of bricks. He just sat on the ground in the park. A few people inquired to see if he was okay, all he could do was nod his head. Milton picked up the bag and ran full speed to his truck. Milton wept and howled until he couldn't cry anymore.

Desiree had made it; she lived. She lived and went on to have twin girls and a husband. Milton could not believe she was alive. He remembered the very night he left he thought about doing a mercy killing. He was going to kill her then himself so that she wouldn't have to suffer through the pain. Milton couldn't understand–she was dead when he left. The nursing staff must have been able to resuscitate her.

What did she think of him? She had to think he was a coward. He could never face her. She had to have thought that he'd abandoned her when she needed him the most. His life had been so empty without her and now that he had seen her alive, it just really showed him how empty his life was and what the drug game had cost him. The love of his life. There would be no one who would ever take her place.

✡✡✡

As the bus crossed the state line into Arkansas, Shea woke from a restful sleep. She looked over at Ira as he slept and thought *if the end of the world is near, should I tell him my little secret.... Or better yet, our little secret.*

Shea had noticed at the end of every month $10,000 would be withdrawn from Ira's bank account. At the first of the month, it was replaced. She never questioned the $10,000 because it always returned with more and she had everything she could ever need and more. She had talked to Keisha about it who asked her given his previous profession as a drug dealer, did she want to know where the money came from. Shea told her no even though she did want to know. Without Keisha, Shea traced the money to a small Jamaican island. She hopped a flight down to Jamaica, told Ira she was going to her parents' house in Syracuse, New York so that he wouldn't be suspicious.

Shea had found the bank where the money was being wired from and wired to each month. She decided to hang around the bank until the first of the month to see who came to pick up the money. A beautiful, young Jamaican woman came every month to pick up the money. Who was this woman; was she Ira's sister? She cashed the money order and deposited over half of the ten thousand into another account at another bank. Following the woman, Shea thought the woman would see her. An Asian woman on a Jamaican island was not so inconspicuous. Tiehera was her name. Shea followed the woman to a nearby fishing village where the woman lived with two small children that she took care of. The little boy can outside to try and fly a kite that the woman had just purchased at a nearby store. One look at the little boy and Shea knew that the child belonged to Ira. It was too much for Shea. She had to go back to the hotel and lay down. She had to get her thoughts together on what to do next. After laying down for some time, Shea knew exactly what she had to do. She had to confront the woman and find out who she was.

Shea decided to go back to the cottage where the little family lived and confront the woman. Shea knocked on the door of the cottage. The entire family came to the door. Shea introduced herself and asked the lady how she knew Ira. The young woman said that she and Ira had been high school sweethearts and that they had married right after high school and the two children belonged to him. The woman was still married to Ira, and he did send her $10,000 a month to support her and the two kids.

Shea didn't think that she would make it through the afternoon after listening to the lady's story about how poor they were and how Ira had to leave to make money for the family. After the first two years, Tiehera said she knew that Ira would never be back, but he made sure that she and the kids were provided for the rest of their lives.

246

The shock of it all almost made Shea sick then she remembered that she hadn't eaten anything all day and needed to go back to the hotel. She bid Tehira goodbye and asked if she could call on her and the children tomorrow before she caught her flight back to America. Tehira suspiciously agreed to meet Shea again.

Shea went back to hotel wondering whether her marriage to Ira was legitimate at all. How could he have kept this from her? After eating dinner, Shea knew exactly what she had to do to remedy the situation.

Shea slept well that night and, in the morning, had an early meeting with a gentleman on the island who would take care of all her problems. Shea returned to the cottage early that afternoon. Her flight left early in the evening, so she hoped the meeting would be quick. It would only if Teihera would oblige her. Shea asked Teihera to sign divorce papers that she had drawn up and in exchange would give her 50,000 then and increase her payment to 15,000 a month. Teihera had no problem signing the papers. She said she knew that she and Ira were over the minute he left the island for a new job.

Shea returned from the island trip exhausted and never mumbled a word to Ira. He never asked about the $ 50,000, he assumed that she spent it on her parents. Shea never told Ira that she knew where the $10,000 was going every month. And, she never told him that he was divorced from Teihera. He had his secrets and she kept hers. One of the stipulations for Teheira to receive the fifty thousand dollars was that she never tell Ira about the divorce papers. Shea decided she would spring it on him if she ever needed to. So far, there had been no need to spring. Just the fact that he had never spoken to her about any of it her know that she was entitled to her secrets too. Shea assumed the grunting in their sleep that they did was all the secrets they kept trying to come out.

✡︎✡︎✡︎

Another hour and a half had passed, and it was Keisha's turned to drive. Bridgette decided to keep her company up front as she drove.

The GPS system was blinking on and off, so Shea cut it off. The guys were in the back playing cards. Bridgette noticed the engine trying to run hot, so she asked the guys if there was any anti-freeze on the bus.

"Pull the bus over and we'll look at it," Ira and Coyote commanded.

"Cut it off but leave the fans on the motor running. I think I can help put the fluid in," Joe said leaning over the front seat.

"Joe you don't know anything about buses," Bridgette said.

"I'll have you know I worked for a cab company for a while back in college," Joe said sticking his tongue out at Bridgette.

"Where are we?" Lorraine asked. "I need to stretch my legs."

"Me too," Ma Williams said.

"Look guys, please stay close to the bus and stay alert to your surroundings!" Coyote said.

"Better yet, stand in the front of the bus," Milton said.

"We are somewhere in Arkansas," Shea answered Lorraine.

"What do you mean somewhere?" Ben asked smelling the baby's diaper.

"Well the GPS tracker burned about a hundred miles ago, so I turned it off."

"Hey, look in the back under those cases and hand me those jugs off anti-freeze," Milton said to Coyote pointing toward the back of the bus.

"Here you go!" Coyote said passing Milton the jugs. "Give it 15 minutes before you crank the bus back up."

"This looks like a nice small town up ahead," Alex said emerging from the bus.

"Let's walk up the road to the town," Alex said stretching.

"Have you forgotten why you are on this trip?" Joe barked.

Just then, a car full of teenagers passed by looking, pointing and staring.

"Ok, what the hell was that about?" Keisha asked going into police mode and writing down the tag number.

"Probably nothing; just not used to seeing strangers in their small town." Alex yawned. "Gabe are you okay? You have been quiet the whole trip," Alex commented.

"My spirit says this is not a good place. There is evil here. Great evil," Gabe answered.

"I feel it too," David said looking toward town.

"Let's get that anti-freeze in and get out of here," Milton said opening the jug and passed it to Joe.

Bazz and Coyote pulled the guns from the back of the bus looking around suspiciously. "Something here is not right. I can't even pull the town up on the GPS. I can't get it on my iPhone. I know that the cell towers are damaged, but the GPs tracker should still be pretty accurate," Bazz said.

"Not if they're jamming the cell towers," Ira said looking up at the towers.

"The satellite phone is saying were one point five miles outside of Harrisburg, Arkansas," Ben said while changing Serenity's diaper and gagging a little.

"Harrisburg, why do I know that name?" Milton said passing the second jug to Joe to pour in the radiator.

Bazz swung around from the back of the bus wide, looking spooked. "You know why you know the name of Harrisburg? It's the K.K.K. capital of the world!"

"How in the hell did we end up in Ku Klux Klan land?" Bridgette asked turning pale.

"Hey calm down. Get back into the bus, and we're out of here!" Bazz squeaked holding the bus door open for Lorraine and Alex.

"Damn, not so fast. The radiator is leaking. I think there is a hole in the hose," Joe hollered back.

"Tape it up and let's move. Dark does not catch black people in this town! They won't even live within a twenty-mile radius," Bazz said looking at Ira. "Yo! Dog nothing good is going to happen here."

"Damn, damn!"

"Yep, it's the radiator hose that's leaking," Joe said closing the hood.

"Look at the anti-freeze leaking out on the ground," Milton pointed out. "Well, we' re going to need two white men. Ben and Joe to go into town and purchase a hose and some anti-freeze before it gets any later in the day. I can install the hose quickly, it's just getting the hose."

"Out of all the towns in America," Coyote said scratching his head.

"We didn't do it on purpose!" Keisha answered hostilely.

"I have never heard of this place," Bridgette said taking the baby from Ben.

"Just because you have not heard of it, doesn't mean that it doesn't exist," Bazz said rolling his eyes. "You do know that the K.K.K. still exists. They don't wear white robes anymore; they wear suits, run companies, and towns. It's a little harder to recognize them. They're like chameleons, but they still exist." Bazz said. "You Americans take everything for granted and live life so laid back and careless. If you don't trip over it and it bites you in the ass, you don't know it exists."

"Hey, hey, hey we're here now! Let's use our energy to get the hell out of here," Ira intervened. "Ben, you and Joe need to go into town and get the hose so we can get the hell out of here before it all goes to pot," Ira said. "We have already been spotted, so let's get out of here as fast as possible."

"We'll take gold, money, and guns, with us," Ben said.

"That's without saying," Ira agreed.

Everyone waited as close to the bus as possible with Milton, Coyote, David, and Gabriel standing watch. Every car that passed by was suspect.

"It feels like they have been gone forever," Bridgette said slumped down, face forward in the bus seat.

"Do you know your daughter makes gas faces?" Ira asked. "Watch, every time she passes gas, she makes this face."

Bridgette sat up in time to see the face. "Oh yeah, her daddy makes the same face when he farts in his sleep!" Everyone laughed quietly. "Well he does," Bridgette said.

"TMI!" Keisha laughed.

"Hey, I'm going to give them another 10 minutes then Brandon and I are going to check on them," Milton said. "Give them another 20 minutes before we start getting upset."

"Mama, I like the blanket you and Miss Lorraine gave the baby. It will be spectacular on the baby's bed. When we get somewhere and settle down," Bridgette said.

"Well baby, you and Ben are still going to Israel with us right?" Ma Williams asked.

"As far as I know, but do we know what is waiting for us in Israel?' Bridgette looked up the road anxiously.

"We don't know what Israel holds, but I'm sure they don't have death squads hunting people down and killing them," Shea said sarcastically.

"I'm not sure what the future holds for us," Bridgette said rubbing her hand across the blanket. "I just pray everything will go back to normal."

"There is no normal left, the seals have been broken, and vials are being poured out of heaven," Gabriel said.

"How long do you think we have left before the end?" Bazz asked.

"No man knoweth the day nor the hour, but I believe it's less than a year. The rapture can happen at any minute, nothing else has to happen before the rapture occurs. Don't worry about how long we have before all things happen, just be ready for the rapture. Confess your sins before God, ask forgiveness and ask Jesus to come into your heart and be your Lord and Savior. Ask that we return to the sky that we be with him. You do not want to be left behind. It's only going to get worse. By worse, I mean all kinds of horrors will be released. They're not just stories, they're prophecies. Be yee ever so ready," Gabriel said shaking his head.

A couple of cars passed by, their occupants staring not hiding their sneers.

"It's been thirty minutes," Milton said looking up the road. "Here they come with bags and stuff."

Just then an SUV with four white men pulled up. Bazz and Ira hid the guns and waited to see what would happen next. Ben and Joe stepped up to the truck and had a few words with men. The truck drove off slowly with the occupants looking back eyeballing everyone.

"Hey, I got the hose. Let's get this on. Please hold this while I climb under here," Joe said taking the hose with him "A few more minutes guys and I will have it on. Okay, I got it on. Now I just need to finish putting the ring on. Coyote, start pouring the anti-freeze while I look under here to see if any is leaking out."

"What was all that about?" Milton asked pointing at the SUV.

"Oh, we were invited to a Klan rally," Joe smirked.

"What?' Lorraine asked anxiously.

"If we're not out of here before nightfall, we're all invited to the rally," Ben said raising the hood. "We got three hours before sunset. Let's get the bus fixed and get out of here."

"Yeah before they decide to come back with company," Ira said.

"I always heard of the K.K.K., I just have never been in the same area they were in. I don't like the smell of threats in the air. I left the south with my family as a child because of racism and the KKK. The KKK hung one of my uncles in Alabama before I was born," Ma Williams said shaking almost in tears.

"Back on the bus, start putting everything back on the bus including people," Joe said moving as fast as he could. Everyone started getting back on the bus. Joe started the bus and let it run 10 minutes so he could check the ground for any leakage of fluids. As the bus sat there running, there was a convoy of SUVs and trucks approaching. The SUV's and trucks sat on the hillside overlooking the bus and its passengers. Gabriel stopped and looked up.

"We are surrounded," Gabe said.

"Yeah, I noticed that," Ira said not looking up on purpose.

"Let's all gather together and say a prayer," Uncle Gabe said.

"Uncle Gabe, I'm almost finished. Can this wait a few more seconds?" Joe asked.

"NO! Now!" Gabe shouted.

Joe got up quickly leaving the cockpit of the bus while it was still running. Joe grabbed Keisha's hand and bowed his head.

"Father God omnipotent and almighty, we come together giving you the glory honor and the praise. We lift our eyes unto the hills from whence cometh our help. Our help cometh from God that created heaven and earth. Lord, we are surrounded by our enemies. With the Angel of the Lord protect and keep us, Lord. Lord you know how to keep and protect your people, we ask for your help and protection. Please assist us now, we ask in your son Jesus' name Amen."

"Rabbi, while you were praying, more SUVs and pickup trucks appeared on the hillside," Bazz said looking up at the surrounding area.

"There are more with us than against us," Gabriel said.

The sun was slowly getting low in the sky. The pink sky of the sunset was closing in. A truck horn blew causing everyone to jump.

"There are another twenty-five trucks pulling up on the hillside," Brandon shouted over the engine noise.

"There are so many trucks, the ground is vibrating," Joe said.

"You can smell the engine exhaust!" Ma Williams exclaimed.

"They're revving the engines to make the noise and smoke," Keisha hollered over the engine noise.

Suddenly a shot from a rifle went up into the air. The drivers started blowing their horns. A few air horns played Dixieland.

"Joe, what's the hold-up?" Milton asked starting to wheeze from the engine exhaust.

"Done. We can go now," Joe said entering the bus again. Milton jumped in the driver's seat of the bus.

"They're just sitting there!" Ira sneered.

"Good, we can get the hell out of here before they start shooting!" Bazz exclaimed slamming the bus doors shut.

The bus pulled off slowly. The trucks blew their horns and gunned their engines. Some of the trucks started trying to follow the bus.

A loud clap of thunder followed by a streak of lightning hit suddenly. Usually, thunder followed lightning. There was a loud rumbling sound. The ridge where the eighty plus trucks and SUVs sat began to crumble. The ground under the SUVs and trucks opened up and swallowed all the vehicles. The hole in the ground was the size of a football field or wider. Then another football field-sized hole opened up and swallowed the remaining trucks approaching the hillside. Another sinkhole opened up under the town. Buildings began disappearing into the ground. The ground closed in over the entire town.

The passengers in the bus wept in shock at the sight. A whole town had been swallowed up in a sinkhole. Milton was driving. He pulled the bus over because he was shaking too much to drive. No one could believe their eyes. The town of Harrisburg was no more, only the base of the Ozark Mountains existed. After sitting for thirty minutes, Milton regained his composure and drove on to the next town before anyone said a word.

Ambulances and a military convoy were headed toward Harrisburg. The area looked like a valley of large overturned boulders. Nothing else, just smoke escaping from the ground.

News Flash

CNN reports that Prime Minister Waleed Aldolho of Jordan has helped Israel and the country of Iran sign a peace treaty. There is finally peace in the Middle East. All countries have signed a cease-fire and peace agreement, that all the countries on the African continent including countries in the southern Congo are at peace.

There is peace on the African continent brokered by Prime Minister Waleed Aldolfo of Jordan, who was raised as a Muslim but recently discovered he has Jewish DNA. In his own words, "We are one!" The Prime Minister has plans on visiting the newly built temple in Israel in the near future.

Also in today's news, Israel announced that they have found the largest oil reserves in the world, in Israel. Israel has also announced that it will not be a member of OPEC.

Members of the organization PETA—People for the Ethical Treatment of Animals—tried to storm the newly built Jewish Temple mount to try and stop the daily sacrifices of animals.

Israeli military troops have been called in to try to keep the peace.

Chapter 39

The next hundred miles passed in silence. No one could believe what they had just witnessed. The ground opening up and swallowing and the whole town. Coyote was the first to break the silence.

"There is a reservation about another fifteen minutes down the road. We can stop and make sure the hose is good and tight."

"Sure, we can do that, does everyone agree?" Milton asked. Everyone agreed.

Pulling into the reservation, Coyote showed his Indian ID and asked to speak to Chief Waterlily. Surprisingly, Chief Waterlily was a female named Abigail Waterlily. She welcomed them to the reservation and asked them to be her guests for lunch at the reservation casino. Everyone obliged, and she gave them accommodations at the hotel-casino.

"Dag Coyote, she must really like you," Bazz said looking around the res and snickered.

"Nah man, me and Abigail, I mean Chief Waterlily go way back. She was there when I took my first vision quest and was able to explain a lot of things to me. Without her, I would have lost my mind. I'll ask her to reveal some information that I received from her at lunch. It will blow your mind that this thing has been hidden since the foundation of the world."

"Hidden from the foundation of the world?" Gabriel asked interestedly.

When the bus pulled up to the casino, Shea jumped out followed by everyone else.

"Wow, this is a beautiful hotel and casino," MS. Williams exclaimed.

"I'm going to take the bus around back and have it serviced. I'll meet you guys for lunch," Coyote said

"We'll go with you," Milton and Bazz said. Coyote drove the bus away.

Entering the hotel, the concierge asked, "Are you guests of Chief Waterlily's? I have your suites ready for you. Welcome to Featherhead Hotel and Casino."

"Wow, a suite for all of us? I wonder how well Coyote knows Chief Waterlily?" Ira asked winking at Brandon. Brandon shot back a grin.

"Here are the keys to your rooms, you may go up. The Chief is expecting you about two o'clock in the executive dining room. Your bags will be brought to your rooms shortly. Please enjoy your stay at Feather Head Casino and Spa Hotel." The concierge smiled and escorted everyone to the elevators.

After a good nights' rest and a wakeup call for everyone, they had a chance to go to the Casino and do some gambling and some sightseeing on the reservation. They explored the historical areas of the reservation learning the rich history of the Native American people. The group was enthralled with the history of the land, their culture, and spirituality. At 2:30 like clockwork, they sat in the executive dining room eating, waiting for Chief Waterlily.

"Hello, how are you? Welcome to Feather Head Casino and Spa Hotel. I am very happy to meet every one of you! I see that you have started lunch without me and that is fine. Is everything to your liking?"

The executive dining room was a large hall with a huge buffet style dinner with all kinds of meats and seafood, the freshest fruits and vegetables. There was a wait staff of six for the group.

After dinner, Chief Waterlily spoke. "I know who you are, and I know where you come from. I don't know what you have been through but know this: that you are not the only ones. There have been many more before who had to use the reservation to escape. The reservations are like underground railroads. If you know your history, then you know that your people and mine are one. So, welcome my sisters and brothers. My ancestors told us long ago that you were coming and that you would need our assistance. We are a very proud and humble people. Because of that, this country tried to break us. We could not and will not be broken. They gave us blankets filled with smallpox and their poisonous firewater. They tried to starve us and took away our lands.

The ghost dance that made the ghost face shirts popular foretold our destiny. He told us that the rocks would cry black tears and it would give our people our pride and humanity back. No one knew what he meant. How can rocks cry black tears? Oh, but they do! The tears are oil deposits in the rocks that produce the largest oil reserves in the world. My people are wealthy, and now we can help our sisters and brothers because we all have some Jewish DNA to prove it.

But first and foremost, we are Native American, and we have helped build this country. We shall help return this country to its former greatness. The prosperity of our people will make it a different country for us because we will no longer be treated as second-class citizens. We have more political power than ever before, and we will use this power to benefit our people and this country.

Those that have the gold make the rules. Those that have the oil rule the world! We have just found the second largest oil reserve. Care to know where it is?" The room was dead silent. "The second largest in the world is in Israel, but they don't know it yet. That's where you guys come in.

We would like for you to be our delegates to Israel to help them understand the oil business. To be able to speak to them and let them know that we are sending our personnel over to help them ease into the transition and also to help with discovery. You are Jewish, and every nation and tribe will be needed to make this a successful transition.

Now, my brothers and sisters, you are home again. Your people are my people, and my people are your people. If you chose to leave, may God be with you, it is rough out there.

The UFOs are busy trying to convert as many people as possible. They have visited my people through the ages. Now that we know who they are and what they want, we don't entertain them as much. Jesus Christ, our Lord and Savior, has revealed who these beings are and what they want.

Do not cross the deserts of Mexico–there are serial killers there who prey upon the weak and feeble. My friend and brother,

Coyote, saved my life in the deserts of Mexico and I will always be grateful to him. My friends, the choice is yours, stay or go. Journey well my friends, journey well.

I must now go and attend to Casino business, but I am humbled and grateful to have been of service to you. Thank you for allowing my people and me this opportunity to return the favor given to my people some many centuries ago. An Indian never forgets who their true friends are. We also never forget our enemies! Thank you and journey well." With that, Chief Waterlily left the room.

All the women were in tears from the beautiful and touching speech. "I never thought about staying on a reservation, but it's nice here," Alex said nodding at Ma Williams and Lorraine.

"Is it safe to stay here? Will the death squads try and get to us?" Bridgette asked.

"This is a reservation and capable of protecting itself. Think of this as a small military base that is willing and capable of defending itself and has the legal right to do so," Coyote said proudly looking around the room.

"Coyote, do you have anything to do with the protection that is here?" Milton and Ira asked together.

"Well yeah. They used me as a security consultant," Coyote said grinning.

"I'm willing to stay!" Milton said lighting a cigar.

"I don't know what to do. I thought we decided to go to Israel? Ma what do you want to do?" Keisha asked.

"Your father said to get to Petra in the last days, at least to Israel," Ma Williams said looking at her wedding ring. "Gabriel, you and David are the oldest and the wisest. What do you think we as a group, should do? Gabriel as a rabbi, a priest, and a man of God, what do you think we should do?"

"I think we should pray and ask God what he wants us to do," Gabriel answered. "Holy God that protects Israel and us, lead and guide us to where we should go. I ask in Jesus' name, amen." Gabriel lifted his head and looked around the table. "Now we must wait for an answer."

"Let's all meet in the morning with a decision," David said. Everyone agreed and said their good nights.

That night everyone enjoyed dinner together and the pleasure of not just having separate rooms, but different suites. Bridgette enjoyed going to the doctor with the baby for a checkup. By the grace of God, all was well medically for mother and baby.

Breakfast that morning was more than euphoric. A hot, all-you-can-eat breakfast bar. Everyone met in the executive dining room. Chief Waterlily and Coyote were already there.

"Good morning," Chief Waterlily said. "I'm glad to see you still have a healthy appetite."

"Appetite has always been good," Keisha said rubbing her stomach with a mouthful of food. "Let's eat because we have a big decision to make."

After breakfast, Chief Waterlily spoke again. "Because of the importance of this mission, no one can know. I have tried to reach the Prime Minister of Israel, but there has been an assassination attempt on his life. Not sure if the phone call led to the attempt on his life, but under the circumstances, precaution is needed. He needs to know that his country is sitting on the second largest oil reserves. I'm sure this will put his country in a volatile predicament; more than ever before.

If other surrounding countries found out that they have the second largest shale oil reserves, it could be the beginning of the end for them militarily. Especially in that part of the world. Israel is at peace. For right now, the world is at peace. This information could start the beginning to the end. No other time has there been world peace on a sizeable stage. So, this information must be kept secret and only be handed to the Prime Minister. He will be waiting for you.

I know you are being pursued by death squads attempting to kill Jewish citizens and that Switzerland had a killing camp that operated for two years. It has been shut down, and the criminals responsible have been executed.

I'm afraid the money taken from the Jewish people is long gone, and there is no way of tracing it. That's why it's so important that Israel knows that they are sitting on this oil, so they can take care of their people and help fortify their land.

Your lives will be in danger, but Coyote has filled me in on your jobs and personalities. We feel that as a group, you are more than qualified."

"What do you mean we are simple people?" David asked.

"First, you are all Jewish. Everyone except Milton and Bazz. You have a Jewish Rabbi, a savvy media personality in Alex, accountants in Ben and Joe, a secretary with chemistry and nursing degrees in Shea, and security with Ira, Milton, Bazz, Keisha, Brandon, and Coyote! You have everything that will be needed to make the presentation. When Israel finds out what their capabilities are, they have no choice but to choose the oil," Chief Waterlily explained.

"Won't this put Israel in harm's way from the other countries?" Bridgette asked feeding Serenity.

"When has Israel not been in harm's way? Believe me, Israel can take care of itself. Better yet, God can take care of Israel," Milton said. There was a long period of silence. Ma Williams spoke up.

"We have nothing to go back to. Ben and Joe, after you get established you can send for your parents. Coyote, you have a family, and you have already decided that you are making the trip."

"I will make sure you get to the boat safely then I will return to my family," Coyote said making his third trip around the breakfast bar.

"I would love to start my new life with my husband in a new country learning new things together," Lorraine said looking lovingly at David.

"It seems we're going to Israel," Shea said smiling from ear to ear.

"Are you going to be able to get some security assistance?" Ira asked Chief Waterlily.

"We have a casino party bus that we reinforced with steel and bulletproof windows. The next best thing to an armored car."

"Now that's what I'm talking about," Joe said slapping his knee.

"It's still dangerous out there," Bazz said rolling his eyes. "We still are knee deep in all kinds of..." Bazz looked at Ma Williams and Gabriel and let the last word trail off. Bazz cleared his throat, "Let's see that party bus," and started walking toward the doors. Everyone followed Bazz.

"Wow, it's huge," Shea said entering the bus first.

"We can all sit here comfortably," David said sliding into a seat.

"It can hold all kinds of supplies and the things we will need to keep us safe," Bazz said looking at the storage bins.

"It's just what we needed to fit the bill," Joe said.

"When are we talking about leaving?" Ira asked.

"Let's stay two more days at least, "Shea and Keisha said at the same time.

"It's no problem for you here at the reservation," Chief Waterlily said. "We will continue to pick up the tab. You all need some rest. We will make sure the bus is stocked with anything you will need."

"Chief Waterlily, how can we ever thank you?" Bridgette said hugging her with tears in her eyes.

"The way to thank me and all my people is to get that briefcase to Israel."

The group oohed and aahed over the bus a few moments longer and said their goodbyes and thanked Chief Waterlily and later decided to go the casinos and spas.

"Chief Waterlily, I have a question for you?" Ben asked politely. "Not to be rude, but how are you running a casino when the national financial institutions have collapsed?"

"Indians have always kept gold. All of our money is backed by gold. We have a gold reserve on the premises, but not like Ft. Knox!" Chief Waterlily said with a wink. "Goodbye!"

Chapter 40

After two days of rest, the team was ready for the next leg of the journey. Gabriel had everyone together at the bus at sunrise.

"God has spoken to me and asked me speak to you about a few things. A lot of things have happened to us and around us, but God has protected us for a reason. He asks as humbly as He knows how, to make a solid commitment to Him, ask Him to come into your heart, and become your Lord and Savior. Give your heart and soul to him and the Father, that he may watch over until eternity. The road we will travel will be new and strange. Your faith and belief in Him must be stronger than ever because there will be more trying times ahead. Your mind, heart, and soul must be prepared for the journey. Everybody hold hands, please. Bridgette, bring April Serenity Zigburgh forth, please." Bridgette and Ben stepped into the inner circle while holding baby Serenity.

"Father God we offer this child to You. We ask that You bless and keep her, watch over her soul, give her parents wisdom, seen and unseen, to protect the anointing and talents that You have placed in this child, so that she may give You all the glory and the praise, for her life, family and accomplishments. We ask these and all things in Your son Jesus' name, Amen.

Repeat after me, everyone. Father, God we also ask You to come into our lives and forgive us of sins known and unknown, that we have committed. We accept your son Jesus as Lord of our lives and Savior. We ask that the Holy Spirit come in and sup with us and reveal your wisdom and knowledge unto each and everyone, as we go on this journey. We ask these and all blessings in your son Jesus Christ's name. Shalom and Amen."

Gabriel raised his head, opened his eyes and looked with concern in Bazz's direction. Did you accept Jesus, with a sincere heart?"

Bazz paused before answering, "I am not ready yet, Rabbi. There are some people I cannot forgive just yet."

"Son, I beg you; time is short. Please do not wait too much longer, it is imperative that you do so," Gabriel hugged him, and everyone hugged each other and boarded the bus.

Coyote hugged Chief Waterlily and thanked her, telling her he would return as soon as he got everyone to the ship. Coyote stepped onto the bus last as Milton closed the door behind him.

"Question man, if you and Chief Abigail aren't involved, could you hook me up with her? She is hot."

"Dude, she is a Tribal Chief. You have to be man enough to approach her yourself. She doesn't want a weakling," Coyote said snickering.

"I was just checking to make sure I wasn't stepping on your toes," Milton said grinning.

"I am a happily married man. And, speaking of happy, let's hurry and get these people to their destination so I can stay married. Don't want to be gone so long that the dog forgets me and attacks."

"Say no more. We will be in Texas about 3:00. Everyone sit back, relax, and enjoy the ride," Milton said lurching the bus forward. Everyone groaned, slipping and sliding, trying to hold on as the bus pulled off.

"My bad folks, thought it would drive like a truck not a sports car. The Indians spared no expense on this baby right here," Milton said by way of an apology.

"Careful Milton, you are carrying precious cargo," Ira said putting his arms around Shea and squeezing until she blushed.

"No problem. Aye, aye captain, full steam ahead."

Everyone chatted amongst themselves and discussed their new lives in Israel. They even watched a little television and heard that some of the members of the death squads of the Brotherhood of the Valkyrie, had been rounded up and jailed.

Gabriel started to teach everyone Hebrew. This would help for a smoother transition and learn the customs along with the language of the Jewish people.

Pulling into Texas port around 2:30 in the afternoon, the sky looked strange. It was orange with very little blue. The scenery was a desert sky, the atmosphere was dry, and there was a strange feeling in the air.

Coyote was asleep, and Bazz kicked the bottom of his boot. "Hey wake up buddy. We might need some Native American insight on this situation."

Coyote sat up and pulled his hood off his head, yawned and took a look around. All the chattering ceased. Everyone was alert and looking out of the windows.

The bus crested the hill and began a descent into a valley and a small town called Medallion, Texas. The gas gauge was getting low, so Milton slowed down. "We're going need gas before we cross over to Galveston. The gas gauge is going berserk. Didn't want to upset anyone so I stayed on this road. It looks orange outside. This comes after a storm, and before another even stronger one blows in behind it. If we're getting gas, let's make it fast," Coyote said looking up at the sky.

"It's a large full-service station. This is our last stop before we get to the port," Milton advised.

Ma Williams was the first to exit the bus. "My, this air is so dry."

"It's Texas Momma," Keisha said getting behind her mother.

"Everybody, you might want to go ahead and stretch your legs," Milton suggested.

"I need to speak to you boys for a minute," Ira said. "I want you guys to know how much I appreciated you guys helping me and my family make this strange and unexpected journey. I thank you for putting your lives on the line for me and mine. I know my wife can be extremely bossy and superficial, I appreciate you for not showing any attitudes. Because of the graciousness you displayed, I will be forever grateful and to show how much, I am giving you guys 6 of my weed dispensaries. You each get two. I will keep the other six for me and wifey." Ira gave Coyote, Milton and Bazz some paperwork. "All you have to do is sign at the bottom and get your attorneys to go over the paperwork, but everything is already in order. Give me a hug. Y'all know y'all my boys. You guys did not just start watching my back on this trip, you been doing it for years. I just wanted to say thank you."

Coyote and Milton were touched by Ira's words and generosity. They even started to cry. Bazz stood with his mouth open.

"Bazz, I know you came in on the end of the deal, but it could be you lying dead instead of Jordan. I want you to give the money in the account in Mexico to Jordan's family. Here is the paperwork for that."

"Ira, we don't know how to thank you," Coyote said.

"Pass the blessings on. I don't have to tell you guys that. We didn't get here without doing some dirt. If you can go back and knock off some of the dirt you kicked up in life, then do that. Money can't change all things, but it will help, it will help." The group of men laughed and cried at the same time. "Now go fill this bus up."

After the gas tank was filled, everyone returned to the bus resuming the conversations they were having when they had pulled into the gas station.

"Ma, don't say that. The end of days are not here yet," Keisha said entering the bus.

"There is such a thing as the end of days," Alex replied wiping her forehead.

"Well, today is not the day," Joe said, "and I don't want to hear about the doom and gloom of it all."

"Don't be a scaredy cat. This stuff has to happen before Jesus comes back," Bridgette said handing Ben the baby. "She stinks again!"

"I just changed her," Ben said huffing.

"Guess what?" Bridgette said. "Everyone, I apologize for my daughter's manners, but I'm not going all the way back in there. So, crack the windows."

"There's a vent fan on this bus," Milton said hitting the switch. "Damn Waterlily!" Milton said. "My kind of woman, classy all the way," Milton said as Coyote shook his head.

"Gabriel is going to be a few more minutes. He got them looking for some pure virgin olive oil." Coyote stepped outside to clean the windows on the bus and stopped in his tracks. Gabriel walked up on him and whispered. "You feel it too, don't you padre?"

"Yeah, just as I stepped off the bus," Coyote said looking directly at Gabriel. "Something here is evil, and it's pursuing us. It has been ever since we left the reservation," Coyote finished.

Chief Waterlily said to stay out of the desert, why?" Gabriel asked.

"Demonic spirits like dry places. There are things that my people have encountered in the deserts that are not of this world. They have been there for thousands of years, since the beginning of time. They didn't see them as often once my people received the Holy Spirit. Only great spiritual ones or wise ones with pure spirits could defeat them. Now they're being unleashed in unfathomable numbers. They're convincing wise people to believe and make foolish decisions. They follow weak and lost souls. We have become targets because we are on a mission to help the Jewish people," Coyote said. "Anytime you help the Jewish people, you become targeted by demons, but the Lord will bless those that bless His people," Coyote said.

Gabriel took a deep breath. "Are they from earth?"

"They were cast down to the earth a long time ago and have made earth their home. They try and convince people that they are from the stars, but they are not. They are not here for no reason," Coyote said.

"Hey, what are you two guys whispering about out there?" Milton asked. "Let's hurry up with those windows. Waterlily won't wait forever for me."

The store clerk came out to give Gabriel the change he forgot. "Here's your change, sir. Are you here to see the space aliens?"

Gabriel shot Coyote a look. "I'm sorry, we're not here for that, we are just passing through."

"The space aliens have been flying in and out not too far from here. It started about five months ago," the clerk volunteered. "They landed in a cornfield and started talking to different farmers, showing them how to grow food and increase their wealth, and when the bottom was going to fall out of the economy. They even told us to switch to gold and get a chip under our skin to improve our health so we won't get cancer."

"I'm sorry, we have to go now," Coyote said pushing Gabe on the bus and shutting the doors.

The girl stood there saying, "Hey you have forgotten your change."

"Milton, pull the bus off now, drive now!" Coyote yelled.

"Okay, man I was just playing about Waterlily."

Coyote and Gabe stood there for a few minutes as the bus started down the road.

"Space creatures?" Lorraine asked again. "They're talking to farmers and you're saying that they are demons?"

"They're helping the farmers get rich and grow all types of food. These people have been eating it for a while, and they've even had chips placed under their skin to keep from getting sick," Coyote said.

Milton kicked up the speed of the bus facilitating a faster exit. Going down the road at top speed, the bus was almost out of the area when it came across a hill and had to slow down because of the crowd. There was a farm that had cars parked up and down the highway on both sides. Milton slowed the bus down to a crawl to allow people to cross back and forth across the highway in front of the bus.

The people had banners and posters, going into the field like it was a parade or concert. They had dazed and confused look on their faces.

"Uncle Gabe, they look a little weird, a little strange. They don't look like they're all there," Bridgette commented.

"They're oppressed by the demons. A few may be possessed, so their thinking and behavior are not normal. I believe in transference," Gabriel answered.

"What's transference?" Lorraine asked.

"It means that through touch, music, or scents, you can be susceptible to the influence of demons." Everyone looked confused. "Certain music attracts demons. Not just rock music, but drums, certain types of chanting and incense can also attract demonic spirits. There are doors you can open that will attract demons."

"Doors?" Keisha asked.

"Horoscopes, Ouija boards certain types of ancient tattoos that people get and don't understand their meaning. It's allowing spirits into the body. That's what spirits want—a body that they can use."

"Uncle Gabriel, have you experienced demonic possession?" Bridgette asked.

"Not on a personal or professional level. I do know that they exist, and I have heard sordid stories of the destruction they can cause."

"My people saw and talked to these beings thousands and thousands of years ago," Coyote said.

"Which people Coyote, your Mexican people or your Native American People?" Bazz asked.

"Both Coyote," said staring out of the windows at the people strolling past the bus. "Okay Dark One, you are from the dark continent. Tell me you have not seen things you knew were straight from the pits of hell. Just living through a genocide, seeing all the death and the way people were being tortured before they were killed, you knew the devil was behind it. You would think that you'd be able to run to the church to get help under those circumstances, but some priest and nuns committed some of the most gruesome deaths. Now, how can you explain that except you say that it was the devil?"

Bazz sat facing the window but not seeing what was going on outside the bus. "That's why I am not trusting of the church. The priest and the nuns killed my first and only love. She was ten years old and had a sister that was twelve. They went to this Catholic boarding school. On my escape out of the area, I stopped by the boarding school to see if I could help my friends escape and the horror I saw there. I have never been able to speak of it again," Bazz said with tears rolling down his face.

"The Azteca and the Inca People have recorded having conversations with the star people, and Native American have also recorded through wall paintings that they have entertained these star people," Coyote said still looking out the window at the strange wanderers.

"You mean the space aliens?" Ira asked scooting up to sit on the edge of his seat to hear better. Milton turned the radio off and rolled the windows up to hear better.

"Some people believe them to be space aliens or water aliens because they have been seen coming and going from earth and the sea. These are the ones that were trying to broker deals on the earth. Without Gods approval. This is why they were kicked out

269

of heaven." No one said a word you could hear a pin drop. Gabriel broke the silence.

"Lucifer, Satan himself. My people believe the space aliens are the fallen angels."

Everybody let out a gasp at the same time. The bus had pulled over a hill, and on both sides of the road, there were at least 10,000 or more people as well as cars in an open field. The people were waving banners and crosses and singing hymns and looking up into the sky. Everyone on the bus looked up and could see shiny metallic-looking disc floating just above the field, slowly descending. Milton slowed the bus down to could see.

"Milton, don't slow down, speed up!" Gabriel yelled.

There were a lot of people crossing back and forth across the road so picking up speed was out of the question, it couldn't be done.

Milton had to wait a few minutes, but as soon as he could, he floored the pedal and the bus accelerated leaving the area.

"How can all these people believe this?" Alex asked looking back at the crowd.

"How could we believe that a bank was going to give fifty thousand dollars to each of us just because we're Jewish?" Joe asked.

"Times are hard, and people are looking for help wherever they can find it, some type of relief. Almost to the point of people forgetting that Jesus said that toward the end times, even the elect could be fooled or tricked," Gabriel explained.

"Let's leave this place. I don't want to see anything crazy," Ma Williams said. "Chief Waterlily said to stay out of the desert."

"So, this is what is going on in the celestial atmosphere," Lorraine asked.

"This has been going on for thousands of years, and no one has figured it out," Brandon said turning around to see it. "I always thought there were things like Big Foot and Loch Ness, stuff you have heard of but could never prove." Brandon sighed.

"Aren't the falling stars called sons of God or…" Keisha asked trailing off.

"Yes, they're thought to be the fallen angels that were kicked out heaven when Lucifer fell and became what we know as demons," Gabriel answered.

Coming over another hill, there was another crowd gathered watching something in the sky. It was the same type of scene they had just witnessed. People were carrying crosses, talking about the return of Jesus and that the space aliens would show America the way. Milton had to slow the bus down again to allow the people to cross the street.

All of a sudden, the crowd slowly moved toward the bus. Coyote and Bazz grabbed the guns and lowered the muzzles onto the crowd. "Wait!" Gabriel grabbed Coyote's arm. The crowd started to rock the bus back and forth violently. "Pray now! They are demonically possessed and are unaware of what they are doing. Look at their eyes," Gabriel said looking at the crowd.

Everyone started to pray. Those who could pray in tongues began to do so. The crowd continued to rock the bus.

"They're going to turn the bus over!" Milton yelled.

"Pray children!" Gabriel yelled. Everyone continued to pray.

Suddenly, the crowd dispersed and walked away from the bus. "Man are you serious? They don't know what they just did," Milton said hysterically.

Baby Serenity started to cry; the entire bus was silent. No one could utter a word. A couple of miles down the road, Alex was the first to speak.

"Our great-grandmother would tell us stories of the falling angels. She said that they had red hair and were 9 and 12 feet tall."

"Is that where the red-headed step-child syndrome came from?" Shea asked.

Everyone was still quiet. Alex continued "I think it is because neither one of the parents had red hair and they assumed that the offspring could have been an offspring of the fallen angels." Everyone laughed at the same time. "Yeah, that was the theory or the assumption. We all thought it was a joke, but there was some truth I guess. You know they have bones of men that stood 9ft tall and taller. Museums have confiscated the bones so they can't be DNA traced to see how much is human."

"You know Darwin's theory," Ben said rocking Serenity.

"Seriously, we as cops have had to guard stuff like that so the public wouldn't find out," Brandon said.

"In other words, regular folks don't need to know. The government has been hiding stuff for years," Keisha said. "Do you think they don't know about the aliens that are landing over in those fields. You did notice that there were no police anywhere to be seen."

"Why are they all of a sudden showing up on the farmlands? They have been testing the farmland with the crop circles, all of those designs were not man-made," Shea said.

"The Native American know what they are now, but people have started to get so lazy in seeking the Holy Spirit, that certain things are not being revealed because people are not listening to the Spirit. How many hours of the day do we have noise on? Television, radio, and internet. Nobody takes the time to sit quietly and listen to what the Spirit has to say. Believe me, this is going to cost people so much wisdom. When we need to know things that the Holy Spirit will be able to tell us, we won't be able to hear," Coyote said.

"This is when the false Prophet comes in and tell us what he has heard instead of trying to hear for ourselves," Gabriel said excitedly. "That's is exactly what's happening over there in those fields!" Gabriel said shaking his head.

"Do either one of you know their connection with Maize or corn because they seem to have a thing for corn, wheat, and barley fields. You never heard of them being in grape vineyards or apple orchards?" Bazz asked.

"I think it is because corn has been here since the beginning of time, and grapes are used in communion," Coyote said shrugging.

"You know, in all the years I have known you, I didn't know that you were this deep," Milton said eyeing Coyote through the rearview mirror.

"Hell, you can't get him to say twenty words at one time. Must be true what they say about still waters running deep," Bazz said smiling.

"Bazz, you could go so much deeper than me, that's why I bug you so much about taking the vision quest. I think it would let all that pent-up hostility out and let more of the Spirit in."

"Man, what did I tell you about dehydration and hallucinating," Bazz laughed nervously.

"I just pray that God takes you deeper and gives you the strength to go deeper, Dark One!" Coyote said.

"If I hear dark one, one more time you're going to be seeing dark," Bazz said shaking his fist at Coyote.

"A few more hours and we will be there. I'm going to get us there in one piece so sit back and relax," Milton said concentrating on the road.

It was almost sunset when they arrived at the port. Everyone said their goodbyes.

"Man, I'm going to miss your creepiness," Bazz told Coyote giving him a quick hug.

"What are you going to do now?" Ira asked Coyote.

"I'm going home to see about my family. I do miss them. Then I'm going to convert my pesos into gold and then check on my stores. Then I plan to build my wife her childhood dream house. You know, they say if you want to make God laugh, make a plan."

"Sounds like you have it all planned out. Just do me one favor, tell your wife everything she wants to know, no secrets. Secrets make shadows look darker than they are. I've decided to tell Shea about Teheira and the kids, so please be praying for me man," Ira said.

"I think Shea has some secrets of her own that she needs to tell you," Coyote said. Ira looked at Coyote questioningly. "Your wife is far from a fool." Coyote winked at Ira and gave him one last hug and went and sat on the bus.

Milton told Coyote, "I will see you in a couple of weeks, so we can take Jordan's family his share of the money." To Ira he said, "Ira I will never be able to thank you for the years and the times we have spent"

"Man, take care of yourself. I'll see you in a couple of months."

"Oh, we will skype a couple times a week, so I'm not totally gone," Ira said.

Milton and Coyote waited until everyone made it up the gangplank before they left. There was a party on the deck of the ship, and everyone started to relax and enjoy.

✪✪✪

Everyone was happy and content as the days went by on the ship. Each took personal time away from each other to have space for personal reflection. The group gathered for dinner the last night onboard. The following day, they would pull into Israeli waters.

A sudden deafening blast of trumpets resounded through the dining room as they ate. The blaring of trumpets was accompanied by great flashes of lightning across the sky from east to west. Diners huddle together out of fear as the trumpet blast grew louder and closer. Then came a great blinding flash of lightning. The passengers closed their eyes and clasped their hands over their ears waiting for the thunder and lightning to pass. Then there was dead silence–no more thunder, lightning or trumpets blaring.

Bazz opened his eyes and looked around the table to find Gabriel and Keisha sitting there in astonishment. There were only the clothes that everyone had on was left behind, their jewelry and rings were rolling around on the table as the ship did a sudden jerk. A dining room that had been filled with 500 people now sat almost empty with the exception of 80 people who stood looking around in utter shock and amazement.

Bazz looked at Gabriel and Keisha and asked, "What the hell, just happened.?"

Keisha started to wail and moan. Gabriel fell back into his chair still holding his iced tea, looking dazed and confused. You could hear a few of the women that were left screaming and yelling over Keisha's own. Male passengers were calling out to their loved ones and looking out to sea trying to see if they could catch a glimpse of their missing loved ones.

Bazz turned around looking out over the dining hall and suddenly ran out to the upper deck. It was almost empty of passengers, except for maybe twelve or more people that were crying and weeping. Those who were not crying were looking for their loved ones.

Just then there was a call out for all available crew members to report to the captain's deck. "All available crew members please report...."

Bazz returned to the dining room were Gabriel was now trying to console Keisha.

"What's happening? What's going on?"

"Sit down my friend," Gabriel said quietly.

Bazz sat down in a bewildered state of depression and confusion.

"What I believe has happened is called The Rapture. Jesus has returned for his people to take them back to heaven with him. We have been left behind, and all others have gone home to glory," Gabriel said with a small cry in his voice.

The music continued to play on the cruise ship as what was left of the crew attempted to keep everyone calm and continue to sail the ship safely. On a ship of more than 2700 souls on board, there are fewer than 400 left. Keisha continued to cry hysterically.

The people who were left behind began to talk and say that the aliens took people to relieve the burden that all the people placed on earth. Keisha stopped crying long enough, to look up at Gabriel. "Why are you still here? I'm sure there is a reason why Bazz and I are still here, but you are a Rabbi."

"Rabbis are people too," Gabriel stated quietly.

Passengers who knew the Rapture had just taken place were calm and sorrowful. Others who did not know, or did not want to know, assumed the aliens had taken their loved ones and were in a state of panic.

The three who were left behind knew the real reason why. It was up to each person to tell why they were left behind.

The only thing that was left for them to do was to deliver the contents of the briefcase to the Prime Minister of Israel. Keisha agreed with the plan to make sure the contents of the briefcase reached Israeli hands. No knew where they would go from there.

The ship was preparing to dock in Israel when Bazz returned to the upper deck where Keisha and Gabriel sat in silence. "Hey, I think we should look in this briefcase. This may have some answers in it for us. Under the circumstances, we need all the help we can get."

"Bazz, that is an official government document," Keisha said red and puffy faced.

"I don't care who it belongs to. Who's to say that there is still a government in Israel or anywhere else for that matter," Bazz said looking at Gabriel for agreement.

"It couldn't hurt," Gabriel conceded.

Bazz found a knife and opened the briefcase. Inside was information on the hidden shale oil located in Israel. There was also information on an item called the GOD BOX.

"What is this God Box?" Bazz question Gabriel.

"Well the God Box…"

"The Ark of the covenant?" Keisha exclaimed. "What kind of information does the Native American government have on the Ark?" Keisha asked grabbing the papers out of Bazz's hand. Keisha started to read the documents and began to weep all over again.

"Why are you weeping?" Gabriel asked.

Bazz took a few of the documents out of Keisha's hand and read. "They're saying that the ark is not where they thought it has been for all these years. They know where the real ark is located. What could this mean?" Bazz dropped the documents back into the briefcase and locked it.

The three sat in silence looking out over the water. Many questions needed to be answered and they had none, only more questions. The number one question was what would happen to them now? Why were they left behind? Why were they chosen to carry the briefcase to Israel in the first place? Where was the real ark? Would the ark even be needed now?

The three had many questions. They knew their journey was not over; they still had to get the briefcase to Israel. No one had the heart to make any major decisions at that point. They stared at the ocean they had just crossed to start a new life. They knew that their lives would never be the same and yet, they knew they still had a job to do.

"I have nothing to go on for," Keisha stated bluntly.

"None of us do," Bazz added. Gabriel said nothing as they stood on the deck watching the distraught passengers prepare to dock.

The Port of Ashdod in Tel Aviv, Israel lay in front of them. They had made it to Israel where just a few hours ago they had nothing but hope and now everything seemed hopeless.

"Let's just keep our word to Chief Waterlily and her people and get the briefcase to the Prime Minister of Israel," Bazz said. "That's the least we can do, and we gave our word."

"In appreciation of Chief Waterlily and her generosity, that's exactly what we will do," Gabriel said.

All three turned to go to baggage claim to pick up their bags and the bags of their friends. All had the same question in mind as they prepared to dock. Bazz was the only one brave enough to ask the question.

"Where is the ark?"

The End

Made in the USA
Columbia, SC
06 July 2019